"I'm no[...]leave the cab[...]"

Laurie's eyes shifted again to the window. It was completely dark now. "Cameron, I'm a police officer. I've worked undercover many times. I've felt afraid before, but never like I did when I was here alone." Her eyes seemed huge as they met his.

Cameron rose and went to the window, closing the drapes and shutting out the night. "Then we'll just have to take care we don't bump into our suspect." He held out his hand. "Let's get some sleep."

She rose, coming to him and placing her hand in his. "Sleep?" There was a trace of disappointment in her voice.

"Among other things."

She rose on the tips of her toes, fitting the contours of her body intimately to his. "It's the other things that have me interested."

* * *

Sons of Stillwater: Danger lurks in a small Wyoming town

* * *

If you're on Twitter, tell us what you think of Harlequin Romantic Suspense! #harlequinromsuspense

Dear Reader,

Covert Kisses is the first book in the Sons of Stillwater series. Thank you for joining me on this new adventure! Stillwater, Wyoming, is a beautiful place. Cradled low in the embrace of a towering mountain range, the town has been largely untouched by time and retains its historic buildings and Western charm.

Cameron Delaney is Stillwater's charismatic mayor and one of the area's wealthiest businessmen. The good fortune he enjoys professionally has not been reflected in his personal life. Cameron is still grieving for his girlfriend, Carla, who died twelve months ago, when his world is rocked by the appearance of her double in Stillwater.

Laurie has come to Stillwater for a reason. She is working undercover for the FBI investigating a drug and people trafficking ring, and Cameron Delaney is her prime suspect. Her likeness to Carla is the weapon she intends to use against him.

The attraction between them is sizzling and instant. On Laurie's part, this is unexpected and inconvenient. She can't afford to have feelings for a man she intends to put behind bars.

Laurie has only been in Stillwater a matter of days when her life is endangered. She is forced to seek help from the very man she has come to Stillwater to investigate.

I'd love to hear from you and find out what you think of Cameron and Laurie's story. You can contact me at www.janegodmanauthor.com, on Twitter, @JaneGodman and Facebook at Jane Godman Author.

Happy reading,

Jane

COVERT KISSES

Jane Godman

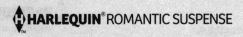

HARLEQUIN® ROMANTIC SUSPENSE

Recycling programs
for this product may
not exist in your area.

ISBN-13: 978-0-373-40208-3

Covert Kisses

Printed in U.S.A.

www.Harlequin.com

Jane Godman writes in a variety of romance genres, including paranormal, gothic and romantic suspense. Jane lives in England and loves to travel to European cities that are steeped in history and romance—Venice, Dubrovnik and Vienna are among her favorites. Jane is married to a lovely man and is mom to two grown-up children.

Books by Jane Godman

Harlequin Romantic Suspense

Sons of Stillwater
Covert Kisses

Harlequin Nocturne

Otherworld Protector
Otherworld Renegade
Otherworld Challenger
Immortal Billionaire
The Unforgettable Wolf

Harlequin E Shivers

Legacy of Darkness
Echoes in the Darkness
Valley of Nightmares
Darkness Unchained

This book is dedicated to Debbie, Dan and Luke. And Gravy. Because, somewhere in the world, there should be a book dedicated to a dog called Gravy.

Chapter 1

Take his breath away.

That was her one and only aim for this first encounter, and Laurie Carter had three things working in her favor as she kept the target in her sights.

First, there was the understated designer swimsuit that molded itself to her curves, while also cleverly drawing attention to the length of her legs.

Then there was the fact that she was wading ashore onto his private lakeside property. As he sprang to his feet from the rock where he had been sitting gazing out across the water, no doubt he was about to point that fact out to her. Laurie did a rapid check, reconciling this man's physical attributes with the photographs she had carefully memorized. Dark, wavy hair, swept back from a broad brow and worn slightly long so that it curled onto his neck. Deep-set eyes above high, Slavic cheekbones. A hawk-like nose and lips that were contrastingly full. She had the right man. There was no mistaking him. Tall and powerfully built, he moved toward her with the grace of an athlete, a frown line pulling his dark eyebrows together.

Judging the distance between them to perfection, Laurie waited until he was close enough. As she fell into a pretend faint, she saw shock and something more register in the hazel depths of Cameron Delaney's eyes. Advantage number three was always going to be the one that clinched it. As his reflexes kicked in and he scooped her up into his arms, Laurie let her head flop back, allowing him a clear view of her face.

His exhalation was an audible hiss. *Mission accomplished.* The fact that she was trespassing on his land had been the thing that made him notice her. The swimsuit had drawn his attention to her curves and kept him looking. Neither of those things had succeeded in driving the breath from his lungs. That had been achieved for one reason only…because she was the mirror image of his dead girlfriend.

Pure adrenaline fired through Cameron Delaney's nerve endings as he gazed down at the head resting against his arm. *It's not her.* His head insisted on repeating that mantra, even as his heart tried to tell him a different story. Her eyes were closed, so he was free to drink in the features he thought he'd never see again.

Subtle differences began to imprint themselves into his brain. Her weight in his arms felt different. She was an inch or two taller, a few pounds lighter than

Carla. Her hair was a tumbling mass. Even though this woman's was wet, he could tell it was the same dark chestnut as Carla's—although Carla's had been longer and artfully streaked with lighter highlights. Carla's skin tone had been a touch closer to gold than the pale porcelain he was studying so carefully now. This smattering of freckles would have been a cause for outrage if it had dared to spoil the perfection of Carla's dainty nose and smooth cheeks. A corner of his mouth lifted in amusement as he imagined Carla's horror at the prospect. *My God, am I finally able to remember her with something other than guilt and sadness?*

The thought was chased away as the girl in his arms stirred. Her eyelids fluttered open, thick eyelashes lifting to reveal eyes that were a brilliant cornflower blue, a shade lighter than Carla's. She fixed him with a slightly unfocused stare, then, apparently becoming aware of several things at once—she was in the arms of a complete stranger, her own state of undress and his naked torso in contact with her body—her eyes opened wide.

"Oh, goodness!" Her voice was husky, deeper than he'd expected, her accent hard to place, but definitely not local. "I'm so sorry. I don't make a habit of trespassing on private land and flopping into the arms of men I don't know. You can put me down now."

"Are you sure you can stand?" It seemed incredible, impossible to be talking to someone who looked so much like Carla, yet wasn't Carla. To not be asking her the dozens of questions that were chasing around inside his head.

"No, but I'll try…if you don't mind lending me your

arm." She smiled as she spoke. In that single instant, the subtle physical differences ceased to matter. That smile was pure Carla. It was like an electric shock to his heart and a karate kick in his solar plexus at the same time.

Carefully, Cameron lowered her to the ground. "Who are you?"

As far as he knew, Carla had no family. Could two people who were not blood relatives bear such a striking physical resemblance to each other? The living proof that they could seemed to be standing right next to him.

She clung onto his arm, testing her ability to remain upright. Apparently satisfied with the result, she let go and held out her hand. "Laurie Carter. It's nice to meet you, Mr. Delaney."

Cameron raised his eyebrows as he shook the proffered hand. "You know who I am?"

She smiled again. He might have to ask her to stop doing that. It was playing havoc with his heart rate. "Surely everyone in Stillwater knows who you are?"

"But you're not from around here." He could make that statement with absolute certainty. Stillwater, Wyoming, was a closely knit community. He and Carla had been together for almost three years. During that time, someone would have mentioned the fact that the mayor's partner had a double living in the county.

"I was born here in Stillwater, but my dad died when I was three, so my mom went back home to her folks' place in California. That's where I was raised. I'm here on vacation...curious to see where I started life." Laurie shivered, wrapping her arms around herself.

Cameron silently cursed his own clumsiness. Were the biographical questions necessary when she'd sustained a severe shock? "Let's go up to the house and you can warm up."

"Oh, hey—" she glanced up at the striking wood and glass structure, just visible through the pine trees bordering the lake, her teeth chattering slightly "—I don't want to be any trouble."

Ignoring her protests, he smiled down at her. "It's an election year. Rescuing tourists who get into difficulties is good for my public image." Turning away for a second, he stooped to pick up the lightweight sweater he'd discarded when he came down to the beach. "Put this on."

"It'll get wet…" Her protests faded at the determined look on his face. Taking the sweater from him, she slipped it on, tugging it down over her swimsuit. "Thank you."

"Didn't anyone warn you how difficult it is to swim across the lake?" He gestured for her to precede him up the steps that were hewn into the rock face. The sight of those long, slim legs beneath his sweater did something to his insides. It was a sensation he hadn't experienced for a long time.

Laurie glanced back at him, a hint of mischief in her smile. "Actually, they did."

"But you didn't listen?"

One slender shoulder hunched in a hauntingly familiar gesture. "I'm a good swimmer. I'm also very stubborn. If someone tells me I can't do something, it becomes the one thing I have to do."

Cameron's heart clenched. Hard. It could be Carla talking. How many times had he cursed her obstinacy?

She'd made him so mad that last night with her refusal to listen to reason…

He realized Laurie was still speaking and forced himself to tune back in to what she was saying. "If I'd known I'd get a cramp and end up trespassing on your private land, I would have listened to the warnings."

He returned her smile. It was impossible not to. "I'm glad you didn't."

So far, so good. The house was amazing. All glass and natural wood, it perched above the rock face, jutting out over the lake so every room seemed to be suspended above the water.

"It's amazing." Laurie stood at the full-length glass wall in the kitchen while Cameron made coffee. She had used the towel he gave her to get the worst of the lake water out of her hair. When it dried, she would look like a wild woman, but that couldn't be helped. She was here, inside Cameron Delaney's house. She'd take successful over well groomed any day. "Who designed it?"

He paused, and she wondered if he was about to tell her the truth. She already knew the answer to her question, of course. Carla Bryan had been one of several architects to submit plans for this beach house. The youngest and most inexperienced, she'd won the contract and Cameron's heart at the same time. It had all been in the file. The one Laurie had spent the last few weeks painstakingly memorizing.

"The ideas were mine. It just needed a professional to bring them to life. Cream and sugar?"

They took their drinks through to a large family room with floor-to-ceiling windows that opened onto a wraparound deck overlooking the lake. Furnished in colors reminiscent of the pine forest outside, the room managed to be elegant and comfortable at the same time. Tucking her legs under her, Laurie curled into one corner of a big, comfortable sofa.

"Are you warm enough now?"

She nodded. His sweater had done the trick. And it smelled delicious. Some sort of expensive cologne lingered in its folds. A woodsy, musky, peppery evocative scent that suited him perfectly. Because, my God, he was a stunning-looking man. *Get a grip, Laurie. You knew that before you came here.* It had all been in that file. No matter how hard she had tried to keep things businesslike during her research, her eyes had developed a tendency to linger a little too long over his photograph. Much in the way his gaze kept straying to her face right now. That was hardly surprising. As far as he was concerned, she was a dead woman come to life.

"You said you're here on vacation. What job do you do?"

Keep it as close to the truth as possible. That was so important in this line of work. Like her name. If she strayed into an elaborate charade, it became too easy to slip up and get it wrong. "I'm an artist." The freelance work she did in her spare time was a hobby rather than a career, but it had always worked well as a cover story.

His raised brows told her she'd hit a nerve. Architect. Artist. She supposed it was close enough to hurt. "Will I have seen your work?"

"Probably not. I illustrate children's books."

"You must be good to make a living from it." Was this the interrogation? So soon?

Before she could respond, footsteps sounded on the hardwood floor and a voice called out, "Cam? That consignment from Pinedale…"

The man who entered the room had to be related to Cameron. The family resemblance was too strong for it to be otherwise. Mentally, Laurie reviewed the contents of the file. There was an older half brother, Vincente, and a younger brother, Bryce. Both men worked for Delaney Transportation. Assessing this man's age in comparison with Cameron and recalling the family photographs, Laurie figured she was looking at Bryce Delaney. Her memory for detail kicked in. Twenty-eight years old. Two years younger than Cameron. An injury in Afghanistan had brought an abrupt end to a promising army career.

Whoever he was, the man stopped speaking, breaking off in midsentence when he saw Laurie, his jaw dropping in an almost comical expression of surprise. His gaze swiveled from her to Cameron and back again.

"C-Carla?"

Cameron's eyes seemed to flash a warning message. "Bryce, this is Laurie Carter. Laurie, meet my reprobate brother."

She smiled at Bryce, who was still gazing at her in shock. "Nice to meet you. But I can't help thinking you mistook me for someone else."

He ran a hand through his hair in a helpless gesture. "You look just like someone we used to know." He cast a glance in Cameron's direction and encountered a frown like thunder. "Sorry, but you must admit it's uncanny. You know what? I've just remembered something I need to do. The Pinedale stuff can keep. Nice to meet you, Laurie."

When he'd gone, Laurie turned to Cameron. "What was that all about?"

Knowing that, if she played her part successfully, he'd have to confront the Carla issue sooner or later— probably sooner—she'd rehearsed this conversation. It was a strange job. One that relied on her ability to play a part 24/7, while those around her had no idea of their roles. Improvisation and fast thinking, those skills were the key to survival.

Cameron rose to his feet and went to the desk that stood in a corner of the room. It looked out over the lake, and Laurie thought what a wonderful place it would be to work. Or maybe not. Maybe that view would distract from doing anything productive. Opening one of the drawers, Cameron withdrew a framed photograph. He brought it over to Laurie and, sitting next to her on the sofa, held it out.

This is it. How you react now is everything. Aware of Cameron's eyes on her face, she took the photograph and scanned it. Although she had seen Carla Bryan's picture many times, the resemblance still took her by surprise. *She has my face. We could have been twins instead of cousins.* She didn't have to fake the widening of her eyes or the sharp intake of her breath.

"Who is this?" She raised her gaze to his face.

"Her name is Carla. She is—was—the love of my life."

"Was?" Suddenly, Laurie wasn't playing a part. All she was doing was reacting to the raw grief in those incredible dark eyes.

"Carla died a year ago."

"Oh, my Lord. I'm so sorry." Without thinking, she reached out a hand and placed it on his knee. "How did she die?"

Cameron covered her hand with his. A warm tingle of electricity spiraled from the point of his touch through to her every nerve ending. *Careful, Laurie. You know feelings are not allowed in this line of work.*

"I killed her."

The lower reaches of the Stillwater Trail were popular with tourists. Higher up was for serious hikers and hunters. Starting out at the river's edge, it wound inland and upward until it reached the highest point in the county, the treacherous climb known as Devil's Peak. Aware she would be gone for much of the day, Laurie set out early, throwing a few snacks into her backpack before she left the rented cabin that sat just at the edge of the pine forest.

Although her mother had lived in this state for only a few years, her short married life had been happy and she'd had fond memories of her time in Wyoming. Laurie's childhood had been filled with stories of the beauty of Stillwater. Laurie herself had always planned to visit one day. How strange it should have happened this way. She locked the cabin door. Not that there was anything inside that would give her away. She was too professional to compromise her personal safety.

If anything, her mother's enthusiastic praise had understated the wild perfection of this place. The air filling her lungs was crisp, clean and plentiful. Which was just as well, because the scenery really did steal your breath from you. Tucked away on the northern-most edge of the state, bordering Yellowstone National Park, West County was still largely undiscovered by tourists. It shared the grandeur and wildlife of its well-known neighbor without attracting the same sort of fame.

The trail started out deceptively flat, and Laurie had time to admire the emerald green of the gigantic trees rising on either side of her, the azure blue of the sky together with the sound of the sparkling stream tumbling alongside the path. After a few hours, she was breathing hard as the gradient increased and, by the time she reached the mountain-encircled body of water known as Wilderness Lake, she was glad of the chance to shrug off her backpack, sit on a rock and take a long slug of water.

She had been there for about ten minutes, drinking in the rugged drama of the granite landscape, when another walker came into view. Although the man wore shorts and hiking boots, he looked as though he would be more comfortable in a business suit. As he got closer, Laurie noticed the sheen of sweat on his face and bit back a smile. Special Agent Moreton had been her partner in a lengthy undercover operation and she knew him well. Even so, if she hadn't seen him in the outdoors with her own eyes she'd have continued in her belief that he was allergic to fresh air.

Moreton carried a map, and as he approached Laurie, he held it out to her, pointing to a spot on it. Anyone observing them would assume he was one hiker asking another a question about the trail. "Were you followed?"

"I don't think so." She bent her head over the map.

"That doesn't mean we're not being watched through binoculars right now, of course."

He followed her lead, covering his mouth with one hand as he spoke. "Lipreading? You think Delaney could be suspicious of you already?"

Laurie shrugged. "If he's who we think he is, he'll take good care to protect himself."

"How did he react when he saw you?"

She shot him a sideways glance. "How do you think?"

"Did he mention Carla?"

She nodded, making a pretense of turning the map and looking up at the surrounding mountains. Anything to buy a little time. When she bowed her head again, her voice was quiet. "He said he killed her."

"That's what he told police at the time. It was the grief talking. What he meant, of course, was that he failed to stop her from taking her boat out that night."

"Are you sure about that?"

Moreton looked startled. "You don't mean…? No, he was at a state function in full view of hundreds of people when she died. Mayor Delaney was the keynote speaker."

"If Cameron Delaney is all the things you tell me he is, would he think twice about getting someone else to kill his girlfriend?"

His round face became even more serious. "If you want out, you only have to say the word."

"You know me better than that, Moreton. When you approached me with this job, I knew what it involved. I'll see it through. I guess if I'm having dinner with a guy I'd like to know in advance if there's a chance he might have killed his last girlfriend."

"Dinner? Tonight?" When she nodded, he whistled. "He's a fast worker, our guy. How will you deal with it if he wants to…" He cleared his throat. "…You know?"

"You mean if he wants to have sex with me?" She almost laughed aloud at his pained expression. "I've done this sort of thing before, remember?"

"I seem to recall you have a few creative ways of keeping them at arm's length. So, now you've met him, what are your initial thoughts on Delaney?"

Laurie hesitated. First impressions were important, and she knew Moreton was asking her because he trusted her instincts. For the first time ever, she wasn't sure he was right to do so.

"You know I had my doubts about this job. Using a man's grief to get under his skin? That has never felt right to me. It was only when you showed me the file about what was going on here—what Delaney Transportation is potentially a cover for—that you convinced me. The evidence against him is about as watertight as it gets." She spread her hands, palms upward. To an observer, she could have been indicating she was clueless about the route. "Initial thoughts? The file you compiled told me he's one of the wealthiest men in the state. Each of the three Delaney brothers inherited a modest amount of money from their father. Cameron used his to set up the business, growing it into a thriving corporation within a few years. He's also a successful businessman and politician. Mayor of Stillwater. The voters love him. He'd get my vote and I don't even know what he stands for. The guy's got charisma. Underneath it all he's hurting like hell. Even when I rocked his world yesterday, the facade stayed in place. I'd say he's going to be a tough one to crack."

"If anyone can do it, you can. Delaney is one of the smoothest operators we've come across. On the surface, he's squeaky clean. He's never had a parking ticket, or filed a late tax return. We have to throw him off balance. The psychologists tell me Delaney will be drawn to someone who looks so much like Carla. He was devoted to her. You'll shake him out of his usual composure. When he's with you he may just slip up, make a mistake, however small, and allow you to get close enough to glimpse the illegal side of the business. It's a long shot, but it's all we have right now. I want to close this bastard down, but so far every attempt we've made to get someone undercover inside the firm itself has failed. This operation has been going on for a long time, but it's only recently we've had the evidence to pinpoint Delaney Transportation."

"Possibly he's started to slip up. There's no doubt that Carla's death devastated him."

Was Moreton frowning because he sensed sympathy in her voice? Even imagining he could detect a moment's hesitation? "Every time that bothers you, think about the drugs and firearms that are pumped onto the streets every day. And we both know that's not the worst part of this operation. Human trafficking. Forced prostitution. A nasty, but very lucrative, business. Many of the girls we're talking about are as young as thirteen. Some are younger. If ever you find yourself feeling sorry for Delaney, think of them."

Laurie felt a flash of anger light her eyes as she raised them to his face. "Are you questioning my commitment?"

"Never." Still in his role as the hapless hiker, Moreton folded his map and turned, shrugging as he pointed back at the trail. "Anything you need from me?" Laurie shook her head. "Next time, maybe we can find somewhere civilized like a coffee shop?"

After he'd gone, Laurie sat a while longer, allowing the peace of her surroundings to soothe her. In six years of working undercover, she had never let her emotions get to her. For a moment back then, she had come perilously close. Why was it so hard to be objective about Cameron Delaney? From the outset, she'd allowed emotion to creep in. It must be the Carla factor. It was hard not to feel a connection to the other woman when she had recently discovered their relationship. The cousin she never knew she had. And Carla had died tragically. Just when she had everything to live for. Sighing, Laurie rose and tugged her backpack into place. She'd have to work a bit harder to fight the feelings in the future. There was a job to be done. Starting with dinner tonight.

Chapter 2

Cameron gripped the steering wheel hard. What was he doing? What had possessed him to invite her to dinner? *You know what it was*, a voice inside his head chimed instantly. *You idiot. Carla is dead. This woman is not her.* Perhaps if he repeated those words often enough, his heart would stop pounding so loudly every time he thought about Laurie Carter.

Twelve months ago, he would have said his heart couldn't pound. If anyone had asked him such a stupid question, he'd have explained it wasn't possible for his heart to do anything. Because the night Carla died, Cameron had been left with a gaping hole in place of a heart. So he supposed the fact he could feel something in the region of his chest in place of the awful, aching heaviness that had been there for the last year was a positive step. He just wasn't sure it should be focused on this stranger who reminded him of Carla. *Reminded him?* He almost laughed out loud at the understatement. Laurie Carter was Carla's double. The resemblance was uncanny enough to be scary. It was frightening the hell out of Cameron. In a spine-chilling yet surprisingly exciting way.

He steered the car up the narrow track that led to the Paradise Creek vacation village. A group of twenty or more log cabins clustered together at the base of the mountain like children clinging to their mother's skirts. More and more of these places were springing up each year as people were discovering that Stillwater had as much to offer as Yellowstone. Some, like this one, were tastefully done and well managed, but there were a few eyesores that caused Cameron and his fellow council members an ongoing headache.

Cameron took his role as mayor seriously. Having been Stillwater's youngest-ever council member at twenty-four and its youngest-ever mayor at twenty-six, he never forgot his duty to the community where he grew up. His four-year term of office was coming to an end, but, in the words of the local radio station, "There's more chance of the Wyoming wind forgetting to blow than there is of Mayor Delaney not getting reelected." That validation would allow him to continue the projects he had already started. Closing down cheap tourist traps was on his list.

Leaving his car in the little parking lot at the end of the road, Cameron walked a few yards to the first cabin and knocked on the door.

"It's open. Come on in."

She doesn't sound like Carla. The thought steadied him, and he stepped straight into the open-plan living space. The place was furnished in traditional vacation-rental style. Polished pine paneling, exposed brickwork and functional furniture had been softened with colorful rugs, cushions and subdued lighting. As Cameron was taking in his surroundings, a door to his left opened and Laurie appeared.

On the drive over he had done his best to convince himself the likeness was not as strong as he remembered. It couldn't be. Unless they were identical twins, two people couldn't possibly look that alike. He'd done a pretty good job of persuading himself. Now she stood before him, a smile just beginning to light the blue depths of her eyes, and his internal lecture became so much meaningless white noise.

Laurie wore tight black jeans, heels and a gray silk blouse. Her hair, which had been wet and bedraggled when he last saw her, was styled now, the chestnut waves falling loose to just below her shoulders. She favored a less-groomed style than Carla, with only minimal makeup and jewelry. Even so, he was stunned all over again at the sight of her.

"I didn't know where we were going. I hope this is okay?"

Aware some sort of response was required, he coaxed his facial muscles so he was able to return the smile. The effort was painful. "You look amazing. And we're going to my favorite restaurant, Dino's."

And what will Dino—one of my oldest friends—say when I walk in with Carla's double on my arm? Will he ask me if I've lost my mind? Tell me I can't turn the clock back? Point out what I already know, that just because she looks like her, it would be unfair to expect Laurie to become some sort of Carla substitute?

"Is everything okay?" The smile in her eyes had faded and was on the verge of becoming a frown.

"Everything is fine." The lie came easily. Despite his misgivings, he wanted to know more about this woman who had the face of his lost love. "Shall we go?"

It was a short drive from the cabin into town, and Cameron was reminded again of the little things he'd lost when Carla died. Companionable silence and the subtle perfume of a beautiful woman were two of them. They were approaching the main street when Laurie shifted slightly in her seat. He got the impression of her bracing herself before she spoke.

"Why did you ask me out tonight?"

Cameron drew into a parking space in front of Dino's and switched the engine off before he answered. He supposed he should have anticipated the question. "You intrigue me and I'd like to get to know you better." Honest, but only a fraction of a complicated answer.

"Because I look like Carla?"

He liked the directness of her approach. It meant he could be equally blunt in return. "I'd be lying if I told you that wasn't a big part of it."

Cameron turned to face her. For a moment something shimmered in the dark space between them. Something that had nothing to do with Carla. He wanted to reach out and grab it, hold on to it, welcome it as the first sign of life going on. In twelve long, empty months, he hadn't once dared let himself believe he could ever feel anything for another woman. Hadn't wanted to. It felt like the ultimate betrayal. Now, like a fragile candle flame in the darkness, there was an unexpected flicker. He wanted to cup his hands around it and shield it. He wasn't sure what it meant. If it meant anything. Wasn't sure he wanted it to mean anything. All he knew was emotions, even conflicting and confusing ones, were better than hollow, gut-wrenching emptiness.

Before he could do or say anything, Laurie smiled. "I'm starved. I hope this place does a good steak."

When your job meant you were constantly playing a part, you had to be prepared for any eventuality. Walking into a busy, brightly lit restaurant and having the whole place fall instantly silent was a new experience. It was one Laurie hadn't been prepared for. In hindsight, she should have anticipated it. Every eye followed their progress as the hostess escorted them to a table at the rear of the room. Cameron nodded and smiled at a few people, apparently at ease with the situation even though she suspected he wasn't. *He's a politician; he's used to the limelight. Even so, this is bizarre. Do they actually think I might be Carla? That she didn't die on the lake that night after all? She faked her death and has staged a comeback? Or I'm her ghost following in Cameron's wake and he hasn't noticed me?* That last thought made her choke back a nervous snort of laughter.

Curious stares continued to be directed their way, even once they'd taken their seats. There was no way she could *not* comment. "So that was fun."

"I'm sorry. Is this too weird for you?"

Those dark eyes were achingly intense, and once again she experienced a pang of guilt. No matter who he was, or what he had done, this man was grieving.

If her mission was successful and ended in his arrest and conviction, would Laurie feel proud of her part in his undoing? She didn't want to explore that question any further. She had a feeling she wouldn't like the answer. "*Just doing my job*" didn't always cut it. Not in response to her own conscience.

"I was thinking more of you. This—" she outlined her own face with a circular motion of one finger "—must be painful for you."

"Not really. I'll admit it was a shock when I first saw you, especially when you emerged from the lake…" Laurie winced. Her plan had been to get his attention. She hadn't thought about the impact on Cameron of her wading out of the very waters where Carla had died in a boating accident. *Take his breath away? You were lucky he didn't have a heart attack.* One more reason for her to lie awake tonight questioning her own integrity. "Now? The resemblance still jolts me, but, believe it or not, I am able to convince myself you are not her."

His smile nearly undid her resolve to keep a grip on her emotions. *You can't trust this man. Every piece of intelligence points to him being the mastermind of one of the most repulsive operations we've seen in a long time.* That was what she had told herself as she read his file and studied his drop-dead-sexy photographs. Face-to-face, it didn't help. One look from those dark eyes and her insides melted.

"Delaney!" A booming voice interrupted her thoughts and made Cameron roll his eyes. "Who let you into my place while my back was turned?"

"You are about to meet Dino. He delights in living

up to his reputation for being larger than life. My advice is to roll with it."

The man who approached their table was of average build, but his personality filled the room. His sharp eyes skimmed Laurie's face before coming to rest on Cameron's countenance. She got the impression some sort of silent communication took place between them, as though Dino was reassuring himself his friend was okay, before he spoke again.

"Aren't you going to introduce me?"

"Dino, this is Laurie Carter. She's here on vacation, and yes, she looks like Carla."

Dino made a pretense of mopping his brow. "I'm glad you mentioned that. Otherwise I'd have spent the whole night wondering if you'd noticed." He winked at Laurie. "You do know every single person in this place is talking about you, don't you?"

She groaned. "Is it that bad?"

"It would have happened anyway because you look so much like her." She decided she liked Dino, liked his bluntness and his warm smile. "Put you together with our esteemed mayor here and you've given our little community the best bit of gossip it's had since—" he scratched his head "—well, I can't remember anything this exciting. Maybe the last time was when Sarah Milligan's daughter took off with that no-good, out-of-town boyfriend of hers. Remember that? We talked about it for weeks."

"*You* talked about it for weeks," Cameron corrected him. "I had other things on my mind."

"That's right. It was only about six weeks after Carla died, wasn't it?" Unabashed, Dino nodded agreement with his own question. "So, what are you guys eating?"

"We haven't decided. Some moron interrupted us before we had a chance to look at the menu."

Ignoring Cameron's deliberate rudeness, Dino grinned at Laurie. "I recommend the steak. And maybe a different companion." With a wave of his hand, he was gone, pausing to talk to various diners as he made his way back to the kitchen.

"I like him." Laurie smiled as she opened her menu.

"So do I, but don't tell him. His ego is big enough already."

She studied the food choices while taking in her surroundings. Stillwater was the county seat. The most densely peopled town in a sparsely inhabited county in the least-populated state in America was still going to be classed as a small town by anyone's standards. Her internet searches had shown her a picturesque place, cradled by mountains, largely untouched by time, reveling in its own Western charm. A website had gone on to expand on how this town was home to cowboy history, an immense outdoor playground, with fine Western dining and friendly faces. It looked like Dino had tried to capture all of that in his restaurant. It worked. The place had a homey, easy feel, and judging by the number of diners, the food must be good, as well.

They ordered steaks, and once the waiter had brought beer for Cameron and soda for Laurie, she decided to kick things up a notch. "Tell me, how do you find time to be mayor and also run a business?"

"I don't sleep." His face remained expressionless for a few seconds, then he grinned. "Seriously? I founded the company with the money my father left me. I'm the person who built it up from nothing, put the hours in to make it a success. I'm still the CEO. But these days my role is strategic, not hands-on. I pay other people, namely my two brothers, to do the day-to-day stuff. Politics is pretty full on." He waved a hand, encompassing the restaurant. "You see quaint, laid-back and charming? You wouldn't believe what goes on beneath the surface."

"So your brothers actually run the company?" This was an interesting piece of information. One that hadn't been obvious from the file. This was why it was so important to get someone in here on the ground. *But don't clutch at straws. What he's telling you doesn't let him off the hook. He's still the one in overall charge.*

"Bryce, who you met briefly, takes care of operations. My older brother, Vincente, is the money man—"

"Did I hear my name being taken in vain?"

Two men had approached the table without them being aware of it. The one who spoke was dark, but that was the only resemblance between the two brothers. Vincente Delaney was tall with a strong, sinewy build, his looks reflecting his Italian mother's heritage. In any other company, his proud features, neatly trimmed beard and olive skin would have been considered handsome. In comparison with Cameron, Laurie decided he didn't quite match up.

"Is the whole town in here tonight?" There was a trace of a groan in Cameron's voice.

"Is this Dino's and is it Saturday? If so, you've answered your own question by coming here." Laurie's attention was drawn to Vincente's companion, a man whose voice rumbled out his reply. She had heard the expression "a bear of a man" without having seen anyone who embodied what it meant until now. This man was huge, blond and imposing.

"Laurie, I guess more introductions are required. As you may have gathered, this is my brother Vincente. And this is Grant Becker."

Laurie studied Grant with interest, and found her gaze being returned by a pair of intense blue eyes. There was curiosity and something deeper in that light gaze. He didn't seem the type to be strongly influenced by her resemblance to Carla, but there was no doubt it had affected him. Then he roused himself and smiled. It was a boyish, charming expression.

The pictures she had seen didn't do him justice. In the flesh the sheriff of West County was younger and better-looking than his online image, although she could hardly tell him so. Moreton had informed her that the local police, both the city police department and the county sheriff's office, remained unaware of the federal presence in Stillwater. It had struck Laurie as a strange move not to involve the local police in the undercover operation. Moreton had explained there were two reasons for the decision. The first was what Moreton described as the "sensitive and unidentified operational radius," by which she assumed he meant there was no way of knowing how widespread the trafficking might be, or how many people might be involved. Secondly, and perhaps more important, Cameron Delaney and Grant Becker had been friends since first grade.

"When Bryce told me you looked like Carla, I thought he was exaggerating." Vincente was speaking, and Laurie turned her attention back to him. "I see now he wasn't."

Laurie wasn't sure she liked the way Vincente's eyes assessed her. Maybe he was being protective of his brother. Cameron had been badly hurt when Carla died, after all. Possibly his judgment of a woman who looked so much like her might be impaired. Also, Cameron was a very wealthy man. For all Vincente knew, Laurie could be a gold digger out to manipulate his brother and take him for all she could get. Even so, those eyes bothered her. They seemed to look right through her.

Grant Becker, on the other hand, had an open, honest expression that invited trust. Having stared long and hard at Laurie, he turned back to Cameron with a slight smile. "I'm guessing you'd like us to leave you in peace?"

Cameron returned the other man's expression with relief. "You guessed right."

Vincente looked as though he might like to protest at this arrangement, but Grant slung an arm around his shoulders, forcing him to walk away with him. "Nice meeting you, Laurie. Enjoy your evening."

When they'd gone, Cameron turned to Laurie with an apologetic expression. "In this town everyone knows everyone else. It makes them think they have a right to intrude on your business."

"I like it. It's very different from what I'm used to."

It wasn't just something to say. She had been here only a few days, but she liked the feel of this town. It saddened her that she was here under false pretenses. *What* is *this? This is what I do. I trap the bad guys. I can't suddenly feel sentimental and regretful about it.*

"Where exactly in California do you live?"

"San Diego." It was true, even though she hadn't been back there in what felt like forever. Lately it had been one undercover job after another. Home felt like something other people had.

The food arrived just in time for her to avoid any further details. While they ate, Laurie turned the talk to what she should see during her vacation. She was an expert at keeping the conversation away from herself. Unwilling to ask too many questions about his business this early in the relationship, she steered Cameron onto the other topic that interested her. She was surprised to find he was quite willing to talk about Carla.

"Can I ask why she was out on the lake at night?"

"Carla was a keen sailor. More than keen. It was her passion. She took part in competitions. She spent every spare minute practicing. The night she died, I was going to a function where I had to stay over. It was a foul night, and there was a storm brewing. She was determined to go out on the lake. There was a big, twenty-four-hour race coming up and she said her night vision was bothering her. I tried to persuade her not to go, to come with me instead." A corner of his mouth creased in an expression of remembered frustration. "She wouldn't listen. We argued. If I'd tried a bit harder, maybe stayed home with her…"

The compulsion to touch him was overwhelming. Reaching out, Laurie covered his hand with hers. "You couldn't have known how it would turn out."

He turned his hand so he could grip her fingers. "It means a lot, being able to talk about her. Other people tiptoe around me, thinking if they don't mention her the pain might go away. Dino, as you may have noticed, is the only one who doesn't."

"What was she like?" Asking wasn't just part of the job. She was curious about Carla the person. Carla her cousin.

He smiled. "Well, I think we've already established she was stubborn. She was also beautiful, clever, talented and witty. She used to tell me I was lucky to have her and I'd have to work hard every day to keep her."

"Yet it sounds like she was as devoted to you as you were to her."

"She was, but that last bit was true." He tossed back the last of his beer. "Carla had many admirers, including a very persistent secret one."

Laurie tilted her head on one side, considering that statement. "Persistent and secret don't seem to go together."

"Whoever he was, he used to send her an arrangement of red roses in the shape of a heart once a week. No message, no other gifts. Just the flowers."

"That's quite sweet, really."

"Carla thought so, too. I thought it was creepy." He laughed. "Maybe I was just being macho and possessive."

"You were together a long time. Did you have any plans to get married?" It felt like an intrusive question, but he'd been open so far and she was curious about why, when he clearly loved Carla so much, they hadn't made their relationship permanent. His face clouded slightly, and it was clear the question provoked a memory that made him uncomfortable. "I'm sorry. I shouldn't have asked."

Cameron shook his head. "It was the one subject on which we couldn't agree. Yet it was such an important one. Looking back now, I wish—" He broke off, taking a moment to collect his emotions. "Carla didn't want to stay in Wyoming, and I could never see myself living anywhere else. I wanted the whole fairy tale. Marriage, kids, big goofy dog, family life, all the things my own folks had. Carla wasn't the maternal type. Her own childhood had been traumatic." He hesitated, and she sensed this was a big part of who Carla was. Even though she had learned recently that she was related to Carla, she knew nothing about her early life. Clearly Cameron wasn't ready to go into details. "We could never meet halfway on it. Now, in hindsight, I think if I'd done it her way, upped and left Stillwater, gone to live in a big city, she wouldn't have been on the lake that night."

His eyes were twin pools of anguish. There was a trace of guilt in his expression and something more. A plea for reassurance. Carla just went down a notch or two in Laurie's estimation. *Sure, cling to your independence. Stick to your principles. But at the risk of losing a man who loved you to distraction? A man like Cameron Delaney? No, Carla, I can't understand where you were coming from. Mind you,* her rational mind kicked in, *let's not forget we are talking about a likely criminal mastermind...even though Carla may not have known about that facet of his life.*

"I'm a great believer in fate. I think there is a time and a place for everything and, while we control some aspects of our destiny, there are other things that are meant to be." Her hand was still in his, and she clasped his fingers tighter. "You may never know what it was, but it's possible there is a reason why Carla was meant to be on the lake that night."

Cameron didn't reply, but she thought some of the tension went out of his frame. Looking around, Laurie was amazed to see the restaurant was empty and they were the only ones left. A glance at her watch told her it was close to midnight. How had all those hours passed without her being conscious of them? Cameron settled their tab and escorted her out to the car.

When they reached the vacation village, Cameron walked Laurie to her cabin. This was always the tricky part. *Make sure he wants to see you again without coming on too strong.* For the first time ever, she felt a pang of regret at that necessity. It would be so easy to give in to her instincts right now and invite Cameron in for coffee. To explore where this attraction might take them. Instead, she rose on the tips of her toes, touched her fingertips to his shoulder and pressed a chaste kiss onto his cheek.

"Thank you for a lovely evening." Determinedly, she ignored the insistent tingle that shimmered through to her nerve endings as her lips brushed his flesh. His delicious scent invaded her nostrils, and she resisted the temptation to press her face into the warm curve of his neck.

His face was in shadow, but she was aware of his eyes probing hers. "Can we do it again?" Somehow she sensed those words didn't come easy. Cameron was fighting an internal battle. Whether he was winning or losing wasn't clear.

"I'd like that."

When he'd gone, she unlocked the door and stepped inside. Years of training had conditioned her. She scrutinized the room, checking for signs that anything might be out of place. The cabin looked exactly as she'd left it. Except for one thing.

In the middle of the table there was a heart-shaped arrangement of dark red roses.

Chapter 3

The city of Cody, in neighboring Park County, looked a lot like the city of Stillwater. It had the same wide main street, historic buildings and backdrop of snow-capped mountains. Laurie parked the rental car and looked out at her surroundings, drawing in a deep breath to steady her nerves. In all her years of working undercover, she had never had to make emergency contact with her handler. She supposed there had to be a first time for everything. And these circumstances certainly were unusual. Grabbing the portfolio of pictures that were her cover story together with the paper bag in which she had concealed the flower arrangement, she locked up the car.

When she found the nondescript attorney's office, she made her way up the steps at the side of the building to the second floor. Moreton, who was leaning back in his chair drinking coffee and reading a newspaper, looked startled when, after a brief knock, she walked into the tiny office he was using.

"Another ten minutes and I'd have been gone." He indicated the clock on the wall. The arrangement was he would be there for two hours each day from 9 a.m. "How are you?"

"Exactly how did Carla die?" Laurie didn't want to waste time on pleasantries.

"In a boating accident. You read the file."

"That's not what I meant. What was the specific injury that killed her?"

Moreton frowned. "It's always been assumed she drowned."

"Assumed? Did you actually read the autopsy report?"

"Laurie, sit down. Take a breath. What's this all about?"

Instead of doing as he said, she produced the heart-shaped flower arrangement from the paper bag and placed it on his desk. His eyes remained on the flowers for a moment or two, before lifting to her face. His expression was blank. "That was left in my cabin while I was out last night."

"Someone got into your cabin?" Moreton pulled a pad of paper toward him and flipped it over to a blank page. "Who else has a key?"

"We can check that out later. How they got in is not the most important thing." Moreton waited for her to continue. "Cameron told me last night Carla had a secret admirer. Someone who sent her a heart-shaped arrangement of red roses every week."

"And you think whoever sent it was the same person who sent these to you? And that he could have murdered Carla?" Moreton was scribbling notes, following her thought processes fast.

"You have to admit it's a possibility."

He remained quiet while he studied the flowers. Laurie knew that look. It meant his analytical mind was weighing every probability. But she caught a glimpse of something else in his expression. A glimmer of acute emotion that looked a lot like excitement. It was gone as soon as it appeared. And it puzzled her. Moreton didn't do excitement. Didn't really do emotion. Maybe it had been a long time since he'd come across such an interesting lead with the potential of opening up a whole new case.

"Okay. I agree it's possible Carla Bryan had a stalker. There's even a chance she was murdered by the person who was sending her these flowers, and her death was mistakenly written off as an accident. Let's not rule anything out. The first thing I need to do is what you've asked, and double-check the coroner's report. I'll let you know the actual cause of Carla's death."

"We could also try to find out where these flowers came from and if any were sent to Carla from the same supplier."

"We?" He raised a brow. "You can't do any investigating. You are not Detective Bryan of the San Diego Police Department. She hasn't been around for a while, remember? You are Laurie Carter, children's storybook illustrator, here in Wyoming on vacation. I don't want you putting yourself at risk."

"Okay." Laurie felt a blush tinge her cheeks. Moreton's reminder put her firmly in her place. In this investigation, she was powerless. In reality, she didn't exist. Even her name was fake. She actually was Amy Carter-Bryan. Her middle name was Laurie, and that was what her family called her. She was an undercover detective in the San Diego Police Department. Two years ago her department had worked alongside the FBI on a series of homicides. Laurie and Moreton had collaborated closely on that case.

When Moreton needed someone here in Wyoming to get close to Cameron Delaney, he had begun his research. Pictures of Carla had instantly made him think of the young San Diego detective he had worked with. Incredibly, further probing had unearthed the information that the two women were related. Moreton had approached Laurie's chief with a request for her to be assigned to the Bureau for this case…and here she was.

Laurie felt obliged to ask the question that had been bothering her since the previous night. "Could Cameron Delaney be wary of me? He might have made up this whole story about the flowers as an elaborate way of scaring me off. He could have had someone plant these in my cabin, in which case, I've already blown the whole operation."

Moreton considered the suggestion, his head on one side. "I checked your credentials before I recruited you. You've never aroused any distrust before. If Delaney wanted to get rid of you, the flowers seem like an elaborate way to do it. He doesn't strike me as that kind of guy. But you tell me what you want to do. If you think Carla's stalker is targeting you, or Delaney's guard is up, don't go back to Stillwater. Come in now."

Laurie had been afraid of this, had actually considered not bringing the flowers to him in case he insisted on ending the operation immediately. At least he was offering her options. "Let's not be hasty. You've been trying for a long time to get someone close to Delaney Transportation. I'm not there yet, but I'm the best you've got. I won't take any chances with my personal safety."

He pursed his lips thoughtfully, then he nodded. She got the feeling she'd given him the answer he wanted. Hell, she was having a lot of feelings today. Most of them uncomfortable. "Let's meet again tomorrow morning. By that time, I'll have had a chance to get the information we need. We'll take it from there. In the meantime, you have your gun with you, right?"

"Of course I do."

Having made arrangements to return to Moreton's office the following day, Laurie headed back to her car. She was surprised and relieved Moreton had listened to her and, having done so, had not insisted on ending the operation there and then. It was a lack of caution that was out of character with what she knew of him, but then, what did she really know of Moreton? She didn't even know his first name. Their interactions were limited to discussions of the case, and this one felt different from any other she'd been on. So different that she was tipped off balance. She had come here certain about her role, but now there was a possible new element to be considered that was throwing everything off-kilter.

She spent the drive back to Stillwater deep in thought, much of it going over the same ground she had covered the night before. She was already convinced Carla's death was not an accident. But, if that was the case, who had killed her and why? The only person who seemed to be in the clear was Cameron. He had a watertight alibi for the night Carla died. Hundreds of people could vouch for his presence at the political function. He was the person who had told Laurie about Carla's secret admirer and the flowers he sent her. And, unless he had an accomplice who had carried out the task on his behalf, he had been with Laurie last night and couldn't have left the flowers in her cabin.

She was so preoccupied she had to slam on her brakes hard to avoid a truck as it pulled across the road in front of her and into the entrance to a concealed track. The black-painted trailer bore the words "Delaney Transportation" in bold red letters across its side. *A timely reminder of the real reason why I'm here. Perhaps I should complain to Cameron about the carelessness of the driver?* She pulled away again, watching the truck in her rearview mirror as it disappeared along the track. Away to her right, a hill shaped like an inverted funnel caught her eye, standing out stark and unusual against the surrounding flat landscape.

Laurie's mother had talked to her about the openness of Wyoming. The vast tracts of unoccupied country through which you could drive and drive without seeing another vehicle. Towns with their population only just creeping into double figures, spread so far apart it took forever to get from one to the other. Scenery so beautiful it hurt your heart to look at it. Traditional ranches stretching beyond the horizon in every direction. Maybe her mother had instilled a love of this land into Laurie with her stories, but it pulled at her. It was a raw, powerful, unexpected feeling, unlike anything she had experienced for any other place.

On her arrival in Stillwater, Laurie stopped for groceries. Pulling up in front of the general store, Milligan's, she tried to recall where she had heard the name mentioned. With her finely tuned memory for detail she recalled Dino saying something about a girl called Milligan running off with an unsuitable boyfriend. Small-town life.

Laurie supposed it was like having an extended family. It was a complete contrast to her own life. She had grown up without a father and was only discovering now that she had a cousin. Who knew how many other family members she had that she was unaware of? For her whole life, it had just been her and her mom. Because she hadn't known any differently, she had accepted their lack of family and close friends as normal. She knew, of course, that her fierce independence and determination not to rely on others stemmed from that isolation. Now, for the first time, she thought it must be kind of comforting to think everyone knew your name and watched out for you.

Laurie was the only customer, and she selected her few purchases, making her way to the single checkout. The woman behind the counter put aside the magazine she had been reading and greeted her with a listless gaze. Laurie's eyes were drawn to the poster at the side of the checkout. It was a photograph of a pretty, smiling girl with blue eyes and long dark hair. Emblazoned across the top in bold font were the words "Have you seen this girl?" Below, in smaller lettering, were details of when and where Deanna Milligan was last seen, a plea for her to contact her mom and a cell phone number. Laurie had glimpsed a few similar posters around town, but this was the first time she had seen one up close.

An icy little worm wound its way up Laurie's spine as she studied the picture. Although Deanna Milligan was much younger than Carla, they both had the same coloring and there were some similarities about their delicate features.

"I'm so sorry." She nodded to the poster while the woman continued to scan her purchases. There was enough of a resemblance between this woman and the girl in the picture for Laurie to make the assumption that this was Deanna's mom. What had Dino said her name was? Sarah Milligan, that was it.

Sarah's eyes instantly filled with tears. "It's the not knowing that's so hard, you know? If she'd just get in touch, tell me where she is. I don't understand why it had to be like this." She withdrew a handkerchief from her pocket and blew her nose into it. "I mean, I didn't like the guy she was seeing—thought he was too old for her—but running away with him? We could have worked it out."

"So you met her boyfriend?" That didn't fit the same secret-admirer approach as Carla. Maybe Laurie was seeing connections where none existed. Lots of girls had blue eyes and dark hair. She did herself. *Things are complicated enough. Don't go trying to make them worse.*

"Once or twice. As I said, I didn't like him. He wasn't from around here. His name was Xavier." Sarah spat the name out as though it was an insult. "Xavier-Quentin Fontaine. He made a big deal of making sure he used his *full* name. Sounds kinda French, doesn't

it? He was a charmer. All that blond hair and those
baby blue eyes. Flashing his big, charming smile at
every woman who came his way. Deanna was smit-
ten. She even started lying to me. Told me she wasn't
seeing him anymore, that he'd left town. But I knew it
wasn't true. Why, he was still sending her those flowers, even though she tried to tell me they were from
a secret admirer—"

"Flowers?" Laurie couldn't help herself. She interrupted the other woman's flow, her voice a staccato
exclamation.

"Every week. Right up until the day she left home."
Laurie's heart gave a sickening thud as she anticipated
Sarah's next words. "Fancy dark red roses in the shape
of a heart."

"Laurie!" Cameron caught up to her as she reached
her car at the front of the store. "You were lost in your
own world. I've called your name twice already."

She turned her head, a half smile piercing her distracted expression. "Pardon?"

"Hey, are you okay?" He scanned her face, amazed
at how he could have become so attuned to this woman's moods in such a short space of time. The slight
crease between those glorious blue eyes told him
something was bothering her. He wanted to reach out
a fingertip and smooth it away.

He had spent the previous night tossing and turning and lecturing himself on the foolishness of getting
too close too fast. Getting close at all, never mind the
timescales. His brain had given his body a lecture. It
was choosing the familiar. Latching on to Laurie because it was easy. If he'd passed her in the street, she'd

have turned his head. The fact she'd fallen unconscious into his arms had thrust her remarkable similarity to Carla right under his nose. Fate had given his sex drive a wake-up call. Her presence had acted like an injection of a performance-enhancing drug directly into his previously dormant sexual urges. It was all wrong. *You want her because of how she looks, not for who she is. No woman deserves that.* That was how his speech to himself had gone last night. Now she was before him again in person, and every sensible, reasonable word flew out of his head again. His body took over, shutting his brain down.

Laurie attempted a smile in response to his question. On anyone else it might have worked. Because, in the short time he'd known her, Cameron had become an expert on her expressions; he wasn't fooled.

"Oh, I'm sorry. I was just talking to the store owner—" she waved a hand toward Milligan's "—and she told me about her daughter. I guess I felt bad for her."

He still wasn't convinced by her reply, but he let it pass. He'd known Laurie Carter for twenty-four hours. It didn't exactly give him the right to worry about her. Hard on the heels of that thought came a question. *Does that mean I want to worry about her?* Last night he hadn't thought beyond the physical wanting. Maybe he should just put any thinking about Laurie aside for another time. Along with the urgent desire he had to draw her into his arms and kiss away that worried look.

"It was a bad business. Sarah was widowed when Deanna was a baby. She devoted her life to her daughter, but they struggled. Making ends meet was always hard, and Deanna had a few problems as she was growing up. She went off the rails when she was in her teens. Now Deanna is gone, Sarah has no one. Loneliness and stress have taken its toll on her well-being."

"That's obvious from the way she talks."

Laurie opened the trunk of her car and shifted a large artist's portfolio case to one side so she could place her groceries inside. As he helped her with the groceries, Cameron eyed the portfolio in surprise. "I thought you were on vacation."

"You should try telling my agent about that." She rolled her eyes. "To be fair, I decided on this vacation after I agreed to a deadline."

"Tell me you're not working so hard you can't join me for dinner tonight?" The words were out before he could stop them. What happened to sensible? He'd convinced himself the logical thing would be to not ask her on the second date he'd mentioned as they parted last night. Now he was practically holding his breath as he waited for her answer.

"That would be nice."

Cameron watched as she drove away. It was probably a good thing Laurie was only here on vacation. The feelings he was developing toward her were threatening to become fairly explosive. And, while he welcomed the signs he was able to feel again, he wasn't sure he was ready for another relationship. Particularly with someone who looked so much like Carla. He knew what other people would say.

My God, I'd say it myself if I was on the outside looking in! You are still grieving. Looking for a substitute. Yes, it's time to move on. Just make sure you get it right. If the time is right—and it seems it is— find a short, plump blonde who bears no resemblance to Carla. Start with friendship and fun. This fierce, burning intensity can't be the right way to go.

Now Laurie had gone, his head was back in control. He knew she wasn't Carla. Apart from her looks, she was nothing like her. Sometime during that meal at Dino's last night—he wasn't quite sure when or how it had happened—he'd stopped thinking about her as the-girl-who-looked-like-Carla and started to think of her as Laurie. And he liked *Laurie*. A lot. Too much for his own comfort. And that bothered him almost as much as all the other stuff.

A hand on his shoulder startled him out of his thoughts. He swung around to face Bryce's laughing features. "You planning on standing there all day gazing into space? Because, if not, you can buy me a coffee."

"How come I get to do the buying?" Cameron asked as they crossed the road to The Daily Grind coffee shop.

"Why change the habit of a lifetime?" Bryce leaned on the counter as Cameron ordered. "Anyway, you owe me."

"Vincente?" They took their drinks over to a table near the window.

"Who else?"

"What's he done now?"

Bryce's expression was long suffering. "Poking his nose in where it's not wanted. When you divided up the responsibilities between us, it was clear I was to take charge of operations. Yet he insists on interfering with the distribution routes and driver's schedules. As soon as I have them organized for the week ahead, I find out he's changed things."

"Why would he do that?" Cameron dragged his mind away from thoughts of Laurie and onto what Bryce was telling him with an effort. Vincente was always difficult. When they were growing up, he had always been conscious of his status as a half brother and jealous of the closeness between Cameron and Bryce. Their mother had done her best to make him feel included, but Vincente had resented Sandy Delaney. He insisted on seeing her as the woman who had usurped his mother's place, even though his parents had been divorced for more than a year when Kane Delaney remarried. And despite the fact Giovanna Alberti—Vincente's Italian mother had reverted to her maiden name as soon as the divorce papers were finalized—couldn't wait to return to her home in Florence, declaring the wide-open spaces and sparse population of Wyoming stifled her spirit.

Cameron guessed that deep down Vincente blamed his father for Giovanna's abandonment and that unhappiness had manifested itself as bitterness. It wasn't the sort of conversation he could ever have with his half brother. They didn't have a close enough relationship, but he sometimes wondered if Vincente recognized those emotions and regretted all those sour, wasted years.

Bryce shrugged. "You know what he's like. He can't help himself. How would he like it if I went into *his* office and started altering the company accounts?"

Cameron stifled a sigh. "You want me to speak to him?" Vincente had always been jealous of Cameron, labeling his brother their father's favorite, and blaming Cameron for his own failings. Despite this, Cameron was the only person his stubborn, hotheaded older brother had ever listened to.

"Would you?" The frown cleared from Bryce's brow.

"I'll stop by the office tomorrow morning."

While she was undercover, Laurie steered clear of the internet. Even when she wasn't working, she adhered to a strict code of conduct. She was scrupulously careful and never did anything that left a trail. On this job, she had an encrypted laptop that she used to keep in touch with Moreton and Mike Samuels, Moreton's boss and her only other FBI contact. Moreton assured her the security on her laptop was cast-iron. No one would be able to trace her, and only someone with specialist skills would be able to get through the firewall. Laurie powered the machine up now, tapping an impatient finger as she waited for it to start.

Xavier-Quentin Fontaine. It was hardly a common name. If Deanna Milligan was with him, it should be fairly easy to find out. Laurie started with Deanna's social media accounts. Chillingly, they hadn't been touched since she went missing. It could mean she didn't want to be found, of course. But, prior to her disappearance, Deanna had been very active online, documenting every detail of her daily life from what she had for breakfast to pictures each time she changed her nail polish. It was most unusual for people to alter their habits so dramatically. And Deanna had been close to her friends and family. Even though Sarah had disliked Xavier-Quentin, there was no real reason for Deanna to completely lose touch with her mother.

And it seemed odd she wouldn't keep in touch with other people she knew.

So, on to the man himself. Laurie did an internet search for Xavier-Quentin Fontaine. What she found was even more disturbing than Deanna's on-line silence. Because, if she had the right man, Xavier-Quentin had been killed in a road traffic accident in Montana two weeks *before* Deanna disappeared. Deanna wouldn't have known about his death at the time she went missing because Xavier-Quentin—if it was him—had been so badly disfigured in the smash it took the authorities another week to identify him.

With a sinking feeling in her gut, Laurie studied the newspaper report that confirmed the victim's identity. The photograph alongside the report showed a handsome, blue-eyed, blond-haired man with a charming smile. Sarah's words came back to her. *Flashing that smile...* Of course Deanna could have gone looking for Xavier-Quentin, discovered he was dead and been too embarrassed to return. It seemed a far-fetched scenario.

It seemed more likely that Deanna had not left Stillwater in search of Xavier-Quentin. Sarah Milligan had assumed that he was the one sending Deanna the flowers, but he was already dead when the last arrangements were sent. Which prompted a new set of questions. *Who was sending the flowers? And what did happen to Deanna Milligan?*

If Laurie's instincts were right—*dear God, let me not be right*—and Carla and Deanna had been stalked and then murdered by the same man, the secret admirer who sent them flowers, was it possible they were not the only ones? If the link between the two of them had been missed, it was entirely possible other connections had been overlooked. How many other local women had been sent a heart-shaped arrangement of dark red roses?

Heart pounding, Laurie started another internet search right there. *Heart-shaped arrangement of dark red roses.* The typed words produced a surprising variety of images. None of them looked like the ones that had been left in her cabin. None of them tied into any of the local florists listed on her laptop screen.

Picking up her cell phone, she started calling the flower stores. Her questions were the same for each. A friend of hers had been sent a heart-shaped arrangement of red roses that she'd loved. As a surprise gift she wanted to send the same arrangement, but she wasn't sure where it had come from. Yes, the same arrangement every week. No? Okay, thanks for your time. Her calls were hampered by an annoyingly intermittent phone signal. It hadn't happened before, and it was just typical that her cell phone connection should keep cutting out now when she was in the middle of these important calls.

None of the florists had made up the arrangement Carla had received. No one seemed to be commenting on social media about how strange it was they were receiving heart-shaped roses from a secret admirer. She didn't know what to make of that result. Good news? That sixth sense she'd developed over years of doing this job told her it wasn't. All it meant was if there was a link, she hadn't found it yet.

Three hours later, and it looked like her sixth sense was right. In the last three years, five women—not including Carla and Deanna—all with dark hair and

blue eyes, had disappeared from Stillwater. When
she widened that search to include the whole county,
the number rose to twelve. With a sinking feeling in
her stomach, Laurie lined up the pictures of the five
women from Stillwater alongside those of Carla and
Deanna on her computer screen. She swallowed hard,
her hand instinctively reaching for her phone. Who
was she going to call? Oddly, her first thought had
been Cameron Delaney. *Good thinking, Laurie. Call
the criminal mastermind who might just be at the heart
of this.* Moreton? If she called in now, she'd be on the
next flight to San Diego and would never get any answers. A glance at her phone told her she had no signal anyway. She frowned. That had been happening
on and off since last night. It had to be the mountains.

She forced her attention back to the laptop screen.
The resemblance between those seven girls wasn't
just a passing likeness. It was striking. *Eight girls, not
seven. My picture should be up there.* Each had dark
curls, bright blue eyes, creamy skin and a dazzling
smile. *This guy has a type, and I'm it.* Her thoughts
kept flying off at disordered tangents. Okay, focus.
Carla. She was the odd one out. The others all disappeared, seemingly without a trace. Although there
was still a long way to go to be sure about that, Laurie's gut instinct was sending her some very strong
messages. But Carla hadn't disappeared; she had been
killed. If Laurie was right, her death made to look
like an accident. Why was that? Carla had to be the
key to this. Laurie scribbled down a few notes in her
unique shorthand, jotting down the names of the missing girls, locations and the dates they were last seen,
together with her observations and questions. Tech-

nology was all very well, but sometimes she liked to do it the old-fashioned way.

A knock on the cabin door startled her, and she glanced around, surprised to see the light was already dropping into late afternoon. It was still too early for it to be Cameron. Quickly closing the laptop lid, she checked the window at the side of the door. When she saw who it was, she knew things must be bad.

"Moreton?" He stepped inside as soon as Laurie opened the door.

"Pack your stuff. As of now, you're out of here."

"Would you care to tell me why?" She couldn't disobey an order from him, but she was sure as hell going to question it.

"You were right about Carla." He turned the key in the lock, removed it from the door and placed it in his pocket. Gesturing to the sofa, he sat down.

Laurie joined him. "How did the police miss it?"

"It was a difficult one. She did drown, there's no question about it. That was the cause of death. It was what happened to her before she drowned that's the issue. The coroner documented a number of injuries that were caused immediately before her death, including—and I quote—'a blow to the back of the head and bruising to the throat consistent with strangulation.'"

"She was murdered." Laurie's heart gave a sickening thud.

"Not officially. *Consistent with.* Those were the key words. It was the water in her lungs that killed her. The coroner's verdict was accidental death."

"Someone was on that boat with her. He killed her." Laurie reached for her laptop and opened the lid, pointing to the photographs. "Each of these women has disappeared from her home in Stillwater over the last three years. Carla is the only one we know for sure has died."

Moreton studied the screen for a few seconds, then his eyes went to Laurie's face and lingered there. Why did she get the feeling he wasn't surprised by what she was telling him? "There's a lot more I need to tell you, but like I said, it's time to go. Right now." His voice was deadly serious. "We'll get someone else in to investigate Delaney Transportation as soon as we can, but your safety is more important."

She rose to her feet. "Does Mike Samuels know about this?"

Laurie had never met Samuels, Moreton's superior in the agency, but she knew his word was final. On everything. Moreton didn't quite meet her eyes, a fact that did nothing for her confidence. "I'll fill you in on everything while we drive to the airport."

Laurie nodded. If there was a serial killer on the loose and her handler was keeping secrets, she wanted out of here. "I'll get my stuff."

As soon as she got into the bedroom, she took her suitcase down from on top of the wardrobe and started pulling clothes out of the closet. After a minute or two, a sound from the next room caught her attention and she paused, listening intently. Moreton must have been moving around restlessly, impatient for her to be finished. Next there was a loud thud followed by silence.

"Moreton?" She tried to keep the note of panic out of her voice. There was no reply.

Was she imagining it, or could she sense a presence just outside the bedroom door? Someone listening on the other side of the wooden panels? Her supercharged perception told her she could hear heavy breathing. Then, just as she thought she might go mad with anticipation, she heard the sound of footsteps moving away. There was a pause, followed by the unmistakable sound of one of the windows being raised. She judged the sound to have come from the rear of the cabin. Quiet descended once more.

With a cold feeling of dread closing around her heart like icy fingers, Laurie moved across the bedroom. With shaking fingers, she reached into the top drawer of the bedside table. Her hand closed around her gun and she withdrew it, willing her breathing into a regular rhythm at the same time. On silent feet, she made her way to the door and opened it a crack. She couldn't see anything. Moreton was out of the line of her vision.

Opening the door wider, Laurie gripped the gun tight and slid through the gap into the other room. The sight that greeted her almost made her heart stop beating altogether. Moreton lay on his back in front of the fire. Blood had formed a puddle around him where his throat had been cut. On his chest someone had placed a heart-shaped arrangement of red roses.

Chapter 4

Cameron pulled up in the parking lot at the vacation village. He needed to do something about this overwhelming craving to see Laurie. No, it was so much more than a craving. It was a need, an all-consuming desire. How the hell had this happened so fast? He had to restrain himself from jumping out of the car and bounding along the path to her cabin like an overeager teenager. He hadn't felt like this since the early days with Carla. He shook his head, trying to clear it. He had *never* felt like this. That was what was so scary. Even with Carla he'd never experienced anything that came close to this restless, burning hunger.

He tried to place what it was that made Laurie different. It was difficult to explain it, even to himself. She was a woman of contrasts. He could say that with confidence, even in the short time he had known her. She was empathetic, yet practical. Feminine, yet strong. Her feelings ran deep, yet her laughter was quick and infectious. All those things drew him to her and made him want to know her better.

Sitting with his head bent and his hands gripping the steering wheel, he allowed himself to think the unthinkable. What if there was something in this? If they let themselves explore these feelings? Maybe he could ask her to stay here in Stillwater once her vacation was over. Her work was freelance and seemed like the sort of thing she could do anywhere.

No! He forced his thoughts away from that direction. He'd come to a decision, and he wasn't going to change his mind. This was all too much. And way too soon. He'd known Laurie Carter for less than three days and already he was planning a future with her? What the hell was this hold she was exerting over him? It didn't matter. He'd come here earlier than they'd arranged to tell her he couldn't see her tonight, and that would be the end of it. No more. His feelings were too fragile. He couldn't put his heart through this sort of strain, not when it was just starting to recover from Carla's death. So why did the decision he'd just made cause a sharp, knife-like pain right in the center of his gut and a fresh ache in his heart? That would be because he'd done something he'd sworn he wouldn't do. He had made himself a promise that he wouldn't risk another heartbreak. Now, he'd let someone get close... and he didn't even know how it had crept up on him.

Purposefully, he climbed out of the car and made his way to Laurie's cabin, pausing for a moment before he knocked. He would keep his distance. Laurie came across as an intuitive, trustworthy sort of person. He thought she'd understand where he was coming from. Raising his fist, he rapped on the door. Even as he did it, a thought flashed through his mind. *Why did you have to come here? You could have called.* There was no response to his knock. He waited a minute and then tried again.

"Who's there?" Laurie's voice sounded different. A pitch higher than usual and slightly shaky.

Cameron frowned. "It's Cameron. We made arrangements to go on a date. Remember?" She didn't reply. "Laurie? Is everything okay?"

"Yes... I mean no." There was definitely a nervous quaver to her voice. "Look, I'm sorry. Something has come up and I can't make it tonight after all."

Cameron stared hard at the door. Wasn't this what he wanted? Maybe she, too, was having second thoughts about the speed with which things had moved. Yet there was that something in her voice, something that worried him. *Walk away*, his sensible self prompted. *She's not okay*, his intuition told him.

Not giving himself a chance to change his mind, he went with his intuition. Reaching out, he grasped the door handle. "I don't want to intrude, but..." The words died on his lips as he walked into the cabin.

What had he expected? Perhaps that Laurie would be annoyed with him for presuming to enter the cabin when she had said she couldn't make their date. That she might be sick. Even that she might be with another man. Never in his wildest imaginings did he expect to be confronted by Laurie standing over the body of a man, holding a gun in her hands. Her white shirt was stained with blood, and her hands were smeared red. Although her face was rigid with nerves, Cameron noticed her stance was that of a professional and the gun was very definitely pointing at him.

"Don't come any closer."

Still working on instinct, he held up his hands. "What the hell is going on here?"

"Close the door, please." Her voice was quite calm now. Cameron followed her instruction. "Did you pass anyone on your way here?"

"No. No one." He glanced at the body. "Is he dead?"

"Yes. His throat has been cut from ear to ear, which means his jugular vein and carotid arteries have been severed. Whoever did this knew exactly what he was doing. They meant for him to die." Although she spoke in a detached way, Cameron noticed her face blanched as she described the horrible way the man on the floor had died.

"*Whoever did this?* You mean you don't know who it was?" He was still standing by the door with his hands up and the gun aimed at his chest.

"No." Her eyes flickered from his face to the body. "My God! Did you think I could do something like this?"

"I don't know what to think. Until a few minutes ago I was here to tell you I couldn't make it later for a burger and a beer."

Laurie seemed to debate with herself. Slowly she lowered the gun. "I was in the bedroom packing up my things. I heard a noise. When I came out, I found him like this."

Cameron stepped farther into the room, allowing his hands to fall to his sides. There was a lot of information in those few sentences. And a hell of a lot of missing information. "Who is he?"

Laurie moved into the kitchen. Placing the gun on the counter, she turned on the faucet and held her hands under the running water until the blood washed away. "His name is Moreton. He's an FBI agent."

Things just got a whole lot more surreal. Cameron had to ask the next question, even though he didn't want to hear the answer. "Why is he here?"

Laurie wrapped her arms around herself as though seeking protection from a chill. Her wet hands left marks on her shirt. "He's my handler. He was here because I'm in danger and he wanted to bring me in from the job I'm on."

"Are you an FBI agent?"

"No, I'm a police officer. I was brought in to work undercover for the FBI on a specific investigation." He thought her eyes were pleading with him for understanding, but it was hard to think straight when something inside him was beginning a slow burn.

"And what exactly are you investigating?"

Laurie drew a deep breath. "The possibility that a local transportation company is being used as cover for a human-trafficking and drug-running operation."

"You came to Stillwater to investigate me?" Cameron's voice was dangerously quiet. The air felt heavier and statically charged. Although Laurie's thoughts were racing, time seemed to have slowed.

"I was sent here to investigate the possibility that your company is being used as the cover for a criminal operation." The cold, hard look in his eyes told Laurie he knew it was a lie.

He muttered a curse under his breath. "That's bullshit and we both know it. If this was about my

company and not me personally, why send someone who looks exactly like my dead girlfriend?" She
winced at the brutality of the words, and he continued,
still with that restrained fury in his voice. "So how
does this work? Were you going to get me into bed?
Wrap those long legs around me? Get me to spill all
my secrets as I was sinking deep inside you?"

Stung by the image, she snapped back sharply, "We
were never going to have sex."

"Oh, I see. You were just going to string me along
and make me think it could happen. Keep me panting after you like a lovesick kid. Was that the plan?"

Laurie could see the pain in his eyes alongside the
anger, and it hurt her. It wasn't meant to be like this.
She wasn't meant to care how Cameron felt. She'd had
enough training to be able to maintain a professional
distance. And didn't she have more important things
to worry about right now? Her handler was lying dead
on the floor. When he had entered the cabin, he had
locked the door and placed the key in his pocket. She
had a potential serial killer stalking her, someone who
found a way to let himself in here. Yet she was concerned because the man she'd been sent to unmask—
*the possible criminal mastermind you were sent to
unmask*—was looking at her with a combination of
contempt and wounded pride. She'd caused this man
immeasurable pain and she wanted to be able to undo
it, but she had no idea where to begin.

When she didn't answer, Cameron gave a short, bit-
ter laugh and turned away. His intention was clearly
to march out of the cabin and out of her life for good.
His hand actually reached for the door handle, when
he saw the roses she'd placed to one side of Moreton's

body when she'd tried CPR. Although Cameron's face was turned half away from her, Laurie saw him flinch. He swung slowly back to face her.

"Is this some kind of sick joke?" He pointed at the roses, a slight tremor in his hand.

"I would never do that." He had no reason to ever again believe anything she told him, but she tried to put every bit of credibility she had into those words.

He must have seen something in her eyes to at least partially convince him because he moved back toward her. Even so, he looked stunned and disbelieving. "What the hell is going on here?"

"Those flowers were left by whoever killed Moreton. They were placed on his body. A similar arrangement was left in here while I was at Dino's last night."

Cameron ran a hand through his hair. Laurie could almost see his mind working. "Does this mean…?"

Could she trust him? Could she afford not to? "I went to see Moreton this morning and suggested to him that meant Carla might have been murdered. He was looking into it." She drew a deep breath. "We were going to meet tomorrow morning. The fact he came here breaks every existing protocol between undercover operator and handler. It was totally unprecedented."

Suddenly the shock of what had happened hit her, and she sat down abruptly in one of the chairs. Cameron remained between her and the door. Laurie's own trauma was reflected in his expression as he scanned her face. "What will you do now?"

She pointed to where the power cable for her laptop had been ripped out of the socket. "Whoever killed Moreton took my laptop. My contact details were stored in there. I need to get to Cody. Moreton had an office there that he was using as his cover. Hopefully I can find contact details for our superior there and call in. This is too big for me to deal with." She drew a deep breath, willing herself onward. Since she was trusting him this much, she might as well tell it all. "Remember Deanna Milligan?" Cameron nodded, the frown in his eyes deepening. "It seems unlikely that she went off with her unsuitable ex-boyfriend... But she was getting the same heart-shaped arrangement of roses sent to her before she disappeared, also from a secret admirer."

He rubbed a hand over his face like a man trying to wake himself from a bad dream. "This can't be happening."

Laurie continued. "Deanna and Carla had similar coloring. Five other women with the same physical characteristics have either died or disappeared in Stillwater during the last four years. There are even more across the whole county."

"Don't tell me—they all got red roses in the shape of a heart?"

"It was on my list of things to have Moreton check out."

"My God, you're serious."

Laurie pointed at the flowers. Her hand shook wildly. No matter how hard she tried, she couldn't control it. "Whoever sent that just killed my handler." She shifted the direction of her finger to a small window at the rear of the cabin. It had been forced open as wide as it would go. "The door was locked, but he had a key to let himself in. That's the way he left. You can see where he damaged the frame on his way out. Yes, I'm taking this very seriously."

"I'm sorry." The words were mechanical. What you said when someone died. He glanced down at Moreton's lifeless form. "Were you close?"

Laurie thought about it for a moment. She had worked with Moreton before, yet she knew nothing about him. "We weren't friends, if that's what you mean. But I trusted him. I'm used to the idea of him being there in the background, looking out for me. Now he's gone—" her voice wobbled and she fought to get it back under control "—and I have to deal with this alone."

"No." The word sounded as though it had been ground out reluctantly. Laurie gazed up at him with a bewildered expression. "You think I'm going to let you go out there on your own, knowing someone could have killed Carla, Deanna and these others, and you might be next?" He shook his head. "I don't know what sort of dirty operation you think I'm running at Delaney Transportation, and I don't care. You clearly believe I'm the sort of low-life scum who abuses women by trafficking them. That's not who I am, and I'm not going to abandon a woman in danger. You may not be my favorite person right now, but I'm driving you to Cody and staying with you until I know you're safe."

Sharp tears stung the back of Laurie's eyelids, and she knew Cameron noticed before she managed to blink them away. She wanted to be proud and refuse his help. To maintain a professional distance from this man who could be one of the most evil and prolific criminals she had ever encountered. But with a serial killer on her tail, pride was a luxury she didn't have. She needed to get to Cody and find a number so she could call Mike Samuels. Her eyes were drawn to Moreton's body. She didn't feel comfortable leaving him here, but calling the local cops would go against the protocols Moreton had instilled into her at the start of this job.

"Thank you." Laurie's voice was husky with emotion. She rose to her feet. "Give me ten minutes to finish getting my things together."

"You've got five." His grim expression told her his chivalry didn't extend as far as making things easy for her.

The tension in the car was like an invisible fog, so thick Laurie felt it threatening to choke her. Somehow, whenever she stole an occasional glance at Cameron's granite profile, it didn't help to tell herself she had only been doing her job. She thought of Moreton, even though it hurt to do so. On their first job together, the FBI agent had told her to trust her instincts. *My gut is telling me Cameron Delaney is an innocent man who is outraged at the allegations I have made against him.* Could Moreton—could the FBI—have gotten this whole thing so completely wrong? It wasn't impossible, but it was unlikely. An undercover operation of this type was not something anyone in the Bureau would sanction lightly. They had to be pretty sure their evidence was cast-iron. *So, how the hell do I start this conversation with a man who is already as angry as if he had just stuck his hand in a wasps' nest?*

The sun was setting now, the night almost upon them as Laurie gazed out the window at the featureless landscape. The sky faded from yellow through orange to dark blue before turning black where it merged into the horizon. The only break in the flat line of which was that curious, funnel-shaped hill she had noticed earlier in the day.

"That reminds me, one of your trucks nearly ran me off this road earlier today. It pulled right across in front of me and turned down that track over there."

Cameron shook his head. "Not one of mine."

"It was," she insisted. "It had your logo across the side."

"Couldn't have been." His voice was dismissive, and still horribly cold. "This is not one of our routes, and there's no way one of our trucks would go down that track. It doesn't lead anywhere. It used to be the entrance to the old Dawson ranch, but that property hasn't been occupied in the last five years or more."

"Have it your way." Laurie had been sure it was this stretch of road where the truck had pulled across in front of her. That hill was unmistakable. Then again, maybe there was another one that looked the same. It had been light then and it was almost dark now. And it wasn't like nothing had happened today to unsettle her. She was hardly going to get into a fight with Cameron over it. Not when she wanted to question him further about his business activities.

Just as she was formulating and discarding questions to try to get him to open up to her, Cameron took her by surprise and seized the initiative. "What evidence do you have against my firm?"

Laurie shifted in her seat so she could see his profile in the light from the dashboard. "I know some of it, but there may be more I haven't been told about."

His lip curled. "It must be pretty damning stuff to go to all this trouble. I'll bet you don't come cheap."

The cop in her resented that. She wasn't some kid playing games, and the word *cheap* had other connotations. Ones that made her feel dirty. "No, I don't. And you're right. There's no way the Bureau would authorize an operation like this unless they were sure they had the right man." Laurie winced at his indrawn hiss of breath. "So why don't you go ahead and convince me otherwise?"

"What happened to innocent until proven guilty?"

"I got the feeling you didn't like the idea of being labeled a criminal, but if you want to play it by the book, that's fine by me."

The car swerved wildly as Cameron pulled off the road and switched off the engine. Swiveling his body around in the seat, he faced her. Laurie was conscious of his size and strength, and the fact that he was very, very angry.

So here I am, alone in a car, miles from anywhere with a man who is likely to be a dangerous criminal, who hates my guts and is as mad as a raging bull right now. Oh, and I packed my gun. It's in my bag. The one in the trunk.

Laurie had been in some tight situations in her time, but right now, she couldn't think of a single one that had been tighter than this.

"I don't want to play it *any* way. Not with you, not ever." He spoke each word very precisely, as though his jaw was clenched just a little too tight. "But I do want to know why you are here so I can show you how wrong you are about me."

Despite all that pent-up fury, Laurie realized she

wasn't afraid of him. It was a fundamental shift. Up until that point she'd questioned her instincts, wondered if she was right to trust this man. Sitting in that car with him, breathing in his anger and power, yet knowing there was no way he was going to unleash it against her—*because Cameron Delaney is fundamentally a good man. I feel that*—she stopped questioning. Instead, she went with what she felt. He was choosing to keep his fury in check. She would choose to share what she knew.

"There was an operation to close down a chain of brothels in Montana. Some of the girls were Mexican. They were underage." Cameron's expression changed, became outraged. "When they were questioned, at first they were too frightened to talk. Then one of them opened up and the others backed her story. They spoke about being transported in trucks with the Delaney Transportation logo. The girls also said the trucks contained drugs and firearms."

"That can't be true." It was as though her words had drained his anger and replaced it with shock in the space of a minute.

Reluctantly, Laurie continued. "There was also a former employee of yours who, around the same time, came forward with some information that corroborated what the girls were saying. Since then, the Bureau has been keeping a close eye on your company. Moreton told me they have tried to get other undercover operators into Delaney Transportation, but it was impossible. Whoever does the hiring and firing wasn't letting anyone past."

"Vincente." It was more an exhalation of breath than a word.

"It seems your company only employs people known to your brother or recommended to him."

Cameron frowned at that statement as though there was something in the words that bothered him. "So they sent you."

"Moreton was researching your background. When he saw pictures of Carla, he was struck by her likeness to me. We had worked together before, and he did some digging. He found out Carla and I were cousins, even though we had never met." It wasn't an easy statement to make. She could tell by his expression it wasn't easy to hear. "That was when he came up with the plan to send me undercover."

"You were related to her?" There was a raw, agonized ache in his voice.

"I didn't know until Moreton approached me about this job." She wanted to say more. But what? Should she offer her apologies? How insensitive would that be? "Our fathers were brothers."

He drew in a sharp breath, switching the conversation back to the trafficking operation, as though he was unwilling to continue the conversation about Carla. "Why would something like that be going on here? Surely the sort of operation you're talking about would be better located in a big city?"

"Why did you choose Stillwater as the headquarters for Delaney Transportation?"

Cameron looked bemused to have his question thrown back at him, but he answered her promptly. "It's my hometown, so I know it well. I know it has cheap and plentiful real estate, quiet roads for heavy freight, easy access to major highways. I-25 will take you south all the way to the Mexican border—" He drew a sharp breath in, making the connection to what Laurie had said about the nationality of the girls in the brothels at the same time he said the words. "And for me, it makes sense because I know this county, and this state, so well."

"The same reasons apply to criminals who are looking for a good place to set up their business. We're talking about transportation here, not a final destination. They are using Stillwater as some sort of depot, bringing the goods—whether those goods are guns, drugs or girls—and moving them on from here to their final destination. There are added benefits for a crime network. Wyoming is a big, quiet state. There are fewer pairs of watching eyes here. Not so many nosy neighbors. The local police have a huge area to cover. Even if they knew of an operation like the one we're talking about, what are the chances of them finding the right truck at the right time?"

"Our headquarters in Stillwater are not being used as this depot. I guarantee it. No way." Cameron's lips were compressed into a thin, determined line.

Laurie tried a different approach. "Could they be using your company, but doing the illegal stuff elsewhere? It sounds far-fetched, but could someone be running an illegal operation alongside your legitimate organization?"

"Behind my back, you mean?" His expression was stunned as he considered the possibility. "My God, that would mean someone deliberately exploited my grief after Carla's death, and used it against me. I wasn't fit to do anything properly after she died, let alone run a company. But this is so cold...so calculating..."

Having planted a seed, Laurie pushed a little further. "Do you have any idea who it could be?"

He shifted position, starting up the engine. His expression hardened and his body language shut her out again. When he spoke, it was as if he was formulating an idea out loud rather than including her. "I can only think of two people within the company who have the means to do this. And both of them are my brothers."

Chapter 5

Cameron had visited Cody regularly over the years. It was a place that celebrated its small-town feel and Old West links, but also enjoyed a thriving nightlife. It was this that he and Laurie got caught up in as they stepped out of the car.

"I feel kind of inappropriately dressed," Laurie commented as they moved along the main street, passing families and groups dressed in cowboy hats, boots and shirts.

"There's a rodeo that takes place every night. Tourists love it. Locals, too." He allowed himself a reminiscent smile. "Bryce and I used to pester our dad to bring us here all the time when we were kids."

He felt something deep inside him clench at the thought of Bryce. Could his kid brother be responsible for the sort of sickening activities Laurie had described? His heart told him no way. Yet he was reluctant to slip into the habit of always thinking the worst of Vincente. Time and again it came back to the same thing. *Vincente hates me. Vincente is jealous of me. Vincente will do anything he can to get at me.* As they were growing up, Vincente had done everything he could to prove it. Lately, his half brother had seemed to have gotten over his unhealthy obsession. He had even started to carve out his own life, instead of craving Cameron's.

How could he believe either of his brothers was capable of the things Laurie had described? Yet he knew what she was saying must be true. He had to accept his company was being used as a front for this vile operation. Laurie wouldn't be here otherwise. There was something about her calm conviction that told him every detail, every sickening fact had been carefully researched. Her tone was regretful, but determined. This was a problem that wasn't going away. And the thought of those young girls—never mind the drugs and the illegal weapons—made Cameron every bit as single-minded. No one was going to use his company, the firm he'd built up from nothing, as a cover for that sort of filth. No way.

The thought almost, but not quite, deflected his attention away from the other predicament. The huge issue of the dead FBI agent and the fact that Carla, along with several other women, could have been the victim of a serial killer. His head still refused to process that information. He was tempted to get on the phone right now to Grant Becker. How could seven women, possibly more, who all looked alike, have gone missing—or in Carla's case died—in a relatively short

space of time in this county and the sheriff's department know nothing about it? Or maybe they did know
and it wasn't public knowledge. But the fact that *Carla*
was one of those women, and the sheriff was one of
his best friends…

With an effort, Cameron got a grip on his emotions. Despite his animosity toward her, Laurie was
a police officer. They were here because of her links
to the FBI. Before they left her rental cabin, she'd
searched Moreton's body, the action clearly causing
her distress. In his pocket, she had found a set of keys,
one of which she was sure would fit the door to his
office in Cody and another the safe she'd seen inside.
Once she called this in, spoke to her contacts in the
FBI and returned to San Diego, then Cameron could
start getting the answers he so desperately needed. To
both the huge questions Laurie Carter's presence had
brought into his life.

She had brought other things with her. Things he
didn't want to examine too closely because, when he
did, he didn't like himself very much. Her arrival had
revived his sex drive. He allowed himself a sidelong
glance in her direction as she walked beside him with
that easy, long-legged stride, her hair swinging. *Revive*
was the wrong word. She had aroused him to the point
where his whole body felt like it had been electrified.
He was thirty years old, for God's sake, and she made
him feel like a horny teenager. It was a sensation that
had nothing to do with twelve months of abstinence.
Since he had met her, Laurie had featured in some
fantasies so vivid and amazing they had interrupted
Cameron's sleep. And with those nocturnal images
had come the inevitable feelings of guilt. Because he

shouldn't be feeling this for someone else. Not when he had convinced himself it would be wrong to feel anything ever again. Even more so when he still wasn't sure whether his feelings were to do with her resemblance to Carla.

Now the initial shock of the real reason behind Laurie's intrusion into his life had worn off, he was left with a residual feeling of disappointment alongside his anger. Frustration that he would never get to find out if the reality was as hot as the fantasy. And that was just one of the reasons he didn't like himself very much right now. He had been gullible enough not to ask questions when a woman who looked exactly like his dead girlfriend fell—yes, *fell*—half-naked into his arms. He had been thinking with his dick instead of his brain when he asked her out, not once but twice.

Just twelve months after Carla's death, he had been enjoying some very erotic imaginings about Laurie. To be brutally honest, he had spent the last few days in a hard-on-powered bubble. And even now, when he knew who she was and why she was here, he was experiencing a pang of disappointment that he wouldn't get to have sex with her after all. The sooner he got this woman, who was Carla's *cousin*, out of his life, the better. He needed to get back to thinking with his brain instead of a more basic part of his anatomy.

Laurie halted on the opposite side of the street from an attorney's office. "Here. It was that building. Moreton was using that second-floor office right across the street from this flower store."

They crossed the street. There was a flight of stairs on the outside of the building, but as Laurie placed her foot on the first step, Cameron caught hold of her arm.

"What is it?" She looked at him over her shoulder, a frown in her eyes. Clearly the cop in her was used to being in charge in these situations and she didn't like him taking over that role.

"Can't you smell it?"

She shook her head, her lips parting as she was about to reply in the negative. Then a light breeze blew in her face and her expression changed. "Gasoline."

As soon as she said the word, the second-floor windows above them blew outward with a loud *whoomph* and the sky lit up. Cameron grabbed Laurie and pushed her to the ground, throwing himself on top of her as glass and other debris rained down on them. Screams and shouts and the noise of people running to and from the scene of the fire filled the air. Laurie squirmed beneath him in an attempt to get free, but Cameron held her down, keeping his body on top of hers. Although chunks of wood and plaster hit him on his back and shoulders, he thanked his lucky stars that they both managed to escape without any injuries.

Laurie turned her head to look at what was going on, and the softness of her cheek was pressed against his face. In spite of the danger and the seriousness of the situation, he gave himself up to the sensation, then cursed his weakness.

So much for the "get her out of his life" pledge of a few minutes earlier. Even with the aftermath of an explosion going on around them, the length of her body beneath his, the scent of her hair in his nostrils, the feel of her skin on his…all of those things were sending the blood pounding to his head. And dangerously farther south. If he wasn't careful, Laurie would soon be aware of his arousal. He didn't want to get a reputation as the man who got turned on by buildings being blown up.

Getting cautiously to his feet, Cameron looked up at the attorney's office. The whole of the second floor was alight. Reaching down a hand, he pulled Laurie to her feet.

"You okay?"

Although she nodded, her face was shocked. "That was Moreton's office."

"Then I'm guessing you won't find the contact details you need in there."

They crossed the street, getting away from the danger zone. Stepping onto the sidewalk on the opposite side of the street, they brushed the dirt from their clothing. A small crowd had gathered to watch what was going on and to await the arrival of the firefighters. Laurie leaned back against the boards of the shop behind her.

"Coincidence?" Cameron raised a brow at her.

She shook her head, her eyes still fixed on the blaze. "There are very few of them in my job. Someone is determined to cover his tracks."

"I think that was obvious when he killed a federal agent..." He was about to say something more when his gaze became riveted on an item in the store window behind her. The words died on his lips, and his blood ran cold.

Grabbing Laurie by the shoulder, he ignored her protest and turned her so she could see what he was looking at. It was a heart-shaped arrangement of roses.

"They aren't the same color." Even as she said the words, Laurie's brain was telling her everything else about the flowers was right. The size, shape, the number of roses, even the type of buds. The only difference was this arrangement comprised soft pink roses instead of the blood-red ones that had been sent to Carla and Deanna. *And to me.*

Tastefully arranged under a single spotlight, a sign next to the flowers read What's Your Message? The words made Laurie shiver. The killer had a message. Every time he sent flowers. And she had received them twice…

"I need to come back here in the morning as soon as this store opens."

Cameron's brows drew together in a frown. "I thought the plan was for you to get back to San Diego as soon as you could?"

"That was before *that*." She pointed across the road to where a fire truck was just pulling up before turning back to look at the flowers. "And before I saw this. I've been getting these flowers."

She raised her eyes to his face. It would be too much to say his expression softened, but there was understanding in his eyes. "Which means you're next."

"Yes, and if I'm right about this guy, do you think he'll let the small matter of a few states between us stop him getting to me?"

He shook his head from side to side slowly. "He's determined, that's for sure. So we have to find him."

"We?" Laurie tried to fight the little flare of hope that ignited deep inside her. Was he offering to help her?

"If you're right, he killed Carla." *Carla.* Of course. For a moment, Laurie had forgotten about her. His girlfriend. Her cousin. "So what's the plan? We go to the police with what we know?"

"Not yet. I want to see if I can find out who has been ordering these flowers first. That way, I have something concrete to take as evidence."

"What about Moreton? The guy is lying dead in a vacation cabin that was leased in your name."

Laurie did some quick thinking. She had no way of contacting Samuels, but Cameron was right. She couldn't just leave Moreton's body to be found by a stranger. And once Moreton was found, the search would be on for Laurie herself.

"I'll find a motel for the night, then call my captain in San Diego. Once I explain what happened to Moreton, he can contact the Bureau and let them take over that side of things. I'll tell him I have a few loose ends to tie up here before I go back. He won't like it, but short of coming out here to hunt me down there's not much he can do about it."

A corner of her mouth lifted in anticipation of Captain Harper's long-distance fury. It had been a while since they'd worked together—she'd moved from one long-term undercover assignment straight to this one—but she didn't imagine he'd changed much in the time she'd been away.

Cameron quirked a brow at her. "Do I get the feeling you may not always play things by the book, Detective Carter?"

"I get results, and my boss appreciates that." She paused, assessing the slight thaw she could feel in the atmosphere between them. "And it's Detective Bryan." She saw his eyes register the name—Carla's name—and moved on quickly. "My real name is Amy Carter-

Bryan. But my middle name is Laurie, and that's what my family and friends call me."

"Are you suggesting we should become friends?" His expression was unreadable. It would help if he wasn't so handsome that simply looking at him took her breath away.

"In spite of a shaky start, I'd like to think we aren't enemies." She inhaled deeply. "That we're on the same side."

He didn't answer. Instead, he just kept staring at her. Then the noises from across the street intensified as the roof of the building started to give way. At the same time, Cameron roused himself from whatever thoughts were occupying him. "Come on—" he paused, and a slow smile dawned, making her pulse race "—Laurie. Let's get you to a motel."

They drove a few miles out of town to a large, ranch-style motel set in its own pine forest. Laurie, used to staying in impersonal concrete boxes that all looked the same, gazed at the charming old building with its golden wood exterior and arched windows. "I wasn't thinking of anything quite so luxurious."

"They know me here. And I'm not sleeping in an uncomfortable bed."

Laurie turned her head to look at him. "You're staying, too?"

"Of course. Did you think I was going to drive back to Stillwater tonight and then out here again in the morning?" His eyes stayed on her face. She didn't imagine it this time. There was a definite softening in their expression. "Besides, while that guy is still out there somewhere, I'm sticking by you. I might not like it, but we're in this together."

The words brought an odd tightness to her throat that Laurie couldn't explain. It must be tiredness. It had been a hell of a day. Cameron got her bags out of the trunk and they made their way inside to a reception area decorated with reminders of the Wild West. A chandelier made of antlers was suspended over the desk and an assortment of guns, cart wheels, cowboy hats and animal hides were hung on the walls. Cameron was recognized and greeted with delight by the female check-in clerk.

Laurie was aware of the clerk's curious eyes on her as Cameron asked for two rooms next to each other and a table in the restaurant for dinner. Had Cameron ever come here with Carla? Was the clerk wondering where he had managed to find such a perfect substitute? What did it matter? There had never been a future for them anyway, but there was even less of one now. He had to feel disgust every time he looked at Laurie and remembered why she had come here. She would never be anything other than the woman who had set out to callously make his grief work against him.

As she was processing those thoughts, Cameron came back to her, his heartbreaking smile lighting the dark depths of his eyes. That was when it hit her. Hard. *Oh, dear Lord, this can't have happened. I can't have fallen for the one man I can never have.*

"Hey, are you okay?"

She forced a smile, despite the fact her heart had just snapped in two. "Fine. A little tired…and more than a little hungry."

He held up the room keys. "We can do something about both of those."

* * *

Because it was so late, the restaurant was quiet. They ate at a corner table. Laurie seemed distracted and Cameron watched her face. He enjoyed watching her face, and not for the obvious reason. The truth was, he'd long ago gotten over the shock of her likeness to Carla. He enjoyed watching Laurie, not a ghost from the past. *A ghost from the past?* How had he reached this point so quickly in a matter of days? He hadn't forgotten that, until the drama of the last few hours, he had actually convinced himself his feelings for her might be real. Now, he was too mentally exhausted to fight the pleasure he got from watching her. He'd deal with that and the whole guilt thing another time. Okay, he hadn't forgiven or forgotten the fact she had come here with the deliberate intention of exploiting his grief. He didn't know how he felt about that.

She was doing her job. It wasn't personal. No, it didn't help to tell himself that. *I was a job.* He had to admit his pride was wounded. She'd been playing a part and he'd fallen for it. *What kind of idiot does that make me? The kind who is going to walk away as soon as I know she's safe and never see Laurie Carter*—or Amy Carter-Bryan or whatever the hell her name is— *ever again.* Even so, he couldn't ignore the troubled look in those stunning blue eyes.

"How did your plan go down with your boss?" he asked casually.

"Pretty much the way I expected. To say he was pissed off would be putting it mildly. My delicate ears are still recovering from the curse words." She laughed. "I've never heard him swear before. The signal was bad, so I used that as my excuse and hung up."

"Will that get you in trouble when you get back?"

"Probably." She shrugged. "When I think about what happened to Moreton, nothing else matters except finding this killer."

"There's something else on your mind." There it was again. Cutting through his chagrin, there was that sense of knowing her, being in tune with her feelings. He decided he might as well just ask her outright. "What is it?"

She looked up, apparently startled by his perceptiveness. "It was what you said about the fire being a coincidence."

"And you said there are very few of those in your job."

"It got me thinking." She pushed the food around on her plate. "It's one hell of a big coincidence Moreton chose an office across the street from that particular flower store, don't you think?"

Cameron's jaw wanted to drop as he followed her train of thought. With an effort he managed to keep it in place. "What are you saying?"

"I'm saying he deliberately chose an office with a window that overlooked the door of that flower store. I'm saying a lot of things that, if they are true, are scaring me half to death." She cast a quick glance around. There were several other couples finishing their meals and a few staff clearing tables. "Can we go upstairs and talk about this?"

Laurie's room was furnished in a comfortable, homey style, with colorful rugs on the floor and woven spreads on the two king-size beds. Lamps cast golden pools of light around the space, but the atmosphere didn't appear to be having a soothing effect on its occupant's nerves.

Laurie paced up and down, her arms tightly wrapped around her body. "This is going to sound crazy."

"Try me." Cameron took a seat in one of the two easy chairs near the window. The drapes had been drawn, adding to the warm, relaxed feel. He experienced an overwhelming urge to go to her, hold her and soothe her nerves. Reminding himself the disclosures of this strange day and their tense relationship really did not allow for that sort of interaction, he stayed put.

"Okay." She took a deep breath. "I did an internet search this afternoon, looking for the arrangement of flowers that were sent to Carla and me. I couldn't find anywhere that sold them, couldn't even find a picture of a similar arrangement. I even called every flower store I could find and drew a blank at all of them. So what are the chances that Moreton just happened to choose an office across the street from the very shop that *does* sell that arrangement?"

She had a point. Hell, it was a good point. This was getting surreal. Cameron tried to inject a note of caution into the conversation. "Just because coincidences don't come along often, doesn't mean they never happen. And, until we speak to the owner of that flower store tomorrow, we don't know enough about that particular arrangement."

Laurie's look told him she didn't think much of that theory. "Before he was killed, Moreton said he needed to tell me all of it. He said he'd explain while we were on our way to the airport. Obviously, he never got a chance to do that. When I showed him my laptop with the pictures of the missing women, I got the feeling he wasn't surprised by what I was saying. If he chose that office because he knew about the flowers, that means he already knew about the murders. Right?"

"Riiight." Cameron elongated the word, keeping it slightly skeptical. He had a number of questions and comments, but he didn't want to interrupt Laurie's thought processes.

She stopped pacing and stopped in front of him. "So what if *that* was the real reason I was brought here?"

"You just lost me." He frowned. "I thought you came here to investigate my company? Because the FBI thinks Delaney Transportation is the cover for this trafficking network you told me about."

Laurie came to sit on the chair opposite him, leaning forward so their knees were almost touching. "Don't you see? If Moreton was investigating these murders, and he saw the similarity between me and Carla, then he discovered our relationship, he would have wanted to get me in here using any pretense he could. And he knew I wouldn't say no once I discovered that Carla was my cousin."

"You mean he wanted to use you as bait?" The idea was so outrageous, Cameron couldn't help feeling incensed by it.

"Even if he wanted to, there is no way the Bureau would have allowed it. Moreton was a seasoned investigator, so he'd have known that. Which meant he had to find another reason to get me here. When the allegations against Delaney Transportation surfaced, he must have seized on it as the perfect opportunity. So he set up the undercover operation, with my role

being to get close to you, to find out about the trafficking operation—"

"When all the while it was really to attract the
killer?"

"Yes!" Her eyes sparkled with triumph at the realization he was finally following her line of thinking.

"My God." Cameron slumped back in his chair. "So
he set up this whole thing, pretending you had been
sent here to get close to me, knowing all the while
Carla's killer would immediately see the likeness and
be attracted to you. Would Moreton really have taken
a risk like that with your safety?"

"Not ordinarily. Which leads me to another conclusion... I think Moreton must have known who the
killer was."

"I need a drink." Cameron went to the minibar
fridge and took out a bottle of beer. Without asking,
he poured a glass of white wine for Laurie and carried it over to her.

She accepted it gratefully. "I'm not explaining myself very well, am I?"

"No," he agreed. The new warmth in his smile took
any sting out of the denial. "What makes you think
Moreton already knew who the killer was?"

"I just don't think Moreton would have risked my
safety on an unknown. This was already wildly out of
character for him. He was usually so careful to play
things by the book. But imagine how it must have felt
to *know* there was a killer out there, and more than
that—to know who he was—yet no one else was prepared to do anything about it. Moreton was a stickler

for detail. He chose that office deliberately. He did it so he could watch the flower store, see the killer coming and going and know exactly when he ordered the next arrangement of flowers. Moreton wasn't undertaking an investigation…he was confirming something he already knew. He was using me to flush this guy out." She took a sip of her wine, sadness washing over her. "He just didn't count on the killer being one step ahead of him."

"If Moreton made a connection between these killings, how come no one else did? Why don't the local police seem to know anything about it?"

"Maybe they do. It could have been kept out of the press for a reason." Laurie felt wrung out with tiredness from thinking about it all. It was like playing some horrible nightmare on a loop inside her mind. "You're the mayor of Stillwater. The chief of police answers to you and your fellow councilors, so it seems safe to say he knew nothing. When it comes to the sheriff's department, Grant Becker is your friend, so perhaps he wasn't able to—or didn't care to—discuss it with you because of Carla."

Cameron looked unconvinced. "If you're right about this, Moreton was taking a huge risk. And look what happened as a result. It could have been you on that cabin floor."

"I wonder why it wasn't," Laurie mused.

"Pardon?" Cameron had raised his beer bottle to his lips, but he lowered it again abruptly.

"I never thought of it until now, but, just before you arrived, I was alone in the cabin with the killer. Moreton was dead and I was in the bedroom. I heard someone coming toward me. Yet, at the last minute, he didn't come in there after me. He turned around, snatched up my laptop and left by the window. Why didn't he kill me when he had the chance?"

"Just be grateful he didn't."

"I am, but there must be a reason. I'm his next target, he had me at his mercy, yet he did nothing about it. If we knew why that was, it might take us a step nearer to him." Laurie smothered a yawn. "Oh, Lord. I'm sorry."

"Don't be. I'm tired, too. Let's get some sleep. We may get some answers in the morning." He rose to his feet, looking down at her. "I don't like the idea of leaving you alone tonight."

Something in the atmosphere had changed. It wasn't just the switch she'd sensed earlier in him from distance to acceptance. This was like there was too much electricity in the air, sucking the breath from her lungs and leaving her giddy.

"Your room is just next door." Laurie's voice sounded husky to her own ears.

Cameron held out a hand, and powerless to resist, she took it, allowing him to draw her to her feet. "That's not what I meant." His sigh was resigned and confused at the same time. She sensed he was waging an internal battle. "I'm supposed to be angry with you, not half-crazy with wanting you…"

He released her, but only so his hands could tangle in her hair. It seemed as though the battle was over. He looked like he didn't know whether to be unhappy he'd lost. Gazing into her eyes, he sought her acceptance of what was about to happen. In response, Laurie rose on the tips of her toes, pressing her body to his, and was caught up in the shimmering intensity of his mouth on hers. Cameron's tongue slid slowly over Laurie's lips, moistening them and urging them to part for him and, with a soft sigh, she opened her mouth, allowing his tongue to enter her body. Warm, intimate, caressing, thrusting, mirroring other movements she dreamed of him making; the touch of his tongue made her moan. Instantly, he deepened the kiss, his hand cradling the back of her head, angling her closer to him. Laurie felt her nerve endings go wild. His kiss told her a hundred things she already knew. He wanted her, but he didn't *want* to want her. More than that. He hated how much he wanted her. Hated that she stripped him of every defense he had and left him breathless. But wanting her was bigger than anything he'd ever known. It was searing him, consuming him, driving every other emotion out of him so all he could think of was her. His kiss told her all of that. When they broke apart, her breath was coming as hard and fast as his.

Cameron ran the pad of his thumb over her bottom lip. There was a trace of regret in his eyes. "I was going to offer to sleep in here tonight, but after that, I think it might be a bad move. I can't imagine we'd either of us get much sleep, can you? And I'm not sure we're either of us ready for more than this."

Trance-like, Laurie shook her head. Part of her wanted to step back into the circle of his arms, but he was right. Even though she knew it cost him every ounce of restraint he had to say those words. This was too much, too soon. They neither of them knew what this attraction was all about. And after the start this relationship had gotten off to, sex was a complication they should probably avoid. No matter how tempting it looked right now.

And, in the form of Cameron Delaney, it looked mighty tempting.

Chapter 6

The store, which was called May Flowers, was just opening when they arrived the next morning. A middle-aged woman with gray hair pulled back in a tight bun paused in the act of unlocking the door to regard Cameron with interest. "I know your face from somewhere."

"I don't think we've met," he said. Laurie sensed he was keeping his voice deliberately noncommittal.

"I know who you are." She nodded in satisfaction. "My sister lives in Stillwater. I've seen your picture in the local newspaper. You're Mayor Delaney." She waved a hand, shooing them inside while she set planters on the sidewalk outside.

On the opposite side of the street, Moreton's office on the second floor was now a burned out shell, and the lower floor had also been vacated. Warning signs had been placed on the sidewalk while a clean-up crew was at work. "I hope her sister voted for you. If not, we're in trouble," Laurie murmured out of the corner of her mouth.

"Have a little faith in my personal charm." If Cameron saw the blush his words prompted, he didn't mention it. They hadn't spoken of the kiss this morning, but it seemed to be there between them, burning up extra oxygen each time they looked at each other.

The woman came back inside. "I'm May King. What can I do for you?"

Laurie stepped forward. "I'm Detective Bryan of the San Diego Police Department. I'm hoping you can help me with an investigation."

May looked her up and down. Her expression was not approving. "You're a long way from home."

"Detective Bryan is assisting the Stillwater police."

"If that's the case, why isn't Sheriff Becker with you?" May put her hands on her hips, her stance becoming ever so slightly belligerent.

Laurie cast a glance in Cameron's direction in an appeal for help. May King had clearly taken an aversion to her at first sight, and she didn't want to jeopardize their chances of finding information by pushing the woman too far. And why was she asking about Sheriff Becker? This was Park County, not West County. It wasn't Becker's jurisdiction. Something didn't feel right about her questions.

"Mrs. King." May turned her attention back to Cameron, her expression relaxing. "Perhaps we didn't explain ourselves properly. Detective Bryan is helping out the Stillwater Police Department. As you know, matters in the city of Stillwater come under my jurisdiction. This has nothing to do with the sheriff's department. I'd appreciate it if you could assist Detective Bryan." Laurie felt a pang of annoyance at the way he could turn on the charm so easily, but there was no doubt it worked. Although May made a slight huffing noise, she nodded.

Laurie smiled at the other woman. "Thank you. I'm interested in the heart-shaped arrangement of roses in the window—"

"Yes, it's one of my most popular designs, especially around Valentine's. Does it really need three police officers in two days to ask me the same question?"

"Three officers?"

May rolled her eyes impatiently. "There was the one who came in yesterday morning. The one in the suit with the official-looking badge. Asked lots of questions about the dark red roses I make up for a special customer."

"Can you remember that police officer's name, Mrs. King?" Cameron prompted gently.

"Morley, maybe? Morgan?" She flapped a hand. "Mor-something."

Moreton. Laurie felt her mouth go dry. "And the second officer?"

May laughed. "Not five minutes after the first officer had gone, didn't Sheriff Becker walk right on in here?"

Even though he was standing a foot away from her, Laurie could feel the tension in Cameron's body. "What did Sheriff Becker want?"

"He said he was working with the other officer on a case and wanted to check his colleague had asked me all the right questions. I got the feeling the sheriff was training the other guy, or something like that. Sheriff

Becker is such a joker, always making me laugh. He was talking about how people from out of state don't get us Wyomingites. He asked if the other officer took away any paperwork about the special customer who orders the dark red roses."

"And did he?" Laurie asked. It was a long shot. Moreton had no paperwork on his body, and anything that might have been in that office would be long gone in the fire.

"No, I don't keep any. It's a private arrangement between me and one of my best customers. And that's what I told Sheriff Becker in case he was worried."

"How do you know Sheriff Becker so well, Mrs. King?" Cameron asked the question before Laurie could. "This isn't his county."

She knew they were thinking the same things: there was a flower store on the main street in Stillwater, and surely one or two others closer to Becker's home. Why would he need to come all this way if he wanted to buy flowers? What was his connection to this particular florist? And why had the sheriff of West County been following in the tracks of an FBI agent yesterday? An agent who had not revealed his presence here to the local police? Of course, it was possible he knew about the murders and was investigating the flowers, just as they were. But why, oh why, would Grant Becker be *worried* about Moreton taking away any of May's paperwork?

"Because he's the one." May's eyes crinkled into a conspiratorial smile. "Sheriff Becker is the special customer who orders the dark red heart arrangement. Regular as clockwork, near enough. She sure is a lucky lady whoever she is."

* * *

They didn't talk until Cameron pulled into a rest stop. By some unspoken agreement, they exited the car, bought cans of soda from a vending machine and went to sit at an isolated picnic bench.

Laurie spoke first. "This is why the West County Sheriff's Department didn't know about me."

"Pardon?" Cameron seemed lost in his own thoughts.

"The other time I worked undercover with the FBI, the local police knew all about it. Even though they weren't involved in the operation, they were aware of a federal presence in their jurisdiction. It makes sense to have no overlap of authority, no possibility of the undercover agent being picked up for a crime and to keep communication open. This time Grant Becker wasn't told I was here undercover. He doesn't know who I am because Moreton knew it was him."

Cameron rubbed a hand across his eyes. "Grant? My God, he used to play in our yard when we were kids. We go on a fishing trip together every summer. Okay, he has been more Vincente's friend than mine in recent years, but he knew Carla. He *liked* her..." His voice trailed away.

Laurie waited, sensing there was more. Overhead, clear blue skies teased them, inviting them to explore the perfection of the surrounding countryside instead of remaining locked in their own private nightmare.

"Looking back, maybe there was something." When Cameron lifted the can to his lips, his hand shook slightly.

"Between Grant and Carla?" Laurie prompted gently.

"Not on her part." He shook his head emphatically. "When Carla first came to Stillwater, she came to my office and submitted her plans for my lake house. That first night, I took her out to dinner at Dino's, and Grant was there. She told me later—months later—he had asked her out, that very first night."

"Even though she was with you?"

He nodded. "It was the first and only time I ever got a sense Grant might not be the stand-up guy I always thought he was. From then on, although she never said much, I got the feeling Carla was wary around Grant. Like she didn't want to be alone with him. I thought it was because she suspected he had feelings for her and she didn't want to hurt him or let it damage our friendship."

"She never said anything more?"

"Do you think I'd have let it go if I thought there was a chance she was in any danger from him?" Laurie could see his pain in the lines of tension in his face and body. He had just discovered the man he thought was his friend could have killed the woman he loved. Acting on impulse, she reached out and clasped his hand. For an instant, he looked like he didn't know how to react, like he didn't know what to do with the unexpected physical contact between them. He stared down at the contrast between her slender fingers and his larger, stronger hand. She was sure he was going to pull away. So sure, she almost moved and did it first. Then he returned her grip. The movement was hard, strong and grateful. It signaled a shift in their relationship, but Laurie didn't have time to examine it or her feelings about it. "So what are you saying? Grant became so obsessed with Carla, he started killing women who looked like her?"

"That's how it seems. Carla's death was always the

one that didn't fit. The other women are missing, so presumably he killed them and had time to dispose of their bodies. Carla's death was made to look like an accident." She took a breath. "I hate to hurt you by speculating like this, but what if—knowing you would be away from home—he seized the opportunity to get her alone on her boat that night? When he came on to her and she refused, he killed her, panicked and made it look like an accident. Carla was too close to Grant. She couldn't just go missing like the others. He couldn't risk the possibility you would remember he'd asked her out. Or maybe he'd tried other things, things Carla hadn't told you about for the sake of your friendship. Grant had no idea what you knew."

"But he still couldn't stop killing, even after she was dead. Only weeks after he killed Carla, he was setting his sights on Deanna Milligan. At least we now know why the local police haven't investigated the disappearances of these women too closely. When the county sheriff is a serial killer, I guess the clues get overlooked." Cameron grimaced. "I wonder how Moreton made the connection."

"His specialty was using technology to look for patterns in crimes. If anyone could have found this link, it would have been Moreton. And he was tenacious. Maybe he didn't know for sure it was Grant, but I think he had an idea." Laurie frowned, a sudden thought occurring to her. "How did Grant find out about Moreton? He must have discovered Moreton was on to him, but how did he know?"

They both fell quiet for a minute or two, pondering the matter. It was Cameron who broke the silence. "He knew about Moreton because of you, Laurie."

Laurie felt her brows draw together in confusion. "I don't understand."

Cameron ran a hand through his hair, his agitation apparent in the gesture. "Don't you see? When I took you to Dino's, we recreated that first night with Carla."

Laurie could feel her jaw drop in what was almost a caricature of surprise. She thought back to that night, saw Grant's light eyes assessing her with a smile. "Dear Lord, for a serial killer that must have been a heaven-sent fantasy. Grant is going to get to kill Carla all over again."

"Now I think of it, Grant and Vincente left Dino's right after they spoke to us. They didn't stay to eat."

"Did he have time to get to Cody, get the flowers and get back again?" Laurie did a quick mental calculation. "If he rang ahead and May King was prepared to open up her shop at night for her 'special customer,' then I think he could just about do it. You and I stayed late at Dino's that night. We were there long after everyone else had gone."

"If Grant hadn't been able to place the flowers in your cabin that night, I'm willing to bet they'd have been left there sometime the next day."

"I still don't see how any of this led Grant to Moreton."

"Think about it. You weren't just any girl. You were his sweetest, darkest fantasy come to life. He wasn't going to let you out of his sight from then on."

Laurie's heart sank. "So you think he followed me the next day when I drove to Cody?"

Cameron nodded. "*You* didn't even know Moreton was onto him at that point, but Grant would have made the connection as soon as he saw you go into that office over the street from May Flowers. He knew right away he was in big trouble."

"I led Moreton's killer straight to him." Laurie swallowed hard.

It was Cameron's turn to clasp her hand. "Laurie, I've spent the last year thinking I killed Carla. Torturing myself with 'what-ifs.' What if I'd stayed home that night? What if I'd insisted she came with me? It doesn't do any good. Only one person is to blame for this. The person who killed Carla and those other girls. The same person who killed Moreton."

"Grant Becker." She nodded. "Although I still don't understand why he didn't kill me when he had the chance. He had me at his mercy in the cabin. Moreton was dead. I'm sure he was on his way into the bedroom, then he just turned around and left."

"Something must have interrupted him."

Laurie frowned, forcing herself to concentrate. "You came along a few minutes later," she recalled. "Did you get straight out of your car when you arrived?"

Cameron looked a little self-conscious. "No, I had some thinking to do. I sat behind the wheel for a few minutes."

"My cabin was closest to the parking lot. I suppose it's possible he was coming toward the bedroom, heard you pull up, went to the window and saw your car with you sitting in it. He must have gotten out through the back window just before you came in. That's why the frame was damaged. He's a big man to fit through such a small space."

She glanced down as Cameron crushed his soda can in his free hand. He barely seemed to notice the action. "My God, Laurie, do you realize how close you came?"

She nodded, feeling the blood slowly drain from her face. "But we still have no evidence for any of this."

"Except for May King's testimony. At least she can testify that he is the person who buys the flowers."

Realization hit them both at the same time, and they were on their feet together, running toward the car side by side. As Cameron gunned the engine into life, Laurie fumbled for her phone. With fingers that were numb with impatience, she found the listing for May Flowers.

Cameron glanced her way, a question in his eyes. She shook her head. "No answer."

"We could still be wrong." Laurie's voice was fretful as the car ate up the miles on the return journey to Cody. "He's your friend, and we could be accusing him of the most horrible crimes, all based on hunches and with no good reason to support them."

"We'll know the answer for sure by what we find when we get to Cody."

They saw the plume of smoke before they reached the town, and heard the sirens as they reached the outskirts. When Cameron tried to turn onto Sheridan Avenue, the road was blocked by emergency vehicles. He pulled over and, climbing out of the car, they joined the little crowd of curiously silent onlookers. From where they stood, the view of the street was clear. The little store called May Flowers was burning, the fire having taken a strong grip on the wood-framed building. While firefighters dealt with the blaze, a body was being carried out.

"Dear Lord, tell me that's not May." The woman next to Cameron raised a shaking hand to her lips.

"Has to be." Her companion placed an arm about her shoulders, his face equally ashen. "She only had help on the weekends."

"Is she alive?" Someone called out to one of the police officers. He shook his head, his expression somber, before walking back toward the burning building.

"What the hell is going on in this town? It was the empty office across the street last night, now a *flower* shop?"

Cameron caught Laurie's eye and jerked his head toward the car. She nodded and they moved away. Once they were back in the car and on the road out of town, Cameron risked a glance at Laurie's profile. She was gazing out the window, her features tense.

"We weren't wrong." He spoke gently.

"No." She turned to face him. "So what do we do now?"

"He'll come for you, Laurie. We have to get you somewhere safe."

Her lip curled slightly. "I'm not scared of him."

"While I…admire—" Had he almost said *love*? Slip of the tongue. "—the spirit that makes you say that, at the moment Grant has the law on his side. He could pull you over on an imaginary offense anytime he chooses. If he does that, he has you in his power. We have nothing except a wild story. Let's go somewhere so we can buy ourselves a little thinking time. Okay?"

"Where did you have in mind?"

"I have a cabin up in the woods, off the Stillwater Trail. It belonged to my uncle. It's a bit run-down. I keep meaning to sell it, but never get around to doing anything about it. It's completely isolated, and the best thing about it is that Grant doesn't know about it." He let go of the steering wheel with his right hand and let it rest lightly on her knee. He didn't pause to examine how right the action felt. Ever since she'd touched his hand back at the rest stop, something had altered between them. Something that made touching okay. "It's the best I can do."

Her long lashes swept down as she looked at his hand. When she lifted them to his face, her eyes were like twin blue headlamps. "Thank you." There was a world of meaning behind those words. It told him she wished they could have started out differently, that she regretted the mistrust that had been the basis for their relationship…and that there was much more she wanted to say.

"Damn." He glanced in the rearview mirror. "We have company. And it's not good news."

Laurie swiveled around in her seat, her face blanching as she caught sight of the patrol car that was gaining on them. "Is it him?"

"Could be." When he'd said Grant could pull her over and get her in his power anytime he chose, he hadn't expected it to be this fast.

"Can we outrun him?" Her voice wasn't hopeful.

"And give him a reason to arrest us, even shoot at us?" He looked in the mirror again. "We are still in Park County. If we were in West County, he could arrest you on a jumped-up charge and put you in a cell. Here, although he can still arrest you, he'd have to hand you over to the Park County Sheriff's Department. I'm going to pin my hopes on him not wanting the explanations that will go along with that. Can you get my cell phone out of my pocket?"

Laurie looked startled, but, as he raised his hip off the seat, she reached into his back pocket and withdrew his cell phone. "Who do you want to call?"

"My brother Bryce. Can you get him for me?"

"You sound way too calm for this situation," Laurie grumbled, as she scrolled through his contacts.

"I want to look Grant in the eye and let him know I'm on to him, shake him up a bit. You need to do the same. Tell him who you are. Make sure you tell him your captain knows your whereabouts." He took the phone from her in time to hear Bryce's voice demanding to know where the hell he had been.

"You said you'd come down here and speak to Vincente about this problem with the routes. He's still being a royal pain in the butt about it."

"I got sidetracked. Listen, this is important. Call me back in five minutes, okay? Don't let me down."

Bryce must have picked up on the urgency in his voice, because he immediately stopped bellyaching about Vincente. "Hey, what's going on? Anything I need to know about?"

"I'll let you know. Just call me."

He ended the call. The patrol car was right behind them now, and Cameron noted with relief there were two figures in the vehicle. Even a desperate murderer was unlikely to try anything in front of a witness. He was going to pin his hopes on that right now.

"Ready?" He gave Laurie a reassuring smile.

"As I'll ever be." She made an attempt to return the smile, but the expression didn't quite work.

Slowing down, Cameron pulled to the side of the

road. He was out of the car before Laurie could leave her seat, closing his door and making his way toward the sheriff's vehicle. He was right. Grant's muscle-bound frame was unmistakable in the driver's seat. As Cameron got closer, he recognized Becker's deputy, Glen Harvey, in the passenger seat. Some of the tightness around his heart eased. Harvey was a decent guy—honest, trustworthy and dedicated to his job. *The sort of thing I'd have said about Grant Becker twenty-four hours ago.*

"Cam." Exiting his own vehicle, Grant came toward him with a smile. Glen Harvey stayed where he was, merely tilting his hat in Cameron's direction. "Where have you been hiding yourself these days?"

Despite the smile, when Cameron looked into Grant Becker's eyes he knew it was all true. There was something behind that genial expression. It was raw and dangerous, reminding Cameron of a wild animal in a trap. There was fear and desperation, but there was a darker edge to Grant's feelings. *You are enjoying this.* The fleeting thought was gone as fast as it came. *And you know I know.* That exchange of glances lasted no more than a second, but it told Cameron everything he needed to know. He wasn't looking into the eyes of his best friend. He was staring down a ruthless killer.

Before Cameron could answer, both men turned at the sound of Laurie's boots crunching on the asphalt surface as she made her way toward them. Her trim figure in tight-fitting blue jeans and white blouse would catch any man's eye. Cameron heard Grant's indrawn breath as, brushing an errant lock of long, chestnut hair out of her face, Laurie smiled. She had the same effect on Cameron, but he managed to contain his reaction. *We both want her...but for very different reasons.*

Laurie held up her phone. "My captain has agreed to let me stay a few more days." She turned the full force of her smile on Grant, ignoring the faint look of surprise on his face. "We weren't formally introduced the other night. Detective Carter-Bryan, San Diego Police."

If Laurie's use of Carla's surname affected him, Grant gave no sign of it. His gaze went from Laurie to Cameron, a frown descending over his handsome features. "I don't understand."

"I was here on vacation, but, by some bizarre coincidence, a crime was committed in the vacation village where I'm staying. I've offered to stay and assist with the inquiry."

The frown deepened. Did Cameron sense a hint of panic behind it? "Why haven't I been informed about this?"

Laurie looked at Cameron, managing to achieve a hint of delicious confusion in her expression. "Have I done something wrong? I was sure I followed all the correct protocols."

"You did." Playing his own part, he went for a reassuring tone. Turning to Grant, he explained. "The crime Laurie is talking about took place at the Paradise Creek vacation village. That falls within the Stillwater Police Department's area."

Throughout his time as mayor, Cameron had never had to make that sort of statement. The Police Department and the Sheriff's Department had always worked so closely together that there had been no need for reminders about their different functions and areas of authority. This was the first time he had needed to point out that Grant was responsible for the law enforcement services within West County, while the city limits of Stillwater itself came under the control of Chief Wilkinson.

If there was a fleeting look of anger in the depths of Grant's eyes, it was quickly gone. "Even so, I'd have expected to be kept informed about something serious happening in Stillwater."

"Because it is so serious, I've been kind of busy this last twenty-four hours," Cameron said, drily. "I've also been trying to avoid any word of a problem during peak tourist season getting out and causing a panic." Just then, his phone rang. "Excuse me." He took the call, listening intently. "Yes, okay. No, I'm just with Detective Carter-Bryan in Park County. Probably ten minutes from the county line. Sheriff Becker is here. I'll be there as soon as I can."

"Developments?" Laurie asked, when he hung up.

"Yes. We have to go." Cameron waved a hand to Deputy Harvey. "We'll speak soon." He addressed the words to Grant, speaking slowly and deliberately. The sheriff gave a curt nod in return. They maintained eye contact, each man sending the same message to the other.

You can count on it.

Chapter 7

Cameron's idea of a "run-down" cabin was not nearly as bad as Laurie had expected. *When you are one of the wealthiest men in the state, you probably have higher standards than the rest of us*, she decided. They had left the car inside a lockup storage unit close to Wilderness Lake and hiked for an hour on a lonely path that took them away from the main Stillwater Trail. Cameron had not been exaggerating when he said this place was isolated. He explained the cabin had been used as a hunting retreat by his uncle, who had died a few years earlier.

"Uncle Frankie loved to get away from it all up here," Cameron said, as he dumped the bags of groceries they'd stopped for on the table. "I'm not a hunter, so I don't know why he left it to me."

"Maybe he thought he could convert you?" Laurie

wandered through the small rooms, enjoying the rustic feel of the wooden furnishings, the bright rugs and cushions and the spectacular views from every window. It was simple, comfortable, yet beautiful. There was only one bedroom, she noticed. Now *that* was going to be an interesting after-dinner conversation. One she wasn't sure either of them was ready for.

"Growing up, none of us ever really showed much interest in hunting. I know that makes us unusual in this state. Vincente was the only one of the three of us who ever had any real interest in it, but I don't think he's taken a gun out in at least a year."

Cameron got the generator working, then lit a fire and made coffee. They took it out onto the porch, even though the temperature was dropping with the sun. Taking a seat on a cushioned bench, Laurie was amazed all over again at the beauty of the Wyoming landscape.

"It's heavenly," she sighed.

"My coffee or the scenery?" Cameron teased as he sat next to her. She took a second to enjoy the feeling. The tenderness in his voice in contrast to the contempt and anger of the previous day was like a warm blanket being draped around her shoulders. Maybe it was sympathy because she had a serial killer on her tail, but she liked to think there was a hint of something deeper in the glorious depths of those dark eyes. Could she be imagining it? It was possible, but for the time being she was going to enjoy the pretense.

"Both. You are very lucky to live here." She wondered if it was a tactless thing to say. His life recently hadn't featured much luck. Carla's death, being framed for human traffic, and now her intrusion into his existence with the news that one of his oldest friends was a murderer. The beautiful scenery didn't make those things any better.

"I know." He shifted position slightly, so he could watch her profile as she drank in the views. "You know all about my life, but I know nothing at all about you. Tell me about Amy Carter-Bryan."

"There's not much to tell. I really was born here in Wyoming, and moved to San Diego when my dad died. That was all true. I've lived there ever since. Joined the police straight out of college." Her eyes flickered across to meet his briefly. "And that's it."

"That's it? What about relationships? You're not going to convince me you've gone through life looking the way you do without dating."

She bit back a smile. This felt a little bit like flirting. It was unexpected. In a nice way. "Of course I've dated. But I suppose, somewhere along the way, my career became my most important relationship. The guys I met didn't seem to know how to handle that… or maybe they didn't want to."

"Jerks. Are you seriously telling me you've never been in love?"

Laurie turned her head to look at him. Big mistake. Looking into those dark eyes was like drowning in melting chocolate. "I've never been in love."

The atmosphere between them went from hot to sizzling in that instant. She had never wanted anything as much as she wanted those big strong hands on her body. Right now. The danger they'd been in added an element of daring to her actions, and she placed her coffee cup down, closing the space between them. She caught the brief flash of surprise and pleasure in Cameron's eyes as she ran her hands over the hard muscles of his chest before reaching up to pull his mouth down to hers.

His hands grasped her waist and jerked her firmly across his body so she was lying half across his lap. He tilted her head and deepened the kiss, his tongue thrusting into her mouth. Laurie's head spun as she realized she had lost control of the situation. Which was exactly what she'd been hoping for. She matched the stroke of his tongue with her own, loving the heat and the abrasive friction. Cameron's hand moved under her blouse, lingering to caress the flesh of her stomach, before moving higher. Tugging aside the lace of her bra, he cupped her breasts, his fingers teasing the peaks into instant stiffness. She could feel his erection pressing hard and insistent against her hip. Laurie squirmed, giving a soft groan of longing.

The sound seemed to rouse Cameron from the daze he was in. Raising his head, he looked into Laurie's eyes. "We are not done here. But you and I have some serious talking to do before we can finish this."

She nodded slowly, sitting up straighter and righting her clothing. My God, how had things gotten crazy so fast? Panting slightly and with her face flushed, she managed to meet his eyes. Just. "Can we talk and eat? We haven't had any food since dinner last night."

Cameron laughed. She was pleased to note his own breathing was not quite regular. At least she wasn't the only one thrown totally off balance by what had just happened. "Let's see what we can rustle up from the cans we bought earlier."

Dinner wasn't exactly gourmet cuisine, but Cameron was happy with the company, even if the conversation wasn't to his taste. Okay, so he'd gone from wanting to get Laurie out of his life as fast as he could to not being able to keep his eyes—or his hands, as the situation earlier had shown—off her. But it wasn't every day you found out one of your closest friends was probably a serial killer. Cameron reckoned he could claim the circumstances were beyond unusual. They were life changing. Yet, when he looked into Laurie's beautiful blue eyes, his head felt surprisingly clear. He wasn't sure how she managed to ground him while tipping his world upside down at the same time.

He could tell himself it was her fault his ordered existence had been thrown into chaos. That, if Laurie hadn't turned up in Stillwater, if she hadn't had the gall to swim ashore on his private beach and collapse into his arms pretending to be in trouble, he would be continuing with his normal life, oblivious to human trafficking and dead women. He could do that. But only for a few seconds. Because that wasn't Cameron Delaney. A man who had fought his way into political office on a social justice ticket at the age of twenty-four was not the sort of person who hid from the truth, no matter how unpleasant it might be. Carla was dead. He had had twelve long lonely months to come to terms with that. More than 365 days and an equal number of sleepless nights to mourn her. How she died mattered. Of course it did. If she was murdered, he wanted justice for her. If Grant was her killer, Cameron wanted to see him behind bars. None of that made him miss her more. He couldn't. It was that simple. His heart wasn't big enough. But the tightness in his chest eased when he looked at Laurie. If that made him a bad person, then he would deal with the hellfire and damnation another time. Because right now he needed to keep looking.

"There are only two ways I can see for us to catch him." Laurie was curled up in a chair, the light from the fire casting a golden glow over her features. "One is that we find the bodies of the other girls."

"Tough call when we have no idea what happened to them." The subject matter might be unpleasant, but watching Laurie wasn't. Cameron let his eyes rest on the delicate hollow of her throat as she turned her head to watch the dancing flames. He wanted to press his lips to the point where he could see a faint pulse beating.

"*He* is our common denominator. If we can figure out more about Grant Becker, maybe we can find out what he did with these women."

"You said there were two ways to catch him. What's the second?" Cameron was fascinated by the intent look on her face as she turned back to face him.

"We set a trap for him."

It took a moment for him to register what she was saying. When he realized what she meant, he shook his head vehemently. "No way. Not a chance in hell, Laurie. I don't care what they teach you in the police academy. Where I come from, you don't set a trap for a man who wants to kill you. Not if what you mean is you want to put yourself in his way."

"Do you have an alternative suggestion? We just wait it out up here? No matter how much I like the scenery, I'm not sure I could stand this sort of inactivity for more than a day or two."

Cameron heard the frustration in her voice, and tried to reassure her. "Hopefully you won't have to.

Now you've let your captain know about Moreton, the FBI will be all over it. One of their own men is dead. His throat was cut. Once they access Moreton's case notes they'll be on to Grant in no time."

Laurie regarded him thoughtfully for a moment or two before changing the subject. "Tell me about your brothers."

Cameron shook his head. "Not so fast. The first time we met you warned me you're stubborn, remember? I knew your cousin well, even if you didn't. She had the same gene. I'm going to need your word that we're in this together and you won't go setting any traps for Grant I don't know about."

A slight smile trembled on her lips, fascinating him into staring at her mouth. The memory of those lips parting beneath his was fresh in his mind, sending a wave of desire surging through him in a direct hit to his groin. Being alone with her like this was the most exquisite form of torture. "If you insist."

He relaxed back in his seat. "My brothers? Why do you want to know about them?"

"Just because we have a bigger problem doesn't mean the investigation into your firm has gone away. Since you're not the one who is running the illegal operation—" Cameron quirked a brow at her, and Laurie had the grace to blush "—and I apologize for ever thinking you were, then isn't it likely one of them must be responsible?"

Cameron leaned forward to place another log on the fire. "It looks probable that's the only answer, but I'm struggling to believe it of either of them. In Bryce's case, just because it would be so out of character." He felt his face relax into a familiar affectionate expression, one that carried years of memories of his younger brother with it. Years filled with laughter and companionship. "I could no more doubt his honesty and integrity than I could my own."

"And Vincente?" Laurie prompted when he lapsed into silence.

Cameron wished his expression didn't have to change at the mention of his older brother's name. Wished he could feel the same sense of certainty and trust where Vincente was concerned.

He sighed. "I just don't know."

Laurie was easy to confide in. How had he gotten to a point where he felt totally at ease in her presence after being so angry with her a little over twenty-four hours ago? Was it simply because they'd been through so much together in that space of time, or was there something more? Could two people bond so easily? It was the strangest way to start something. Could anything lasting be built on such awkward foundations? And what was the "something" he was thinking of? It certainly felt like more than friendship.

"It had to be hard for him when we were growing up. Vincente was the outsider, but he never tried to be anything else, you know? He delighted in being the stereotypical half brother. He was always so jealous of everything. But particularly of me. Jealous of my relationship with our father, jealous of my closeness to Bryce, jealous of my success in business and jealous of my political career."

"He sounds like a good candidate to be the one using your company for illegal purposes," Laurie commented. "Even if he isn't doing it for personal gain, he could be doing it just to get at you."

"It would be so easy to think that, but I honestly believe he's turned himself around. These last few years, since he's been working for Delaney Transportation, Vincente has been a changed personality. He's worked harder than anyone I know to develop the company's financial systems, and he's really tried where our relationship is concerned, too. I hate to think the worst of him just because he's not Bryce."

"Could it be someone else inside the company?"

"I suppose nothing is impossible, but it seems unlikely. Given what you've told me, I need to get in there and check things out." He slumped in his seat. "I'm too tired to think straight about any of this right now."

Laurie fixed him with that direct blue gaze. "Is this where we need to have a conversation about our sleeping arrangements?"

Cameron rose to his feet, holding out his hands. Laurie placed her own hands in his and allowed him to draw her to her feet. "I guess it is."

"You said we had a lot to talk about before we finished what we started earlier." Her voice was husky.

"I'm all talked out. The most important thing to say is how much I want you." He drew her slightly closer, exulting in the warmth of her body and the clean, floral scent of her hair.

"I got that message when we were on the porch." Her lips were tantalizingly close.

"No. What I'm trying to say is, I want *you*, Laurie. I'm not using you as a Carla substitute. You have to believe that."

He felt the shudder that ran through her at the

words, as though some final, invisible barrier had been broken down. "I'm glad."

"And finally, however forward it might have been of me, I went shopping for more than food before we came up here." He reached in his back pocket and withdrew a pack of condoms. Buying them had been the test. If it had felt like a betrayal, he wouldn't have gone through with it. Would have known it was too soon. Instead, it had felt—he searched for the right word—*different*. There had been the frisson of anticipation, the thrill of something new, the wondering if he was doing the right thing. The sensation of stepping over a chasm from the past to the future. But betrayal? No. To his relief, that hadn't featured in his thoughts. "I knew being alone here with you would be tempting. After the kiss we shared last night, I thought—maybe even hoped—you might feel the same way."

Laurie didn't reply. His heart pounded. Had he got it hopelessly wrong? He was thirty years old and he felt like he was doing this for the first time. Then she took hold of his hand and led him toward the bedroom.

Cameron took Laurie's face between his hands and bent his head to hers. Her lips parted readily. His tongue gently met hers before he crushed her mouth in a kiss that melted them into one another.

"Sure about this?" He raised his head to scan her face.

Laurie loved that he could ask her that question in spite of his raging desire for her. Sweet, molten heat surged through her. "More than I've ever been about anything in my life."

Sweeping her up in his arms, Cameron carried her

over to the bed. Placing her on its surface, he lay down with her, covering her body with his. His leg moved between hers and, as he parted them, he brought his knee up, applying pressure at the apex of her thighs. Laurie stifled a groan as his lips moved to kiss the hollow of her throat. With her stretched out beneath him, Cameron pushed himself harder against her, his mouth closing on hers.

At first the kiss was light and teasing, then something shifted so it became rough and hungry, wild and abandoned. One of Cameron's strong hands fondled a breast through her shirt, finding the hardened peak, as his knee continued to press against her, driving her into a frenzy. Shifting his weight to one side, he undid the buttons of her blouse, dragging the cup of her bra aside. His hand was warm on one breast, exposing it to his gaze before he bent his head and suckled, his lips and tongue feeling maddeningly good on her sensitized flesh.

Laurie's hands gripped his shoulders, and held on to him as she pushed her body up toward his, bucking and writhing against that insistent knee. Soft, pleading sounds escaped her lips, sounds she had never heard herself make before. Wanton, demanding sounds she never would have imagined issued from deep within her throat.

With an answering groan, Cameron raised his head. Swiftly, he helped her out of her blouse and bra, then flung them aside. His own shirt followed, and Laurie drew in a sharp breath at the sight of the muscled perfection of his chest and shoulders. His biceps flexed as he worked her jeans over her hips and helped her wriggle out of them. When her underwear was gone, she lay back on the bed.

"My God, Laurie, you are exquisite."

"Your turn." She reached for his zipper, sliding it down. She slipped a hand inside and wrapped her fingers around his shaft, exulting in his hot, hard flesh beneath her touch.

Cameron's whole body jerked as though from an electric shock. "Laurie…" His voice was hoarse.

With the last barrier of clothing gone, they were free to explore each other's bodies. Cameron ignited fires all over Laurie's skin with his mouth and hands as he alternately touched, stroked, licked and kissed. There was too much urgency between them for restraint. Too much wanting for waiting. Although they had known each other for only a matter of days, it was as though they had packed a lifetime's worth of desire into those hours. It erupted now into a torrent of touches and tastes that quickly grew out of control.

Shifting his weight, he eased himself on top of her. Laurie was burning for more. Lifting her hips, she wrapped her legs around his waist, rubbing herself against his hardness, letting him feel how much she wanted him. Her heart hammered wildly as she felt his erection pressing hard up against her entrance.

"One second." She heard the rip of the foil packet and felt him reach between their bodies to get the condom on.

Then he was slowly pushing into her, and everything else was lost except red-hot sensation. Cameron held on to his control, maintaining eye contact, those glorious eyes darkening as he drove home in one long, searing push. Laurie gasped, gazing back at him as she dragged her nails up his back.

She bit her lip. "God, that feels so good."

He gave a shaky laugh, easing his hips back until he almost pulled out of her completely, before pushing all the way back inside her again. "Feels even better now."

She didn't know how he could stand to take it so slow. Not when she could see in his eyes how desperately he wanted her. Dragging back, pressing forward. Keeping his gaze fixed on hers. She knew that was important to him. He wanted her to know he wasn't thinking of anyone else. Laurie certainly wasn't. She was lost in Cameron, wrapped around him, feeling every hot, hard inch of him. Pleasure so intense it was painful rippled up her spine and made her cry out his name.

His patience and control snapped then, and he drove in and out of her. Fast and frenzied. Cameron slipped a hand between them, using his thumb to stroke, circle and tease. Pressure built through her core, a wild mix of pleasurable tension and tingling ache. She had handed over control of her body to this man, and now she was moving in time to his rhythm, matching the pace he was setting, and she couldn't get enough of it…couldn't get enough of him. Her body strained to draw him closer, her tongue tangled with his, her hips bucked beneath him, her breasts were hot and aching as they pressed against his hard chest.

Cameron's kisses grew more demanding as he picked up the pace. He rocked faster and faster, driving deep as Laurie began to moan and cry out. Stars floated in front of her eyes, and she gasped for air. Frenzied pleasure built to a peak until Laurie's body exploded and she clung helplessly to Cameron. As his own body jerked in time with hers, he pressed his face into her neck, murmuring her name over and over.

Reeling with a series of aftershocks, she lay back until the world finally righted itself. When they drew apart, Cameron pulled her into his arms and she snuggled into his hold as if it was the most natural thing in the world. For that moment, this was all there was. Just the two of them. No serial killers on their tail. No murdered FBI agents. No human trafficking. No dead lovers.

Sunrise had always been Cameron's favorite time of day. Here, high in the forest above the Stillwater Trail, the early morning light was just poking its golden fingertips between the trees. A faint mist lingered over the ground, and the scent of pine was a fresh, clean wake-up call.

He had left Laurie sleeping, easing away from her gently as he slid from the bed. She looked so beautiful, lying there with her hair tumbling over her naked shoulders; it had been tempting to stay where he was and maybe wake her with a kiss…just as he had done in the night. Instead he had pulled on his jeans, fixed himself a cup of strong coffee and came out onto the porch. He needed some thinking time.

They had made love again during the night. Slower, that second time. Exploring each other's bodies, each taking the time to find out what the other one liked, drawing out the pleasure so it became an exquisite agony. And, in Cameron's case, confirming what he already knew. He was doing exactly what he had sworn he wouldn't. He was getting in too deep.

This had all crept up on him too fast. He didn't know what the rules were about grief and mourning, but he was fairly sure the town gossips in Stillwater would be able to tell him. He could picture the whispers behind the hands, the shaking heads, the sour expressions. *Twelve months? Not nearly long enough. It isn't seemly*, they would say. *He should still be grieving.* Add in the complication of Laurie's looks, her relationship to Carla...

Thinking like that made it seem like he was somehow trying to distance himself from what had been an earth-shattering night. He knew how Laurie made him feel. He had never experienced a connection like the one he had felt to her. *Never.* And that scared him. He wasn't going to devalue Carla's memory with comparisons. Even now, the thought of Laurie was doing things to his body he'd never believed possible. Just thinking about her was making him hard as all hell. He shook his head, giving a soft laugh. He wasn't in control of his own body anymore. It was a strange and new phenomenon, one he was surprised to find himself enjoying.

Cameron had never been a love-'em-and-leave-'em guy. Even before Carla, he hadn't been into one-night stands. He had to feel an emotional connection to a woman before he engaged in a physical relationship. He wasn't vain, but he knew his looks attracted women. He could have had affairs, before and after Carla, if he chose. He just didn't choose. It wasn't him. Now he was faced with a new and intriguing situation. He'd found a cure for the pain of his grief. The problem was, he might already be addicted to the remedy.

A sound behind him made him turn. Laurie was

standing there, dressed just in his shirt, her hair tousled and her long legs bare. She smiled. "The lack of phone and internet signals is going to kill me."

He slid an arm around her waist, the action feeling comfortable. "Why? Do you think you might get bored?"

She chuckled reminiscently. "After last night? Not likely. But I wish I knew what was going on with this investigation."

"I have to go and check in with Bryce today. His pleas for help were getting increasingly frantic when I spoke to him briefly yesterday. And I need to pack a bag with some clean clothes. I'll see what I can find out while I'm in town." Her lips parted and he shook his head, anticipating her question. "It's too dangerous for you to come with me."

Laurie sighed. "I suppose you're right. How will I stop myself going crazy on my own up here without you?"

"There are a few books and magazines, so you will stay inside and keep your gun right next to you." The thought of Grant finding her here, alone and vulnerable, was unbearable. *He can't know where we are,* his rational mind insisted. *He's never been here, and even Bryce or Vincente would struggle to find this place after all these years.* He tried to remember the last time his brothers had been up here. They must have been kids, Bryce no more than eight years old, Cameron ten and Vincente two years older. A memory, bright and clear, of the three of them playing in the snow while their dad and uncle watched from this very porch came back to him. How could he possibly broach the subject of one of his brothers betraying him?

"Now you know what you're looking for, it will be easy, because you'll know the right questions to ask them." Laurie's voice was sympathetic.

How had she known what he was thinking? He gazed into those clear, blue eyes and marveled at the chain of events that had brought them to this point in time. It felt so right holding her at his side like this, yet there was a trail of death and flames behind them and a madman lurking in the shadows. Not to mention someone using his firm for trafficking underage girls. Was it wrong to feel happy in those circumstances? In any circumstances? And what was Laurie feeling? What did this mean to her? There was no question in his mind last night meant *something* to her. The raw emotion between them had been incredible. Could she be experiencing the same wild roller coaster of emotion that was sweeping through him?

"Are you thinking what I'm thinking?" Her smile was mischievous.

His heart gave a thud. "What might that be?"

"Breakfast."

Chapter 8

Bryce Delaney was definitely not one of those people who subscribed to the view that a tidy office also meant a tidy mind.

"This reminds me of when we were kids and all the times Mom used to yell at you to straighten your room," Cameron commented, as he moved a pile of paper, a takeaway container and an old boot from a chair so he could sit down. "Now I know how she felt."

Bryce's grin was unrepentant. "My mess, my problem. I know where everything is."

The sad fact was, Cameron decided, Bryce was telling the truth. If his brother's secretary came in right now and requested a file or docket from six months ago, Bryce would be able to put his hand on it immediately.

"So at the risk of sounding like I'm not pleased to

see you…where the hell have you been?" Bryce's eyes, several shades lighter than his own, scanned Cameron's face, with a trace of concern in their golden-brown depths. "And what can I do to help?"

He wouldn't double-cross me. The thought was fierce and certain. Of all the people in the world he might suspect, Bryce was the last on the list. An Explosive Ordance Disposal (EOD) officer in Afghanistan, his promising army career had been brought to an abrupt end two years ago by a roadside bomb. Although his physical injuries had healed fast and he was left with only a slight limp as a result, it was the mental wounds that had taken their toll. Since Bryce never spoke of that time, Cameron could only guess at how deep they went. Now and then, he caught a flash of something dark and tortured in his brother's eyes and knew the damage had scarred his soul.

"I'll let you know if the time comes."

Bryce hesitated. "Tell me to butt out if you want to, but has this got anything to do with the girl who looks like Carla?" Cameron remained silent. "Because she's not Carla." When Cameron still didn't reply, he plowed on, his face reddening slightly. "And it would be weird."

Cameron held up a hand, indicating enough was enough. Until he had this clear in his own mind, he wasn't ready to talk it through with anyone else. Not even Bryce. "Thanks for your concern." He felt the need to add something more. "For the record, she's Carla's cousin. And it's not weird."

"Your business." Bryce shrugged.

"Exactly. Which brings me to why I'm here. What's going on with you and Vincente?"

A scowl crossed his brother's handsome features. It was an expression he reserved uniquely for Vincente. "When is he going to stop treating me like the baby brother?"

It was a question Cameron had heard many times. "Bryce, I don't have long. Can we skip the preliminaries and get straight to the details?"

Bryce pointed to a set of maps on the wall. Starting out with West County, they widened to include the state and then the entire country. Every map included a complex network of colored roads and symbols. Attached to each was a detailed, color-coordinated chart.

"You know how much work I put into the planning process. I have to maximize fuel costs, driver time and depot space when I put each of these routes together. Then there are all the other factors such as arrival times at ports and airports, scheduled delivery times, third parties we outsource to and how many long- or short-haul trips each driver is doing. I've worked up a computer program to get this right so each driver gets his, or her, schedule at the start of each week."

"Her?" Cameron raised a brow. Something about Bryce's voice when he said the word hinted at a problem.

Bryce's scowl lightened long enough to laugh. Was it Cameron's imagination, or was there a trace of self-consciousness in the sound? "We have a few female drivers on the payroll, but only one of them is a chronic thorn in my side."

"It sounds like you have the perfect system." Cameron gestured to the wall.

"Had. I *had* the perfect system. For the past few weeks, all I've had is a constant series of phone calls from truckers calling me at all hours of the day and night, demanding to know why their schedules have been changed with only a few hours' notice."

"Let me guess." Cameron knew his voice conveyed intense weariness. "Vincente?"

"Did someone say my name?" A drawling voice drew his attention to the open doorway. Vincente had a knack for arriving at the perfect moment.

Cameron could never see his older brother without thinking of all the things Vincente could be, if he would only put his mind to it. Strikingly good-looking, Vincente was the artistic, intellectual one in the family, yet he could still outrun, outshoot and outswim his more openly athletic brothers if he chose. And that was the secret to Vincente. *If he chose.* Although Vincente had potential in abundance, he never seemed to choose the easy route. Life on Vincente's terms was never simple.

Cameron got straight to the point. "We were discussing the problem with the drivers' schedules."

"I don't have a problem with the drivers' schedules." Vincente's smile was deliberately insolent as it flicked over to Bryce. He had always known exactly which buttons to press to send his younger brother into overdrive. He still used them to his advantage, and he did it now as skillfully as he had done when he was eight and Bryce was four. A furious expletive burst from Bryce's lips as he rose to his feet.

"Easy." Cameron waved him back down. "Why have you been making changes without consulting Bryce? You know operations are his territory."

Although Vincente had been born and raised in Wyoming, some of his gestures unconsciously betrayed his Italian heritage. The shrug he gave now was as Italian as the taste of Chianti or the roar of a vintage Vespa's engine. "Just trying to be helpful."

Cameron knew that look in Vincente's flashing dark eyes. It was the look he had seen so many times when they were kids and Vincente had been caught in some wrongdoing.

"Maybe you could confine your helpfulness to those times when it's asked for in the future?" Cameron kept his voice level. Arguing with Vincente was like wresting an eel.

He could feel Vincente's rage in the air between them, darker, quieter and more brooding than Bryce's stormier display. But there was a flash of something more in his older brother's expression. Behind the anger, there was hurt. Just for a second, Cameron thought Vincente was about to say something. It was quickly gone and Vincente's expression returned to neutral.

Then, with a curt nod, he turned and left. A feeling of unease lingered in Cameron's mind. He wanted to go after Vincente and ask him what the hell was going on, but he knew his brother too well. He would get nothing out of Vincente in this mood.

"Think he'll listen?" Bryce asked.

"If he doesn't, I'll take it up a notch." The prospect was not something he relished. Cameron rose to his feet, getting to the other reason for his visit. "Anything else before we go down to the depot?"

"While you're here, I don't suppose you can get rid of that creep Vincente has hired."

The feeling of disquiet intensified. *I've stayed away for far too long.* "What creep would this be?"

"Name of Zac Peyton. I have no idea what his job

is meant to be, but the guy seems to spend most of his time snooping around. I even found him on his way into this office the other day. He claimed to be lost, but I don't like the look of him." Bryce's face was serious. "I'm worried, Cam. I think Vincente could be up to something."

"I think you could be right."

Was it really only a few days since he'd first pulled into the Paradise Creek vacation village for that first date with Laurie? If he'd known then what he knew now, would he have kept walking and still knocked on her door that night, or would he have turned tail and run for his life? Cameron had never run out on a challenge. And—wherever the future took them— he would not have missed this chance to get to know Laurie for all the world. A flashback to last night hit him. The intent look on her face as they made love, the soft gasping sounds she made, her fingernails clawing his back, the velvet warmth of her muscles gripping him... Yeah, he was glad he'd hung in, even though this was turning out to be one hell of a week.

He'd toured the transportation depot with Bryce and come away with one certainty. Whatever was going on at Delaney Transportation, it was not happening at the main depot here in Stillwater. Operations there, under Bryce's eagle-eyed supervision, were running like clockwork. Cameron would have been happy to invite a dozen FBI special agents in to subject the place to a detailed scrutiny. He was certain they would not find anything untoward. So why, after that awkward encounter with Vincente, did he still feel uneasy?

The vacation village was curiously quiet for a major crime scene, and that caused another uncomfortable feeling to settle in his gut. He had so many of these feelings chasing each other round inside him today, it felt like he'd swallowed a barrelful of butterflies. But he wasn't wrong about this place. It was *too* quiet here. There should be local law enforcement and federal agents crawling all over this scene right about now. Instead, the only sounds were a faint breeze ruffling the trees and the distant warbling of a vireo.

The door to Laurie's cabin stood open, but there was no crime-scene tape stopping him from crossing the threshold. Even so, he paused, standing outside and leaning in to avoid contaminating the scene. The only person inside was a tall, thin man in dungarees. He was whistling to himself as he brushed the floor. *What the hell is going on here?*

"Hi there." Cameron raised his voice to be heard above the sounds of whistling and brushing.

The man paused, a smile dawning as he recognized the intruder. "Oh, hey, Mayor Delaney. Are you looking for the owner, Mr. Johnson? He's out at one of the other sites this morning."

The normality of the whole situation was getting to Cameron. Clearly he wasn't going to contaminate anything. With another check to make sure he had the right cabin, he stepped inside.

"No, I was looking for the woman who was staying here. A Miss Carter."

The guy, Cameron had seen him around town doing odd jobs in various places—what was his name? Ben? Bob? Bobby, that was it—shook his head. "Weirdest thing. Mr. Johnson said she just upped and left, even though she was paid up until the end of the summer. She even left her rental car out front."

"When was this?"

"Last night." How did Bobby know that? Particularly since he was wrong. Cameron should know. Laurie had actually left the night before. He had been with her.

"How do you know she's gone for good? She could be staying somewhere else for a few days. Maybe she went to Yellowstone for a visit. Lots of tourists do that."

"Some guy called Mr. Johnson on her behalf. Said she'd had to go away. Urgent business back home. Asked if Mr. Johnson could arrange the return of the car. There was some damage to this window. She left the cash to cover the repairs." Bobby scratched his head. "Place was spotless. Like she'd cleaned before she left. Really cleaned, scrubbed the floors and all. Who finds the time to do that when they get an urgent call?"

Who indeed? Cameron felt his hands shape themselves into fists, and he wished Grant Becker was here so he could pound them into that handsome face. Once again Grant had been one step ahead of them. The fake call pretending to be on Laurie's behalf was all very neat, but what had he done with Moreton's body? And why, when Laurie had rung her captain in San Diego to tell him what had happened to the FBI agent, had there not been at least some sort of law enforcement interest in this place?

"Did anyone else come by here today, Bobby?" Cameron did his best to keep his voice casual. He wanted to ask if the police had been around, but that would be too obvious.

"Not that I know, but I only stopped by to fix the window. I'm just finishing up. Been here about an hour."

It was close to noon, roughly forty-two hours since Moreton had been killed. Three or four hours after his death, Laurie had rung Captain Harper in San Diego. What had been happening here since that time? It looked likely Grant had been back to this cabin, disposed of Moreton's body and cleaned the place, before calling Johnson to say Laurie had left. But how had he managed to throw the police off the trail? Even if the FBI had been here and found nothing suspicious, they still had a missing agent *and* a missing undercover police officer. Something just wasn't adding up.

Nodding a quick goodbye to Bobby, who seemed eager to get on with his sweeping, Cameron returned to his car. The Stillwater Police Department was located in City Hall, the same majestic building that housed the mayor's office. Cameron typically spent two or three days a week in his office, more if he was needed. His role was very much one of public relations and, as the city's leader, he was prepared to devote as much time as necessary to the job. That was why the voters of Stillwater loved him. They could get to see their mayor with their problems pretty much anytime they wanted to. He hadn't planned on a detour to this office in downtown Stillwater, just off Lakeview Drive, but, in view of what he'd just seen, he desperately needed to make some inquiries.

Conscious he hadn't been around for a few days,

he paused at his secretary's desk first. "Anything I should know about?"

Alberta Finch regarded him over the top of her half-moon spectacles. "And who are you again? Just remind me…"

Cameron grinned. "Don't give me a hard time."

Alberta's usually harsh features softened. Despite her formidable exterior, she was genuinely fond of Cameron and had been fiercely protective of him when Carla died, guarding his well-being and privacy like a gray-haired bulldog in a hand-knit sweater. She cast him a sidelong glance. "Seems like the whole town has been talking about a girl who looks like Carla."

Cameron groaned. "I was a fool to take her to Dino's."

"Is she nice?"

How was he supposed to answer that? A picture of Laurie's face, eyes half-closed and head thrown back as he entered her, rose unbidden in his memory. Yes, she was nice. And a whole lot more. In the end he opted for a noncommittal reply. "Too soon to say."

"Your face tells me she's nice." There was no fooling Alberta. Her tone became gruff. "I'm glad."

This was one conversation he wasn't having. "Is there anything you need me to look at?"

"There's been some graffiti out on the town welcome sign. I won't damage your ears by telling you what it says."

Cameron groaned again. "Can you get someone out there and have it cleaned up?"

She flapped a dismissive hand. "Already taken care of. There's nothing else I can't handle."

"Good. I have to go away for a few days." He avoided her searching look. "Is Chief Wilkinson in?"

Alberta snorted. "Since it usually takes nothing short of a minor earthquake to pry him out from behind that desk of his, I expect so."

She was being unfair to the man who had been the Stillwater chief of police for as long as Cameron could remember. Bradley Wilkinson was an administrator, rather than a hands-on cop, which was where the impression he didn't budge from his office came from. But he was an astute police chief, and Cameron had a great deal of respect for him.

"I'm too old for this job." It was Wilkinson's usual refrain, and the first words out of his mouth as Cameron entered his office.

"Trouble?" Cameron had been wondering how to play this. Walking in here and pouring out the whole story wasn't going to work. The city police department and the County Sheriff's Office worked closely together. If he marched in and accused a well-respected police officer like Grant Becker of being a serial killer... Well, he could picture the looks that would signal the end of his political career, and likely his permanent exit from Stillwater. The gossip mill would start up. *Never been the same since his girlfriend died, poor man.* Or, *Just when he seemed to be getting back to normal.* And the worst of all. *Appearances can be deceptive. You never can tell.*

But maybe, just maybe, Wilkinson was about to tell him what was going on without any prompting.

Wilkinson waved the sheaf of papers he was holding. "Mrs. Martin."

Cameron slumped into the chair opposite Chief

Wilkinson, his optimism fading fast. Mrs. Martin was the chief's least favorite person, but her letters rarely involved any actual crimes. If she was uppermost in the police chief's mind, it seemed probable there wasn't much else going on. "What is it this time?"

"Strange goings-on out at the Hope Valley coal mine. Seven pages. Count them with me, Cam. Seven of the damn things."

Cameron was barely listening. *Why* didn't Chief Wilkinson know anything about a dead body out at the Paradise Creek vacation village? Because it was obvious he sure as hell didn't. If he had, Cameron knew the other man would have come right out and told him about it. Hell, Cameron's phone would have been ringing nonstop the minute Wilkinson got word of the murder. The excuse Cameron had used to Grant about preventing a panic had been a valid one. As the mayor, his role would be to do what he did best and manage public relations. Right now, there was nothing to manage. Not for the first time this morning, he wanted to put his fist through the wall in frustration. The thought of Laurie back at the cabin, counting on him, kept him calm.

"Everything seems quiet around here."

"You're right, it does. But not so quiet I'm tempted to drive out to an abandoned coal mine and investigate Mrs. Martin's mysterious lights and spooky noises." He eyed Cameron hopefully. "I don't suppose you'd care to go out there and work your charm on her? Reassure her the police department has everything in hand?"

Laughing, Cameron declined the offer. "I'm going

away for a few days. Call me if you need me for any-thing. Doesn't matter what time of day or night."

"Any problems and yours is the first number I'll call. I have you on speed dial, just like always." With a wave of his hand, Chief Wilkinson returned to his perusal of Mrs. Martin's letter.

What the hell is going on here? The question sur-faced again, and Cameron's overwrought brain still refused to provide any answers.

His last stop was the lake house, the home he and Carla had shared. All at once, it seemed like some-one else's place, like it belonged in another lifetime, the familiar things suddenly unfamiliar. Hurriedly, Cameron packed a bag with clothes and other essen-tials, threw a few more groceries into another bag and dashed back to the car.

The problem of Laurie's phone conversation with her chief in San Diego gnawed away at him constantly as he drove. He couldn't believe her captain would not have instantly responded to a call of that type from one of his officers. Or that the FBI would not have immediately mobilized at the news one of their agents had been killed. Had Grant managed to get to them? Persuade them Laurie's call was a hoax? Even so, wouldn't someone have tried to contact Moreton or Laurie for reassurance, and when they failed to reach them, at least have checked things out? And would Grant be stupid enough to implicate himself that way? The guy had been pretty good at covering his tracks so far.

The thoughts kept coming on an endless loop until he reached the lockup near Wilderness Lake. It was impossible to get a car any nearer the cabin than this.

Cameron had been checking his rearview mirror for the last few miles and, as the road narrowed and became more remote, he hadn't seen any other vehicles. Nevertheless, he wasn't taking any chances with Laurie's safety. The cabin was an hour's hike from where he left the car, but he took a circuitous route, doubling back on himself several times. By the time the cabin was in his sights, he was high above it, looking down on the wooden building through the trees.

Nothing stirred around him. The silence and stillness were no consolation. Grant Becker was a skilled hunter. If he was close by, he would be at ease in these surroundings and quite capable of stalking Cameron through the pine trees the same way he would hunt a deer. The thought sent a chill up his spine. Laurie was down there waiting for his return. He had to get to her.

Cameron held his breath as he moved stealthily out into the open ground, half expecting a shot to ring out and catch him in the spine. Nothing happened and he exhaled in a long, grateful sigh as he reached the cabin door. His imagination was working overtime. Just one more score he needed to settle with Grant when he got the chance.

"Laurie?" He called out her name as he stepped inside and closed the door behind him. There was no reply. It took about thirty seconds for him to ascertain that the cabin was empty.

Chapter 9

Laurie glanced at the screen in frustration. Her phone had stopped being a means of communication. Now it was just a clock, and it was exactly two minutes since she'd last checked it. Cameron had been gone for much longer than she'd anticipated, and rather than risk going completely stir-crazy, she had come outside and wandered a little way from the cabin into the forest. Her gun was tucked firmly into the waistband of her jeans, but she didn't feel afraid out here. She felt more comfortable than in the cabin, where every creak of the wooden frame had her eyes skittering left and right, making her fearful Grant Becker had found her hideaway and was on his way inside to get her.

She was in danger of allowing him to dominate her through fear even if he couldn't get to her in person, and she decided she'd rather risk a face-to-face con-

frontation in the open than cower in a corner. Sitting
on a rock, looking down the majestic valley, Laurie
wanted this thinking time to review what she knew
of the murders and Grant's part in them. Instead, her
mind stubbornly refused to shift away from Cameron
and the events of the previous night.

How did this happen? How, in the space of a few
days, had she gone from being the ultimate professional, married to her job, to being so utterly, hopelessly attracted to the man she had been sent here to
investigate? She tried to analyze it. Was it their unique
situation? She'd never been in this sort of danger before, and he had come to her rescue. Was she seeing him as a modern-day knight in shining armor?
Was it because they'd been unexpectedly thrown together? Was she—heaven forbid—subconsciously trying to step in and replace Carla because she sensed
that might be what he needed?

This isn't reality. She had to keep reminding herself of that. *We've never been granted the opportunity to get to know each other. The person I think I've
fallen for doesn't exist. If we met under normal circumstances, I probably wouldn't look at him twice.*
Okay, that wasn't strictly true. Any sane woman with
a pulse would look at Cameron twice. *But I wouldn't
be feeling like this. I wouldn't be driven to distraction by this restless, burning longing for a man I met
a few days ago.*

"Laurie." Cameron's voice jolted her back down to
earth. Whom was she kidding? As she rose from her
rocky seat, she knew she was in deep trouble. It didn't
matter how long she'd known him, what the circumstances were or what was coming in the future. This

man held her in the palm of his hand, and there was no chance she was getting away anytime soon. "What the hell are you doing out here?"

Although she smiled up at him, he didn't return the expression, and she saw the depth of his concern in his eyes. For a second, she put herself in his place. He'd lost Carla to Grant, and now Grant was coming after Laurie. *I don't mean as much to him as she did—no one could—but it must hurt like hell to be reminded.*

"I'm sorry." She tried to keep her voice upbeat but failed miserably. "It felt claustrophobic in there on my own."

His face softened. "Let's go back and get a drink while I tell you about my strange morning."

Once they were back inside the cabin, Laurie listened with a growing sense of disbelief as Cameron recounted the story of what he'd seen at the Paradise Creek vacation village and his subsequent conversation with Chief Wilkinson.

She felt the color draining from her face. "I don't understand. I spoke to Captain Harper myself. Even though he wasn't happy with me when I told him I wanted to stay in Stillwater for a few days, he told me he was going to inform the FBI about Moreton as soon as he got off the phone."

"Talk me through that conversation. Start to finish." Cameron carried the coffee cups out onto the porch. Laurie sat on the bench, tucking her legs under her in a defensive position. "How did he sound when you spoke to him?"

"It's hard to say. The reception was so bad." She frowned. "In fact, I couldn't hear anything at all that first time."

"First time?" Cameron's gaze became intent.

"Yes, I didn't really think much of it with everything else that was going on. I called Captain Harper's number, but the line was so bad all I could hear was a buzzing noise. I ended the call and a few minutes later he called me back." Lifting a hand to her mouth as a thought struck her, she turned wide eyes to Cameron's face. "Oh, dear Lord. It wasn't him, was it?"

"Check the call log on your phone."

With fingers that weren't quite steady, Laurie checked the last number to make an incoming call to her phone. She held it up to show Cameron. "No caller ID."

Cameron took a sip of his coffee. "Interesting, but it's not conclusive. When the signal was bad, your captain could have called you back from another phone rather than using his own cell. How did he sound?"

"It was hard to say. His voice was faint. There was still interference, like there was static on the line." She looked up, her brow furrowing as she concentrated on the memory of that call. "I told you about the cursing, right? That was unusual. The captain has a temper, but I've never heard that sort of language from him before. He's usually always professional. Is it possible Grant intercepted my call to Captain Harper somehow?"

"From what you've told me, I'd say it's not only possible, it's highly likely. If he was hacking your phone, he'd have been alerted as soon as you tried to make your call to Harper. All he needed to do was use some sort of jamming equipment so you couldn't hear anything and were forced to hang up. Then he called you back, pretending to be Harper."

"I've been having problems with my phone signal."

Laurie did her best to remember when it started. It came back to her now. "Ever since the night we went to Dino's. The night I first met Grant. He could have been hacking my phone since then, but to do that he'd have needed my number."

"I've been thinking about that. Did you give your number to the vacation rental company?"

"Yes, they needed it for housekeeping and to give me directions when I first arrived. But surely they wouldn't give it out, not even to a police officer."

"No, but Grant must have found a way of getting into their office on the vacation village site. He had to have a key to your cabin. He got in there to leave the first arrangement of flowers and then he got in the second time to kill Moreton," Cameron reminded her. "He could have found your number at the same time."

Laurie took a moment to think about that. About her sleeping in that cabin while Grant Becker had the key to the door in his pocket. About him turning the key over between his fingers as he planned how he was going to kill her. Then another thought took over. She turned wide eyes to Cameron. "So we are still the only people who know Moreton is dead?"

"It looks that way." His face was grim as he sipped his coffee.

Laurie assimilated the impact of those words. The bottom line wasn't good. Two days ago, when she had believed she was calling Captain Harper, not only had she told him Moreton had been murdered, she had also told him where the agent's body was. Now the body had vanished and she was back to having nothing except allegations and hunches. Her captain had no idea what she was doing here in Wyoming. The exact nature of her undercover work for the FBI was a closely guarded secret.

The only people she knew for sure she could trust were Moreton and Mike Samuels. One of those was dead, and with her laptop gone, she had no way of contacting the other. If she called Captain Harper now and outlined her suspicions against Grant Becker, she knew he would listen to her, no matter how wild her story sounded. He had known her since she joined the force, had nurtured and supported her as one of his most promising junior officers. But there was no way he would respond with a knee-jerk reaction to what sounded—even to Laurie's own ears—like a crazy accusation against a well-respected sheriff from another state. No, the captain would do what he always did and play by the rules. Which would involve Laurie coming out of hiding and exposing herself to danger. The situation would be exactly the same if she tried to call the FBI. And, anyway, how the hell was she supposed to start *that* conversation with a telephone operator in the nearest field office?

She was aware of Cameron watching her as though he was attempting to follow the thoughts flitting across her face. "I don't know what to do," she confessed.

"Grant has had his own way for too long over all of this. It's time to take the fight to him."

"The common denominator is how these women look, right?" They had eaten dinner and were sitting across from each other at the table. Cameron was making notes on a pad. Laurie nodded. "So it seems likely he sees them, they have the right look, he sends them flowers and then he snatches them and kills them?"

"That seems the most obvious scenario." Laurie took another surreptitious glance at the darkening window.

"Stop worrying. He isn't out there," Cameron assured her. "Back to our scenario. What if there is more to it? What if he needs to have some interaction with them, as well?"

Her smile peeped out, making his heart give that extra beat it reserved just for her. "I thought I was meant to be the cop around here?"

He threw out his chest, striking a macho pose. "I've watched a lot of movies. I know how these things work."

She laughed, and he was pleased to see her starting to relax. The realization she had no credible way of contacting the authorities about Moreton's death and the missing girls had hit her hard. "Okay, continue with your theory, Detective Delaney."

"If he did have some interaction with them before he killed them, we might be able to link him to at least one—hopefully more—of them."

"There's just one problem with that. None of these women are officially dead."

"I've thought of that." Cameron held up his pad, pointing to the words he'd just underlined. *Find the bodies.*

Laurie slumped in her seat. "Just like that? In case you hadn't noticed, this is a very big state. Searching it would take longer than forever. Particularly as we have no way of knowing where to start."

"Nobody has been looking until now. At least not

officially. And nobody has been looking for bodies," he reminded her. "Grant has been safe because no one has made any link between him and these girls. Now he has a double problem." She raised a questioning brow. "You're a cop and I know him just about as well as anybody does."

"Okay." She took a sip of the wine he'd poured for them both. It was a bottle he'd snatched up from the lake house before he left, one of his favorite vintages, and the mellow flavor was helping Cameron relax. He hoped it would have the same effect on Laurie. "Tell me about our suspect."

Cameron thought about Grant Becker. Big, dependable Grant. That was the way he'd always viewed him. Yet, even as a child, he'd known there were things in his friend's life that were troubling. He tried to find the words to paint Laurie a picture of the man he'd more or less grown up with. "We met in the sandbox on the first day of school and have been friends ever since. My mom would bring him home from school with us and he'd stay for dinner two, maybe three, times a week. I never went back to his house."

"Why was that?" Laurie's eyes were fixed on his face.

"At first I never questioned it. You don't as a kid, do you? You just accept things. As we grew older, I realized his home life wasn't good. His dad was a drunk. Grant would have bruises. Oh, he always had an explanation for them. He walked into a door…fell down a stair."

"You think his dad beat him?"

"That was what I figured at the time, when I was old enough to think about it at all." Cameron took a slug of wine. "I was wrong. His dad left home when we were ten and the bruises continued. That was when I knew it must have been his mom who was beating him."

"Didn't anyone do anything?"

"I know my own mother went to see the school principal a few times." Cameron's lips quirked into a smile at the memory of the fiercely protective woman who had reared him. With enough maternal love to spare for every child in Stillwater, Sandy Delaney hadn't been able to bear the thought of her son's friend being subjected to cruelty. "But while Grant stuck to the story his injuries were caused by accidents, there was nothing anyone *could* do. Short of sending him on summer camps for underprivileged children and hoping he might open up to someone, of course. And I know what you're going to say. If Grant was abused by his mother as a child, that placed him at risk of becoming an offender—potentially a killer—as an adult."

Laurie lifted her wineglass to her lips, sipping the light-colored liquid slowly. "It's not my area of expertise. While I know most serial killers have experienced childhood trauma of some sort, not all victims of child abuse go on to kill. Many grow up to lead fulfilling lives. But abuse can impair self-esteem, interfere with the ability to function adequately in society, succeed academically and form healthy relationships. Take that to the extreme and serial killers will often fail to keep a job for any period of time and rarely have a successful intimate relationship."

"Academically, and in the workplace, Grant has always been an overachiever. In school, his grades were consistently well above average, in spite of anything he might have been dealing with at home. When he left school he joined the police force and was fast-tracked onto a criminal justice degree program. Once he'd completed his degree, he pretty much straight away ran for office. That about sums up his determination. And you've seen how he looks. Muscles like those don't come easy. He's a big guy anyway, but he works hard to maintain all that physical strength and endurance."

"What you're describing isn't necessarily someone who *is* functioning adequately in society," Laurie said. "It sounds to me like Grant has always had a hell of a lot to prove."

Cameron considered that statement. "I never really thought of it like that. I guess you could be right, except…well, couldn't you say the same thing about me? I worked hard at school, got a degree, built up my own business and got elected to public office at a young age. How is Grant so different from me?"

"That brings me to my next question. Does he have the ability to form healthy relationships?"

"Growing up, I think I was his only friend. In recent years, he and Vincente have become friendly. They are both single guys with a few interests, like hunting, in common." He considered the matter. "Although when we saw them together at Dino's, I was surprised. I thought the friendship had fizzled out recently."

Laurie shook her head. "The question was not so much about friendships, although they are important. I meant intimate relationships."

Cameron gave it some careful thought. He couldn't remember Grant ever forming an attachment to a woman. Even during their teenage years, his friend had never seemed to experience the highs and lows of the agonizing crushes that gripped his peers. He shook his head. How had he missed this?

"As far as I know, he *never* had a relationship. Never even dated. The first time I saw him pay any attention to a woman was when he asked Carla out that first time he met her. If I hadn't been so mad at him for hitting on my date, I might almost have been pleased he was finally relaxing and taking time off from his job long enough to pay attention to his personal life."

"Except we now know his interest in Carla wasn't normal." Cameron's fingers tightened around the stem of his wineglass at the words, and Laurie placed her hand on his arm, her face sympathetic.

He relaxed slightly under the pressure of her fingers. "So we can look at the missing girls and see if we can make a link to Grant that way, or we can look at possible places he may have disposed of their bodies."

Laurie jumped up. "The lack of internet is a hindrance, but I made some notes about these girls. You may recognize some of their names." She headed into the bedroom and emerged with a notepad. Flipping over the pages, she bent her head over what appeared to be a series of hieroglyphics.

"Did a spider crawl over the page?" Cameron teased.

Laurie frowned in mock annoyance. "If you can't read it, neither can anyone snooping. Let's start with the first girl to go missing. Lisa Lambert vanished two and a half years before Carla died. Age twenty-two, she was a clerk working at Palmerston Insurance in Stillwater, although she was barely clinging on to her job. She shared an apartment, had some problems with drugs and alcohol. She didn't come home after a night out, which wasn't unusual. When she'd been gone a week, her roommate reported her missing."

Cameron shook his head. "I didn't know her. Don't even remember anything about her disappearance, but—" he looked stunned "—my God, Laurie, that was only six months after Grant met Carla."

"If Carla had the sort of effect on him you described, who knows what that did to an unbalanced mind? He could have seized on anything about Lisa that reminded him of Carla. We know their coloring was the same. Eight months after Lisa disappeared, Kathy Sachs, a waitress working at the Stillwater Heights Hotel, didn't turn up for her shift. She'd only been there a month or two, wasn't local, had said she wasn't happy in her job. She was quite open about the fact that she only came to this area to escape an abusive marriage, but she missed her family back home. No one took much notice when she didn't show, except she left all her stuff behind, even her cell phone. The hotel manager decided to report her missing."

"Don't tell me—she never got in touch to claim her stuff?" Cameron grimaced. Somehow, hearing there were five missing girls wasn't as bad as hearing their individual stories.

"If she did, there's no record of it." Laurie went back to her notes. "The next girl who definitely fits the physical type I was looking for is nineteen-year-old Tanya Horton. She was due to meet friends at the cinema in Stillwater. When she didn't turn up, they went in without her. After the movie, Tanya's best friend rang her mom to check if she was okay. Tanya was known to be something of a wild child, and it wouldn't have been out of character for her to have gone off somewhere without telling anyone where. On this occasion, her mom confirmed she had left on time to meet them. She didn't live in town. Her folks had a place out near Elmville. Her car was found on the road between Elmville and Stillwater. The keys were still in the ignition. Like Lisa, Tanya has never been seen since."

"I vaguely remember that in the news. When did it happen?"

Laurie squinted at her scribbled notes. "A year before Carla was killed."

"And no one was linking these cases?" Cameron couldn't believe what he was hearing. "These young women all went missing months apart in a specific geographical location and nobody was asking questions?"

"Cameron, there are seven hundred and fifty thousand people reported missing every year in the United States. At any one time, there will be about ninety thousand people still unaccounted for. Some of those people will be dead, some don't *want* to be found. The police do all they can, but the sad fact is, unless bodies start turning up, no one is going to make these sort of links."

"Moreton did," he argued.

"Moreton was a geek, a one-off. He found patterns where no one else did, and he used sophisticated technology to help him. Your local police don't have that sort of equipment, and, don't forget, they were actually hampered by the fact one of their own was doing all he could to throw them off the scent."

He was reluctant to let it go, but they could spend all night arguing over past mistakes. They needed to move this forward. "Who was next? Carla?"

"No. The next one is intriguing and possibly doesn't quite fit the pattern of a missing person. I added her to the list because of how she looks, but she was never reported missing. Not in this country, anyway."

"You've lost me."

"Marie O'Donnell was a young Irish woman who had been visiting her boyfriend on a tourist visa. When Marie's visa expired, she had to go home to Ireland. The plan was she would return when she could get another visa. She never came back, and he never heard from her again. The reason her case made the headlines is the boyfriend was quite vocal about a system that could break up relationships. He became quite the campaigner."

Cameron had been doodling on his own notepad as he listened, but he looked up sharply at that. "What was the boyfriend's name?"

Laurie shook her head regretfully. "I didn't make a note of his name. Is it important?"

"If I'm right, I know it anyway. He chained himself to the railings outside the council offices, even though we explained to him the laws governing visas are national, not local. Ever since then he's dropped into my office once in a while to tell me where I'm going wrong. Alberta, my secretary, even knows how he takes his coffee." He grinned reminiscently. "His name is Toby Murray."

"Can we go and see him?" Laurie's eyes sparkled.

"I'm not sure it's safe for you to leave the cabin."

Her eyes shifted again to the window. It was completely dark now. "Cameron, I'm a police officer. I've worked undercover many times. I've felt afraid before, but never like I did when I was here alone." Her eyes seemed huge as they met his.

Cameron rose and went to the window, closing the drapes and shutting out the night. "Then we'll just have to take care we don't bump into Grant." He held out his hand. "Let's get some sleep."

She rose, coming to him and placing her hand in his. "Sleep?" There was a trace of disappointment in her voice.

"Among other things."

She rose on the tips of her toes, fitting the contours of her body intimately to his. "It's the other things that have me interested."

Chapter 10

"How do I look?" Laurie tilted her head so she could peer at Cameron from beneath the oversize baseball cap she was wearing. Her hair was tucked up inside the hat and she wore one of Cameron's sweatshirts over her jeans.

"Disturbingly sexy." He ducked his head and kissed the tip of her nose.

They had reached the lockup storage and were waiting for Bryce to meet them. Cameron had managed to get a phone signal here and had called his brother with instructions to bring them a rental car. To Laurie's relief, Cameron had been right when he said Bryce wouldn't ask any questions. Instead, his brother had promised to be with them as soon as he could. Before long, they heard the crunch of tires on the track outside.

"Wait here." Cameron went to the door and looked out. He nodded. "It's Bryce."

Laurie trailed behind him out into the bright sunlight. She wasn't sure how Cameron's brother would react to this situation. Even if he didn't know the details, it must be obvious there was a problem and that she was the cause.

Bryce brought the SUV he was driving to a halt and jumped out. He regarded his brother thoughtfully before his eyes moved to Laurie. "Is there any point in me asking what this is all about?"

Cameron held up his car keys. "I need you to take my car and give me that one."

"That tells me what we're doing. It doesn't tell me why." Bryce waited, and when Cameron didn't elaborate, he sighed. "This makes me think you don't want to be recognized by your vehicle. But that would just be odd, because who would be following you around the state highways...and why?"

Cameron placed a hand on his shoulder. "If I told you, you wouldn't believe me."

"That's unfair." Bryce shot the words back at him. "You're my brother. You know I'll believe what you tell me because *I* know you wouldn't lie to me."

Cameron held up his hands in an apologetic gesture. "Let's just say, I don't have the time right now to explain it in any way that would sound credible."

Bryce exhaled, releasing some of the tension from his frame. For the first time, Laurie appreciated just how close the two brothers were. Bryce's genuine concern for Cameron shone through in his expression. "Promise me you're not in any danger?"

"I promise I won't put myself in unnecessary danger."

Bryce's handsome face clouded over even further. "Goddamn it, Cam, that's not the same thing. You know it isn't."

"I swear I'll give you the full story when I can. I just can't do it now." Cameron held out his hand.

"But you'll come to me if I can help in any other way?" Reluctantly Bryce handed Cameron the documents and keys to the rented SUV.

"Absolutely."

Obviously feeling something more was required of him, Bryce turned to Laurie. "Nice to see you again." Even though she got the feeling he had to work at injecting a note of enthusiasm into the words, she appreciated the effort.

"You, too." She tipped her head back to look at him. If he noticed her strange outfit, he didn't comment.

Cameron held the passenger door of the SUV open, and Laurie stepped up into the vehicle. When he had taken his place in the driver's seat, Cameron pulled on his own baseball cap before starting the engine. Bryce watched them as they pulled away.

"He pretty much said he knows you're trying to avoid the police," Laurie said.

"Possibly he thinks we've robbed a bank or something."

"He's not that stupid." *Stupid* was just about the last word Laurie would have applied to any of the Delaney brothers.

Cameron sighed. "You're right, he's not. But we both know the truth is just too far-fetched for anyone to make a wild guess at."

They continued in silence with Laurie alternating between watching the side mirror for signs of traffic behind them and checking her phone. The road was quiet, and although they did occasionally see other vehicles, none of them were patrol cars. Her phone was a different matter. After she had skimmed quickly through her first few messages, the screen suddenly went blank. From then on, nothing she did could restore it.

"I don't know what happened," she said, gazing at it in frustration. Her final link with her true identity had just quietly died in her hand.

"I don't know much about these things, but I've heard about viruses being sent from one phone to another by SMS. Did you open any links?"

Laurie groaned. "Yes. The last message I looked at seemed to be from the car rental company I used in Stillwater. There was a link to their website asking me to confirm closure of my account. I clicked on that and the screen went blank. Now I've lost everything. All my contacts, photographs, music, messages." She gazed at her phone in frustration. Now it wasn't even a clock.

Cameron took his hand off the wheel and rested it briefly on her knee. "Once we get the evidence we need, we'll find your captain's number and call him direct."

Although he was right, she couldn't help feeling another tie had been severed. Grant had won another battle. He knew which car rental company she'd used, because he had access to the vehicle itself back at the Paradise Creek vacation village, along with her records there. He seemed to constantly be one step ahead of them. He was deliberately cutting her off from the world, making her vulnerable. There had to be a way to shake him down from the superior perch he'd placed himself on. Gloomily, she slumped in her seat, lost in thought.

After a while, she noticed the strange, funnel-shaped hill on the horizon, and it triggered a memory that still bugged her. So much had happened that she'd almost forgotten it.

"I know you told me this isn't one of your routes, but it was definitely one of your trucks that almost ran me off the road when I was driving back from Cody the day I went to see Moreton."

Cameron took his eyes off the straight highway for a second to glance at her. "You seem sure about that."

"I know what I saw." Her eyes challenged him to disbelieve her.

He frowned, scanning the road ahead and the rocky terrain to either side of it. "Let's pick this up again after we've spoken to Toby Murray." A few miles farther on, he took a right turn off the main highway and they bumped along a track that was uneven enough to make Laurie glad Bryce had chosen to hire an SUV.

"How come Toby brought his case to you when he doesn't live in Stillwater?"

"He did at the time Marie left. He only moved out here quite recently."

"What does he do for a living?" As a series of low-level buildings came into view, it was clear Toby Murray had elected to live as far from other people as possible. This was taking getting away from it all to extremes.

"Toby is a musician. He writes music for other people, to be exact. Quite successfully, I think. He certainly seems to make enough money to keep this place going."

When she alighted from the car, Laurie was able to see for herself what Cameron meant. The largest of the group of buildings was a house. Built on one level, it formed a semicircle, allowing each room to look out over a shallow valley where a number of beautiful horses had been turned out. Most of the other buildings were stables, although the purpose of some smaller units was less clear.

A tall, fair-haired man with an easy smile was waiting on the step to greet them. Laurie had built a mental image of Toby from Cameron's description, and she had expected someone uptight and intense. This good-looking, charming man was the complete opposite of what she had imagined he would be.

His eyes quizzed Cameron good-naturedly. "Let me guess. You've either got a message from Alberta to tell me to stop hounding you over the proposed changes to the river road industrial complex, or you want to buy a horse?"

"Neither." As Cameron strolled forward, Laurie pulled off her baseball cap, and Toby's eyes widened slightly as he watched her shake out her hair. "This is Laurie Bryan."

For a moment or two Toby didn't speak, he just stared down at her. Then, as though rousing himself from a trance, he spoke directly to Laurie. "I'm sorry. Just for a moment, you reminded me of someone I once knew."

"I think that brings us neatly to why we're here. Can we go inside?"

"Of course." He gestured for them to enter into the house before him. "Can I get you a drink?"

They opted for soda, and Toby brought cold cans through to the open-plan seating area. "This view is incredible." As they sat down, Laurie indicated the panorama of the valley.

"It's why I chose this location," Toby explained. "Cameron already knows horses are my passion. One of my twin passions. The other one is my music. But what's the point of breeding horses if you can't actually see them, if you tuck them away somewhere? This way, I get the best of both worlds." He leaned forward, elbows on his knees as he gazed at Laurie. "Are you related to Marie? Do you have news about her? Is that why you're here?"

Laurie shook her head. "But we do want to talk to you about her, if that's okay."

Toby quirked an amused eyebrow in Cameron's direction. "Okay? Hasn't Cameron mentioned that, once I get started on the subject of Marie, it's difficult to shut me up?"

It was impossible not to like him, and Laurie continued with a smile. "How did you and Marie meet?"

"We met in Dublin. As part of my master's degree, I did a placement at one of the universities there. When I came back home, we kept up a long-distance relationship for a few months until Marie finished her course. Then she followed me out here. We knew we wanted to get married, but she needed to go back to Ireland and tie up a few loose ends there. She had an apartment she needed to pack up, friends she wanted to say goodbye to. The next time she came back to Wyoming it would be for good. That was the plan."

"But she never came back?"

"She never came back." His eyes were gray, and Laurie thought they resembled a stormy sky as he said those words. Theirs had not been some casual relationship.

"Apart from starting a campaign to change the law, what did you do?"

"I went over to Dublin to look for her, of course." Toby seemed surprised at the question. "I've been back four times."

"Tell us what you've found out."

"Nothing. I've found out nothing." He got to his feet, going to the window and gazing down at the valley. Laurie got the feeling he wasn't seeing the sweeping valley and the horses. He seemed to be staring into the past. "Marie had no family. She was an orphan, raised in a convent children's home. So there was no one to turn to, no one to ask. She didn't go back to her apartment. She never contacted any of our mutual friends. If I hadn't been one hundred percent sure she got on the plane at this end, I could almost believe she never arrived in Ireland."

Laurie sat up a little straighter. *One hundred percent.* That was very certain. "Did you take her to the airport yourself?"

He shook his head. "Right at the last minute, I had car problems. Isn't that just typical? The old Jeep I had back then had never given me a minute's trouble, then, the day before I need to take my girlfriend to the airport, the damn thing refuses to start."

Laurie felt a crawling feeling begin to trace its way down her spine. She sensed Cameron's eyes on her profile and knew he was thinking the same thing as her. "Who drove Marie to the airport?"

"Marie had become friendly with Grant Becker, the sheriff. You know him, right?" He turned to Cameron for confirmation. Cameron nodded, his jaw tense. "They had a shared interest in Irish literature, of all things. The sheriff doesn't look the type, does he? Although, to be fair, Marie used to tease him and say he didn't know as much as he liked to think he did. Anyway, he happened to stop by to give her a book for the journey. She told him about the problem with the Jeep, and he offered to drive her. Problem solved. He stepped in like a knight in shining armor. That was what Marie said to him at the time."

Problem solved indeed. And so neatly.

"Why didn't you go with them to the airport?" Laurie managed to keep her voice calm. Was this it? The link between Grant and one of the missing girls they had been seeking? But they still didn't have a body...

"The sheriff's personal car was a two-seater. A sporty little number he'd only just taken delivery of." Laurie's eyes flicked over to Cameron for confirmation. He gave a slight shake of his head. This two-seater sports car was clearly news to him. "There was barely enough room for Marie's luggage. We said goodbye at our apartment." Toby's voice was quiet. "It didn't seem like a big deal at the time. We thought we'd be together again soon."

"Did you report Marie missing to the Irish police?"

"Of course I did. They filed a report, and I've checked in with them each time I've been back. There haven't been any developments. It's as if she vanished that day." Toby came to sit back down. He looked from

Cameron to Laurie and back again. "Why have you come here to ask me about Marie now?"

Laurie glanced at Cameron. He nodded. Toby could be trusted. "Laurie is an undercover police officer. While she was in Stillwater on an unrelated investigation, she stumbled on evidence that my girlfriend, who was also Laurie's cousin, Carla Bryan, may have been murdered. You never met Carla, but she also had dark hair and blue eyes. This is all unofficial, but there is a chance other women may also have been targeted by the same man. We're looking into the possibility he chooses women who look alike."

Toby was clearly trying to absorb what he had just been told. "But Marie was taken to the airport..." His face paled as the truth hit him. "It was him? Are you here to tell me Marie was murdered by Grant Becker?"

"We don't know anything for sure right now." Cameron had to repeat the message as Toby paced the room. There seemed to be a real possibility of his friend storming out of the house in search of Grant.

"Was anything out of the ordinary happening just before Marie left?" Laurie asked, and her calm tone had a soothing effect on Toby, drawing his attention back to her. "Anything that made her feel uncomfortable, or made you think someone might be paying her unwanted attention?"

Toby frowned. "You're talking about the flowers, right? We laughed over them at the time. I said she was sending them to herself to make me jealous. She said it was me, and I should just be up-front and tell the truth, confess to being a hopeless romantic instead of pretending she had a secret admirer. It was only after she'd gone that I wondered now and then if there really was a mystery man. I've tortured myself wondering if she went off with him instead of coming back to me."

"These flowers she was getting, were they a heart-shaped arrangement of dark red roses?"

"My God, that's exactly what they were." Toby slumped back onto the sofa. "I can't take this in. What happens next? You're a police officer—you must be able to arrest him."

Cameron knew Laurie would have liked nothing more than to assure Toby she could do just that. But what did they really have? They might just be able to persuade someone to take an interest in the fact that Deanna, Carla and Marie had all been sent the same arrangement of flowers and two of those women were missing while one was dead. Yes, Carla and Marie had both known Grant, but it was a huge step from knowing them to killing them. Stillwater was a small town. There was no such thing as a stranger. Cameron himself had known Carla intimately and he'd shopped in Milligans, so he knew Deanna well enough to pass the time of day with her. Okay, there was the interesting issue of Grant driving Marie to the airport. If they could prove she didn't get on that plane, their suspicions might have more weight.

As if she was reading his mind, Laurie was asking Toby that very question. "Did you ever try to find out if Marie actually boarded her flight?"

"No, because it never occurred to me until today that she might not have."

"Can we start there?" Cameron asked. "Get the

airline to confirm whether she actually did fly with them that day?"

Laurie sighed. "I wish it was that easy. I know from experience that getting airlines to part with that sort of information requires a warrant. I could have tried pulling strings, used my police contacts—" she held up her dead phone "—if I still had any." She sent a sympathetic glance in Toby's direction. "As far as the police are concerned, unless we find a body, or Grant comes after me, I know what the response will be. As it stands right now, we are just making up stories about this guy."

"If we can find their bodies, we will be in a position of strength to let the police know the rest of our suspicions." Cameron rose. "Do you have any binoculars we can borrow?" As Toby left the room, he was aware of Laurie regarding him in surprise. "Just something that occurred to me."

Toby returned with the binoculars. "I feel so helpless. You'll let me know as soon as you find something out?"

"Of course. In the meantime, I know we don't have to ask you to keep this to yourself." Cameron paused on the doorstep, scanning the area around the house. He didn't know what he was looking for exactly, maybe some sign he and Laurie had been followed here. Nothing disturbed the tranquility of the surrounding scenery.

"That goes without saying. But, my God, I'd like to get my hands on that bastard." Toby's eyes misted over, and Cameron understood how he felt. Hadn't he experienced the same emotions at the thought of what Carla must have gone through? Both of them had been suffering, making assumptions about what had happened to the women they loved, when all the time there was a common denominator. A serial killer who chose them because of their dark hair and blue eyes.

He glanced at Laurie, at *her* dark hair and blue eyes, and felt something lurch inside him. This last year had been as if his heart was wrapped in barbed wire with someone tightening and loosening it at will. Since meeting her, it had been getting looser. Slowly, steadily, the tightness was easing up. He almost hadn't noticed it at all today. His heart had felt normal.

Laurie hesitated before stepping out into the sunlight. Keeping her safe was his priority now. Cameron had even more reason than Toby to make sure Grant Becker got what was coming to him. He had to keep Laurie alive.

"I'm ahead of you in this line," he told Toby.

"You said there were five women matching this description who had disappeared in West County over the last few years, not counting Carla and Deanna," Cameron said as they drove away from Toby's home. "Lisa, Kathy, Tanya and Marie. That's four. Who was number five?"

Laurie had checked her notes again last night, so she knew the details without needing to refer back to them. "This was the most recent one. Four months ago. She was an attorney called Bethany Wade."

"Beth Wade? I thought she just left town."

Cameron's quiet tone seemed at odds with his words. Surely the fact he knew one of these women was helpful and, therefore, worthy of a little more enthusiasm?

"You know her?"

"Yes." That was it? He remained silent for a moment or two. His next words explained his hesitation. "She and Vincente had an on-off relationship for a while."

"Bethany Wade isn't officially a missing person, but there was a report about her leaving her law practice very suddenly. Clients were left in the lurch, and it made the local press. When I read the reports, I saw her picture and she fitted the profile for how the missing women look. When she was dating Vincente, didn't you notice that she looked like Carla?" What Laurie had picked up on when she was doing her missing persons search was the similarity in the women's coloring. Only someone who knew them could say for sure if they were truly alike.

"Not so you'd notice," Cameron said, after giving it some thought. "I suppose there were similarities. But I'm looking at these women now in hindsight. I'm not sure I'd have noticed if this link between them hadn't happened. There's something he sees in them that we might not."

The thought made Laurie shiver, but there was something else troubling her. She drew a breath. There was no way to be diplomatic about this. "I can't help noticing Vincente's name crops up a lot in our discussions about Grant."

"That's just what I was thinking."

"Maybe we need to talk to him?" Cameron's profile was annoyingly inscrutable.

"I was thinking that, too." He turned his head slightly to look at her. "We'll do it after we've taken a look at the old Dawson ranch."

"How will we do that? It's broad daylight. If there is something going on at that disused ranch, we can't very well just drive on up there and ask what it is."

"Trust me."

For the time being, she had to be content with that, because he didn't elaborate further until they were within sight of the funnel-shaped hill once more. She did trust him. In the short space of time she'd known him, Laurie had come to trust Cameron more than any other person she knew. More than she thought she had it in her to trust another human being. It was as exhilarating as it was scary.

Turning off the main highway just before the point where Laurie had seen the Delaney Transportation truck, Cameron took the SUV along a narrow track that climbed steeply upward until they were at the top of a narrow, tree-lined ridge. Leaving the vehicle behind the cover of the trees, he led Laurie with him, until they were crouched at the edge of the sheer, rocky drop. Below them, the old ranch buildings looked like dollhouses set in a patchwork of red earth and green grass.

Cameron held up the binoculars Toby had lent him. "Forward planning."

Lying on his stomach, he commando-crawled forward until he was right at the edge of the cliff. With a glance of resignation at the red earth and her sweatshirt, Laurie followed him. Training the binoculars on the scene below them, Cameron viewed the old ranch buildings in silence for a few minutes. Unable to see anything herself, Laurie started to feel impatient.

"What can you see?"

"There's nothing going on right now, but there is

an old barn that's big enough to take one, maybe even two of our trucks." He handed her the binoculars.

Laurie focused on the building he was referring to. It was huge, dominating the smaller structures around it. "Why would a ranch need a building that size?"

"Movement of livestock. When this place was a thriving business, old Culver Dawson was one of the most successful ranchers in the area. He kept several trailers in that barn for transporting his cattle to market."

"And how long has this place been empty?" She moved the binoculars over the area around the barn.

"Culver died about five years ago. He had no family, and no one bought the place. It's been standing empty ever since. Why?"

"For one thing, it's tragic such a beautiful place should go to waste, but I'm also wondering why there are fresh tire tracks leading to that barn." As she spoke, a car came into view along the track leading to the ranch. It halted in front of the barn, and a tall man with shoulder-length hair tied back in a ponytail slid out from behind the wheel. Laurie handed the binoculars back to Cameron. "Recognize him?"

He muttered a curse under his breath. "As a matter of fact, I do. His name is Sam Nichols, and he's the safety compliance officer at Delaney Transportation."

"Isn't he a little far from where he should be if his job is to ensure the safe compliance of your trucks?"

"He's not the only one who has strayed." Cameron handed the binoculars back to her. Another car had pulled up, and a red-haired man got out. He and Nichols entered the barn together. "That was Jesse Warren, one of the depot managers. Both these men were hired within the last twelve months." His expression hardened. "By my brother."

"I guess we have even more reason for that talk with Vincente?"

Cameron's voice was grim. "It's starting to look that way."

Chapter 11

Vincente lived in a new apartment complex in the downtown area of Stillwater. It was the sort of development Cameron and his fellow local politicians were keen to encourage, even though traditionalists like Bryce sneered at the modernization of their hometown.

"There was nothing here," Cameron explained to Laurie as they pulled into the parking lot of the riverside development. "As long as it's done tastefully, anything that keeps young, professional people in the town has got to be a good thing. Otherwise, these traditional communities start dying out."

"You love this place, don't you?" She'd overcome her fear of encountering Grant on the journey between the Dawson ranch and the town, and was glad to stretch her limbs as they walked toward the elegant apartment block.

"Is it so obvious?" His smile was slightly sheepish.

"I like that you feel such a strong sense of loyalty to your hometown. It's something I've missed out on, living in a big city." She drew a breath as he pressed the buzzer to Vincente's apartment. "Will this be tough?"

He nodded. "I'm not going to lie to you. If Vincente feels cornered, *tough* is likely to be an understatement."

Vincente's voice crackled over the intercom. "Who's there?"

"It's Cameron. Are you alone?" On the drive over, they had discussed the frightening possibility he might have Grant with him. If that was the case, they would hightail it out of there in double time without explaining the reason for this visit.

"Yeah, what do you want?" Even through the medium of electronic communication, Vincente's voice was unwelcoming.

"I need to talk to you." There was a lengthy pause, then—could Laurie actually sense his reluctance, or was her imagination working overtime?—Vincente buzzed them in.

Vincente's apartment was on the second floor, and he was waiting at the door as they mounted the stairs. His eyes registered a brief moment of surprise as he took in Laurie's presence, but he made no comment, merely gesturing for them to step inside. The views from the full-length windows across the river were incredible, and Laurie was momentarily mesmerized again by the raw power of the Wyoming landscape. She envied these people who got to see it every day.

"This is an unexpected pleasure." The sarcasm in Vincente's voice was unmistakable.

"I wish it was about pleasure." Cameron had clearly decided to get straight to the point. "There are a few things bugging me, and I need to speak to you about them."

Vincente gestured for them to sit down. Laurie, taking a seat on a leather chair, decided to let Cameron do the talking. They had agreed he should start with the situation at Delaney Transportation. Maybe they could lead into their questions about Grant from there. Always supposing the conversation went well.

"Who is Zac Peyton?"

Vincente's smile was easy, untroubled. The switch from his antagonistic starting point was dizzying. Laurie decided he was a man who could be very charming. When he wanted to be. He answered without hesitation. "My assistant. Why?"

"What exactly is he assisting you with?"

Some of the easy manner slid away. "Do you want a copy of his job description?"

Cameron maintained his calm approach. It was obvious this give-and-take was something the brothers were used to, a veneer both of them knew was a pretense. Like poker players, they were waiting to see who would fold first. "An outline will do."

Vincente grew tired of the bluff first. "Stop pretending, Cam. Just tell me what the hell this is all about." There was a flash of Italian fire in his dark eyes.

Cameron cast a glance in Laurie's direction and she nodded. *Tell him.* "Laurie is a police officer working undercover for the FBI. She was sent here to investigate the possibility that Delaney Transportation is being used as part of a human- and drug-trafficking operation."

Vincente ran a hand through his hair. "Damn. I was hoping to shut it down before you found out."

For a few moments, Cameron seemed incapable of speech. Laurie could tell from his stunned expression that he had expected more of a fight from Vincente. Maybe denials, excuses or pleas for leniency. Not this bland, unblinking approach. Her cop instincts told her something wasn't adding up. Vincente Delaney wasn't acting like a guilty man.

"To be honest," Vincente continued as though unaware of the lowering thundercloud of his brother's anger, "it's a relief you know. At least this way we can sort this problem out together."

"Together?" The word was loaded with stupefaction. "You expect me to get involved in this?"

"Hey." Vincente held up a conciliatory hand. "I'm trying to do you a favor."

Before Cameron could explode out of his seat in rage, Laurie placed a hand on his arm. Her training had taught her to keep an open mind. After everything she'd heard about him, she hadn't come here expecting to like Vincente Delaney, but her gut reaction told her she wasn't looking at an out-and-out villain. "I don't think Vincente is making a confession."

"Confession?" Now it was Vincente's turn to look stupefied. He stared at Cameron and then muttered a curse. "You thought I was capable of something like that? I'm your brother, yet you thought I could treat young women that way, let alone smuggle drugs and firearms? And that I would do that to the firm...to you? Well, thanks a million."

"But you said—" Cameron broke off, drawing in a deep breath, struggling to get his feelings under control. "Can we rewind and start this conversation over? At the point where you said you were hoping to shut this operation down?"

Vincente nodded, going up in Laurie's estimation once again. Cameron had come just about as close as he could to accusing him of running the illegal operation, yet, as soon as his brother asked him to start the conversation over, he was willing to do so. That took a strength of character she hadn't expected from him.

"Look, I don't have any evidence. All I know is there has been something odd going on. I figured it out a few months back, but I wanted to find some actual proof. There were trucks taking much longer than they should over certain routes, an increasing number of drivers not available if we called them to do overtime, even when they weren't scheduled to be working, invoices coming in for gas and repairs from places we shouldn't have been visiting. I started to get suspicious there might be something illegal going on. That was why I employed Zac Peyton. He's a private detective."

"Why didn't you come to me?" Cameron asked.

"Isn't it obvious?" There was a hint of bitterness in the twist of Vincente's lips.

"My God." Cameron stared at him. "You think Bryce is behind this, don't you?"

Vincente lifted one shoulder defensively. "I knew it wasn't me. Who else could it be? I thought maybe he was in trouble and needed money. There have been times, since he left the army, when I've wondered if he might be struggling to come to terms with civilian life. But I knew there was no way Bryce would talk to me if that was the case."

"That's why you started interfering with the schedules."

"I figured it would be harder for Bryce to plan whatever it was he was doing—I had no idea what it was until you told me just now—if I kept shaking things up." Vincente laughed. "It didn't work. It just made him mad as hell."

"I know." Cameron grinned reminiscently. "How much are you paying Zac Peyton?"

Vincente visibly bristled. "Peyton's salary is coming out of my personal savings. I never put him on the payroll. Why?"

"Whatever it is, it's not worth it. Laurie and I have found out exactly who is responsible for the illegal operations. If Peyton was any good at his job, he'd have had no trouble doing the same thing. It's not Bryce, but we'll need the two of you to help us shut it down."

"You can count on me," Vincente said without hesitation.

"I know that now." Cameron looked at his brother with regret in his eyes. "I should have known it all along."

While they waited for Bryce to come over, Cameron filled Vincente in on the details of what they had seen out at the old Dawson ranch. All the while, he was cursing his own bullheadedness. Why had it needed Laurie, who didn't even know Vincente, to point out the obvious? He watched her as she talked to Vincente, marveling again at the way she made him feel. He'd known her a few days, yet in that time she'd fundamentally changed his life. He could argue it was because of the situation they'd been thrust into, but Cameron knew this went way deeper than that. The effect she had on him was profound and moving. He only had to look at her for his whole world to shift off course. The feeling was scary and exhilarating, and he didn't know what the hell to do with it.

When he'd met Carla, he had been ready to fall in love. It seemed a strange thing to look back and think about himself now, but it was true. He'd been young, rich, handsome and successful. All that was needed to complete the picture was a beautiful woman on his arm. Prior to Carla there had been plenty of willing partners, but no one had attracted him the way she had. Attracted? Carla had enchanted him. From the moment he saw her, he had tumbled headfirst in love with her.

The only issue they had ever had was exactly what he had told Laurie. Carla didn't want to stay in Stillwater. She had hated Wyoming, and three years of being back in the place she had been born in, and living here with Cameron, had done nothing to change that. At the same time, Cameron could never see himself moving anywhere else. It was too early to think long term about Laurie—*we spent one night together, for God's sake!*—but he couldn't see how things would be any different with her. Her home, her work, her whole life was in San Diego.

It's different this time. I'm not looking for someone to complete the picture. I've learned that appearances don't matter. He had learned the hard way not to take love for granted. Love? *Hold on, where did that thought come from?* It was way too soon to think about loving Laurie. Having fallen so deep and hard once, he knew his heart was too fragile to put it through anything that might cause it to relapse. And the emotions he felt when he looked at her were not the same as those he had experienced when he had looked at Carla. Then it had been bells and whistles. He had been driven to constantly impress Carla, to earn her love, to make her proud of him.

With Laurie, he felt easy, comfortable. His thoughts tried to take him down the route of *meant to be*, but he dragged them ruthlessly away. *Not going there.* He forced himself to think of Alberta and the other Stillwater gossips, of pursed lips and shaking heads. Of the mayor making a fool of himself. Putting himself through pain for something that was doomed from the start. Then he looked her way again, and all his good intentions scattered into a million tiny pieces...

Bryce looked thunderous when he arrived. "This had better be good. I had a date."

Since Bryce generally had a date every night, usually with a different woman each time, this was not news to either of his brothers. "Sam Nichols and Jesse Warren have been using our trucks to run an illegal human-trafficking and drug-smuggling operation out of the old Dawson ranch." Cameron summed up the reason for bringing him there in one concise sentence. "Probably arms, too," he added, as an afterthought.

Bryce uttered a curse and sat abruptly down on the sofa. "In that case, I need a beer."

"I guess we could all use one," Vincente said. "Laurie, are you okay with beer?"

"I'm fine with beer." She smiled up at him, and Cameron noticed Vincente's expression soften as he responded. Vincente? His older brother was the most hard-hearted person Cameron knew, yet, minutes after walking into his apartment, Laurie had him melting like a puppy dog with a new toy.

Once they each had a drink placed on the large oak coffee table in front of them, Cameron quickly recapped what Laurie was doing here in Stillwater and outlined what they had seen out at the old Dawson ranch. His brothers listened in silence, Vincente remaining expressionless while Bryce's face grew increasingly thunderous.

When Cameron had finished, Bryce turned accusing eyes to Vincente. "You hired Warren and Nichols. What the hell were you playing at?"

Although Vincente's dark eyes flashed, he didn't rise to the challenge. "They both came highly recommended and had great references. I had no reason to question them."

"Bullshit. They must have been looking for a company like ours to use for this operation, which means they've done this sort of thing before. You clearly haven't checked them out properly."

Vincente slammed his beer down on the table in front of him hard enough to cause the liquid inside to froth over the top of the bottle. Before he could respond, Cameron spoke up. "Fighting among ourselves isn't going to solve this."

"The solution seems straightforward." Bryce's body language remained uncompromising. Stretching his long legs in front of him, he took a long slug of beer. "We go to the police." He directed a frown at Laurie. "Come to think of it, isn't that what you're here for?"

Cameron had been over and over this in his head. If only it was that simple, but going to the police wasn't going to be an option. Not yet. "We can't involve them."

Vincente frowned. "I don't usually find myself agreeing with Bryce, but he's right on this. These men are using our trucks, and some of our drivers, to commit a felony. It's a no-brainer."

Before Cameron could speak again, Laurie cut across his thoughts. "Tell them what they need to know."

He frowned. Even with that permission, he was unsure what to do. Although Vincente was a couple of years older than Grant, the two men had become close friends. Lately, he wasn't so sure the bond was as strong as it once had been. The bottom line was... how far could he trust Vincente, Grant's friend, with Laurie's safety? If he didn't get the answer "one hundred percent," he didn't want to go there.

"Laurie's assignment has hit a problem, which means she is no longer in contact with the FBI or the police." He shrugged his shoulders slightly at Laurie as he spoke. It was the best he could do, and he was well aware it was woefully inadequate.

Bryce spluttered on the beer he was drinking. "You mean she's been fired?"

Laurie started to laugh, her lovely features reflecting genuine amusement. "Cameron, we can't do this properly by giving your brothers half a story."

He relaxed back in his seat. "Okay, we'll tell you

all of it. But first, I want to deal with the problem of Warren and Nichols. Leaving Laurie out of this, if we went to the police with the problem, what do you think would happen?"

"Those two low-lives would be arrested," Bryce said promptly. "And put behind bars for a very long time."

"That's all? You don't think there would be any investigation into our company? You think we'd be allowed to continue trading normally? That we wouldn't lose money? Our competitors wouldn't be waiting to step in and pick up our business while we were closed? There'd be no adverse publicity for Delaney Transportation? That this couldn't close us down, even cost us the company?"

They fell silent for a few minutes while the full force of what Cameron was saying sank in. It was Vincente who broke the silence. "Do you have any suggestions for what we should do instead?"

"I do have an idea—" Before Cameron could outline his plan, the buzzer sounded.

Vincente frowned as he rose to answer it. "I'm not expecting anyone."

As he pressed the intercom button, some sort of sixth sense got to work so Cameron knew exactly whose voice he was going to hear. Sure enough, the easy, pleasant tones he had dreaded intruded into the silence.

"Hey, it's Grant."

Vincente, completely oblivious to the change in Cameron's mood, laughed delightedly. "Come on up. You may be just the guy we need."

"No!" Cameron leaped to his feet, but it was too

late. Vincente had already pressed the button releasing the door and admitting Grant into the building.

Cameron could almost see the blood drain from Laurie's face. She was pinned to her seat with panic. His own heart was pounding so loud it felt like it was making a determined effort to break out through his chest.

He moved fast. "Don't ask any questions. Just go along with everything I say." He glanced from Vincente to Bryce and back again. They both looked slightly alarmed, but nodded their agreement. "Laurie was never here. You don't know where she is. If Grant asks, you don't know anything about her. Vincente, show her through to the master bedroom. Whatever happens, don't let Grant go back there."

Bryce was regarding his brother with concern on his face. "Cam, is everything okay?"

Cameron strode over to Laurie, pulling her to her feet and drawing her close. Wishing he could hold her for longer than a few seconds, he tried to warm her with his body, to give her the injection of courage he could see she desperately needed.

"No, everything is not okay." He bent his head closer to Laurie's, speaking softly to her. "But it will be. Go with Vincente. I'll keep you safe."

She nodded, her eyes wide with nerves. Before she left the room in Vincente's wake, she cast another scared glance over her shoulder, and Cameron nodded encouragingly.

"What the hell is going on?" Bryce sounded even edgier now.

"I'll explain it all later."

Vincente returned just as Grant knocked on the

apartment door. Ignoring the bemused expressions on his brothers' faces, Cameron sat down and took a long slug of beer.

"Shall I get that?" Vincente asked.

"I guess you should." Cameron took a deep breath, preparing to come face-to-face with the serial killer he had grown up with.

Grant's ready smile faded as he entered the room just ahead of Vincente and took in the scene.

"Cam, Bryce." He nodded at them each in turn, his eyes lingering a fraction too long on Cameron's face. Cameron knew exactly what he was thinking. Just how much information had Cameron already shared with his brothers? "I didn't know I was interrupting something."

"Just hanging out, having a few drinks with my brothers," Vincente said.

Cameron tried not to wince, both at the false joviality in Vincente's tone—Vincente didn't do jovial—and at the words themselves. Anyone who knew the Delaney brothers as well as Grant did would know they didn't socialize. Not together. Cameron and Bryce might hang out, but the three of them? There was more chance of hell freezing over.

Grant's boyish smile remained fixed in place, but Cameron could see a hint of tension in the lines around his eyes.

"If there's any of that beer going spare—" His eyes narrowed as he took in the fourth, almost full, bottle of beer on the low table in front of the chair Laurie had speedily vacated. "—or were you expecting me?"

Cameron cast a warning glance at his brothers, but he was pleased to see that, although clearly bemused, they were waiting to take their cue from him. He let his anger carry him over the initial nervousness he had felt when Grant's gaze landed on Laurie's drink. *You have no right to ask the questions around here.* Leaning over, he snagged Laurie's beer bottle. Maintaining eye contact with Grant, he took a drink from it. Setting the bottle down next to his own, he looked at Vincente.

"Get Grant a beer."

"Thirsty, Cam?" As he took a seat next to Bryce on the sofa, Grant raised a brow in the direction of the two bottles of beer.

"No, pissed off."

As he stared into the eyes of his childhood friend, he got that same sensation again. The feeling he got when he had met Grant out on the highway two days ago, just after May King's shop had been torched. The feeling that a savage killer was very close to the surface and the veneer of respectability was wearing thin.

You're enjoying this. It was the same thought he'd had back then. It made him want to lunge across the table and pound his fists into that smiling face. Over and over until the smile disappeared and the truth surfaced. *The difference between us is I'm not feral.* It was a much-needed reminder.

"Any particular reason?" Grant accepted the beer from Vincente with a nod of thanks.

Cameron could feel his brothers trying to pick up on the undercurrents between him and the man they knew only as the respectable, hardworking sheriff. Grant was their friend. He'd been pretty much a permanent feature in their lives. Now they could obviously sense something had gone very wrong in his relationship with Cameron. Since Laurie was hiding out in the bedroom, it didn't take any great test of ingenuity for them to work out it was to do with her. She was the unknown in this equation. Would they trust Cameron to know what he was doing? Or was it possible they might believe he had been bewitched by this stranger with the face of his dead lover? That Laurie was driving a wedge between him and his friend for no good reason? Whatever they might be thinking, Cameron just needed them to keep their thoughts to themselves until Grant was gone.

"Oh, you know. Just a little tired of things that aren't what they seem."

Grant tilted his beer bottle toward Cameron with a grin. "I'll drink to that." Ignoring the flash of anger in Cameron's eyes, he took a long swallow. "What happened to your police officer friend? What was her name? Detective Carter?"

It was a good act, but not quite good enough. The relaxed question was at odds with the sharp look in Grant's light blue eyes. Cameron shrugged, noticing the way Bryce sat up a little straighter in his seat. "Carter was her undercover name. I'm surprised you remembered that."

Grant's eyes registered his annoyance at the slipup. "What can I say? I have a good memory."

"It's clearly not that great. Not since her real name should be an easy one for you to remember. It's Bryan. You know, the same as Carla. Her cousin. My girlfriend. The one who died."

Grant drew a breath. "I'm sorry, Cam. I shouldn't have got that wrong." *Bastard.* He was too good at this. He'd played the part of the good guy for too long to be tripped up by one small slip of the tongue. "Is she still in town?"

"I assume so. Why?"

"No reason. By the way, that murder at the vacation village you told me about when I saw you the other day—I still haven't heard anything about it. I even stopped by Chief Wilkinson's office and he didn't mention it." There was a wolfish hint of triumph in Grant's smile now.

Cameron returned his stare. "I don't remember mentioning a murder."

He knew he hadn't. When they had met Grant on the highway in Park County, he and Laurie had both talked about a serious crime that she was staying in Stillwater to investigate. Neither of them had been specific about what that crime was.

Grant's smile vanished in a heartbeat to be replaced by a cold, hard, dangerous look that needed no interpretation. The intent behind it was so clear that Bryce shifted in his seat as though preparing to make a move to get between Grant and his brother.

Then, with a short laugh, Grant drained his beer. "It's been nice, but I can't stay. Can I use your bathroom before I go, Vincente?"

"Sure. You know where it is."

Vincente cast a worried look in Cameron's direction. The bathroom was along the hall, close to the bedroom where Laurie was hiding. As Grant made his way out of the room, Vincente held his hands palms up and shrugged in a helpless gesture. "What could I do? I couldn't refuse." He whispered the words.

"When he's gone you need to tell us exactly what this is all about." Bryce kept his own voice low. "That look he gave you was more venomous than a rattlesnake about to strike."

They fell silent, listening for Grant returning. When the bathroom door opened and they heard his boots on the wooden floor, Vincente leaped to his feet. "He's not coming this way. He's heading for the bedroom."

The three brothers dashed along the hall and through the open door of Vincente's bedroom. Grant paused with his hand on the door handle of the en suite bathroom. "I heard a noise in here."

Vincente stepped forward, drawing himself up to his full height. "Don't you need a warrant to search my property, Sheriff Becker?" Cameron had heard that chilly tone in Vincente's voice many times, but he had never been glad of it until now.

Grant gave a blustering laugh. "Come on, Vincente. This is me. We're friends."

Vincente didn't answer. Just stood there with his arms folded across his chest. Bryce stepped up and stood next to him, adopting the same stance. Cameron felt a lump rise in his throat. His brothers were coming through for him. He moved into place next to Bryce. The three Delaney brothers.

It took us long enough to get to this point, but when we work together, we make a formidable team.

Grant's hand dropped from the doorknob, and he shrugged. "Just trying to help a friend."

"I'll show you out." Vincente stood to one side, making room so Grant could walk past him.

Grant moved slowly toward the door. As he passed

Cameron, he looked him fully in the eye, all pretense gone. His gaze was pure malice.

"I'll see you around." He raised his voice slightly so it would carry through the bathroom door. "Both of you."

Chapter 12

Laurie braced herself against the narrow walls of the bathroom. With her hands pressed up against the tile, she was ready to kick out with both feet if anyone came through the door. When she had heard those booted footsteps coming toward the bedroom, some deep-seated instinct had told her it was Grant, and with lightning-fast reflexes, she had taken refuge in this room.

Why the hell did I leave my gun back at the cabin?

Moreton's murder had unsettled her more than she had initially recognized, throwing everything she thought she knew about herself off balance. She felt like an amateur, a rookie, a kid playing at being a cop. Leaving her gun behind was a stupid mistake. Now she was holed up in this tiny bathroom and on the other side of the door was a man who, if her instincts were correct, had killed at least seven other women. Grant had her backed into a corner like a frightened animal.

Cameron is out there. He won't let anything happen to me. She clung to that certainty, forcing herself to think rationally, calming her quivering nerves and biting back the cry that rose to her lips as a hand tried the door. Grant could hardly murder her here in Vincente's bathroom, or drag her out by her hair with the three Delaney brothers standing by. Her rational self knew he wouldn't try.

She suspected what he wanted to do was to intimidate her by looking her in the eye or putting his hands on her when no one else was around. To show her what was to come when he finally did get her alone. Possibly he hoped to drive a wedge between Cameron and his brothers by convincing Vincente and Bryce that Laurie was unstable, that she wasn't a cop at all. Maybe he would try to convince them she wasn't even Carla's cousin, that she was an impostor who had duped Cameron into believing Grant was some sort of villain for her own reasons. Probably because she was out to get her hands on Cameron's money by using her likeness to Carla to play on his grief.

Laurie had no doubt Cameron was right when he said Grant would arrest her on any trumped-up charge if he got the opportunity. With no badge, no ID and no way of contacting her captain or the FBI, she couldn't prove who she was. Not fast enough to get her out of his clutches before he could spirit her away to wherever he had taken the other women, anyway.

She heard Vincente's voice on the other side of the door, although she couldn't make out what he was saying, then Grant's mumbled response. Finally, his voice rose on an aggressive note so she could hear him. There was no mistaking the threat in those words when he said he would see them around. Silence followed, then the door handle turned again.

"Laurie, it's me. Open up."

She realized her arms were shaking with the effort of supporting her body weight against the wall in preparation to lash out if Grant should appear in the door frame. When she released the lock and Cameron's dark head appeared instead, she relaxed her stance, swaying toward him.

He caught hold of her. "It's okay. He's gone."

"He knew I was in here." The words were muffled as she pressed her face into his chest, inhaling his scent, assuring herself that he was here, that he was real and she was secure in his arms.

Her hands tightly clutched the front of his shirt, and he held them gently, pressing a kiss onto her knuckles. The action grounded her, restoring her confidence that she was safe.

"We owe Vincente and Bryce an explanation," Cameron said.

Laurie nodded, even though she wanted to stay here with him, wrapped in the reassuring bubble of his nearness. She lifted her head, scanning his face, seeing strength and understanding. It stunned her all over again that he was prepared to forget why she had come here and help her.

He is my white knight. The thought flitted in and out of her mind, fleeting and troubling. She tried to catch hold of it, sensing it had a deeper meaning, possibly one that had nothing to do with Cameron, but it was gone. He was right. It was about time they told his brothers what was going on.

Vincente and Bryce both looked shocked at what had just unfolded before them. Their expressions grew increasingly more astonished as Cameron explained what he and Laurie had discovered about Carla's death and the other missing women. His brothers listened in silence while he summarized everything they knew. Laurie's eyes went from Vincente's expressionless face to Bryce's stormy one. Did they believe what he was saying? Or would they come down on the side of their childhood friend, Grant? Would they choose instead to believe she had brainwashed Cameron in attempt to come between him and his friend?

Bryce spoke first. "You think he is selecting these women because of how they look?"

"You believe us?" Laurie felt the tension ooze out of her muscles. She hadn't realized how tightly coiled her body had been until now, when she allowed herself to relax.

"I'm not sure I would have been able to accept what you're telling me, if I hadn't seen that look on his face. It didn't last long, but I have no doubt he wanted to kill you in that instant, Cam."

"And he had no reason to go into my bedroom unless he was looking for Laurie. If he really did hear a noise, why not just come back in here and tell me?" Vincente nodded his agreement. "Of course we believe you."

"Thank you." Laurie felt a sudden sting of tears at the back of her eyes, and blinked them away. "I'm not sure I believe it all myself sometimes."

Cameron took over, returning to Bryce's question.

"There's no doubt he chooses them for their looks. All of these women have dark hair and blue eyes, but many women have that coloring. There has to be something more to it than that. Something else about them appeals to him." He shifted position slightly, so he was facing Vincente. "We think Beth Wade could be one of the victims."

"Beth?" Vincente sat up straighter, and Laurie could see the name had a profound impact on him. "What makes you say that?"

"She disappeared suddenly four months ago. At the time it looked like she just up and left town without a word to anyone. You knew her well. Was that the kind of thing she'd do?"

Vincente shook his head. "Hell, no. Not Beth. She's the most conscientious person I know. It was totally out of character for her to leave her clients in the lurch like that. Everyone said so at the time."

He slumped in his chair with his chin sunk down onto his chest. Cameron exchanged a meaningful look with Laurie. It looked more likely than ever that Beth was one of the victims.

"So Grant is the reason we can't go to the police about Warren and Nichols?" Bryce drew their attention neatly back to the other problem facing them.

"He's the main reason, but, like I said, the publicity fallout from this could ruin us. I'd rather deal with it ourselves. For now," Cameron said.

"How the hell are we supposed to do that?" Vincente dragged himself back into the conversation with a visible effort. "Sounds like these guys have quite an operation going."

"Bryce summed it up earlier when he said Warren

and Nichols must have done this before. They didn't just meet up when they started working for us and think this whole thing up over a few beers. They targeted Delaney Transportation," Cameron said. "Where did they come from? Who recommended them to you?"

"They both came from a firm called Monroe Haulage in Colorado. I hired a few drivers from the same company around the same time. Monroe was laying men off. Like I said, Warren and Nichols came with great references." Vincente's expression clouded over. "You think I was set up?"

"I think it's likely Monroe Haulage never existed, that it was a front for whatever dodgy activities Warren and Nichols were into." Cameron leaned forward, his expression sympathetic as he looked at Vincente. "It's possible the police were onto them in Colorado and they were looking for a legitimate business where they could shift this venture, keep it going and be less obvious. We were the unlucky firm they chose."

"You mean I was the lamebrain who fell for it." Following on from the revelations about Beth Wade, Vincente looked to be in danger of sinking into a pit of despair.

"You couldn't have known," Cameron insisted. "The important thing now is we put a stop to it."

"How?" Bryce's single word cut across the room like a gunshot. "If we can't go to the police, how are we meant to close this down and still make sure these bastards get what's coming to them?"

"The first thing is to get rid of Warren and Nichols. I don't care what made-up charge you use. Fire those guys tomorrow along with any drivers who came from this Monroe Haulage along with them."

"If we fire them, they'll walk away and find somewhere else to start up their evil business. Plus, they get away with everything they've done in the past." Bryce's frown summed up exactly what he thought of Cameron's plan.

"I'm not proposing we let them walk away unscathed. I think the three of us should pay them a little visit." Cameron glanced from Vincente to Bryce, securing their agreement. "Just to be quite sure they know we're onto them. And when this business with Grant is over, Laurie will be free to file a full report." He flashed that devastating grin her way. "I hope you'll be able to minimize the damage to Delaney Transportation once Warren and Nichols no longer work for us. I don't want to be in a position where we don't cooperate with the police—this whole business Warren and Nichols have been operating is too big and too nasty for that. I just want to buy a little time before our involvement becomes necessary."

Laurie nodded. "It will be the least I can do." *If we get through this in one piece.* Somehow, her mind refused to let her imagine the future. Having just escaped Grant's clutches, she couldn't picture anything beyond the next ten minutes. "What about the old Dawson ranch? They could still use that place as their base."

Cameron laughed. "I'll tell Chief Wilkinson there's a rumor a group of local kids have been driving over there to drink and make out. He'll have someone checking the place out on a regular basis like a shot."

He looked at his brothers. "You both know what an old puritan he is."

Bryce appeared to be turning things over in his mind. "I don't like it, but I guess until the bigger problem of making sure Laurie is safe gets resolved, it will have to do."

"On the subject of Laurie, what happens next?" Vincente asked. "You can't hide from Grant forever."

"We need to find something that links him to the disappearance, and presumably the death, of these women. We wondered if you might be able to help with that," Laurie said. "You're one of his closest friends. Is there anywhere you can think that he might have taken these women, either to kill them or to dispose of their bodies? Some place to which he feels a connection?"

Vincente was silent for a few minutes, frowning in an effort to concentrate. When he spoke, his voice started out hesitant. "I'm not sure if this is important. I used to go hunting with Grant, but I lost interest in it over recent years." He gave a soft laugh. "Funnily enough, it was Beth who convinced me to give it up. She was fiercely against any blood sports." He seemed to make an effort to shake off a memory. "Anyhow, around the same time Beth was campaigning for me to stop hunting, Grant was starting to act weird."

"Weird in what way?"

"It was like he had a ritual. No matter what we were hunting, or where we were heading, we had to meet in the same place. Even if we were going fishing up on Wilderness Lake, he'd insist on starting out miles away, out by the Hope Valley coal mine—"

"What?" Cameron's interruption startled Laurie into turning her attention away from Vincente.

"I know." Vincente nodded. "It's crazy. You have to go five miles out of town to get to the old coal mine, then double back in the opposite direction to head toward Wilderness Lake. So much easier to just take a direct route…" He trailed off. "But I get the feeling that's not why you interrupted me."

"When I saw Chief Wilkinson yesterday, he was complaining he'd received a letter from Mrs. Martin about mysterious lights and spooky noises. Mrs. Martin has the last house along the Hope Valley road. It runs close to an abandoned coal mine," Cameron explained to Laurie.

"I guess we know where we need to start looking tomorrow." Laurie didn't know whether to feel excited or dispirited. "Although a disused mine doesn't sound the easiest place to search."

"It could be worse. This was a small mine, and following a campaign by myself and the council members, it was cleaned up and the mineshaft made safe about five years ago. Its advantages to anyone looking for privacy are going to be its remote location and the fact the only people who go there are mine-exploration enthusiasts. It's not the prettiest place. Although when we were kids, it had the element of danger that the more scenic locations nearby couldn't offer."

Cameron gave a nostalgic shake of his head before he continued. "Dad threatened to tan our backsides until we couldn't sit down for a week if we ever went out there, but Grant didn't have anyone to impose those boundaries on him. He was always boasting about how far down into the mineshaft he'd been and trying to get me to go with him."

Vincente laughed. "I'm guessing Dad's threat kept you away?"

"You guessed right." The three brothers shared a sentimental smile.

"How long ago was it that Grant started insisting you went out there before you went on your hunting trips?" Laurie asked Vincente.

"That's the strange thing. He didn't always do it. It was a habit that must have started around three and a half years ago."

"About the time Lisa Lambert went missing," Laurie said. "We think she was the first girl to disappear," she explained to Vincente and Bryce.

"You mean he could have been going there as some sort of *celebration*? Knowing her body was there?" Vincente's face paled. "And taking me with him? My God, was he hoping that on some level I'd share his sick enjoyment?"

Cameron placed a hand on his brother's knee. "He's a killer, Vincente. He can't help himself. Probably your presence was unimportant." He glanced at the clock, then at Laurie. "We'd better get going. If we're going out to the Hope Valley mine tomorrow, I want to make an early start."

"Where are you staying?" Bryce asked.

"Uncle Frankie's cabin."

"I'd forgotten that old place existed. You're certainly well hidden up there." Bryce laughed. "I'll walk out with you." He turned to Vincente. "We have a busy day tomorrow, as well. Let's nail those bastards Warren and Nichols."

Vincente nodded, gripping his arm briefly. He turned to Cameron. "Look after yourself."

Cameron nodded. "I intend to."

Laurie sensed a shift in mood between the three brothers. In the few hours they'd been together in the apartment, the antagonism between them had been replaced by a new camaraderie. She hadn't known them long, but she hoped it lasted. Walking out into the darkness between the two tall figures of Cameron and Bryce, she felt comfortable and protected.

They said good-night to Bryce in the well-lit parking lot. His car was closer, and he was already driving away as they approached their rental. Just before they reached it, Laurie tucked her arm into Cameron's.

"I like your brothers."

He turned his head to look down at her with a smile at the precise instant that a shot rang out and Cameron dropped to the tarmac.

Cameron hit the ground hard, searing pain shooting through his upper left arm. Even though it was bad, he was able to think rationally. *Flesh wound. Blood loss will be the biggest problem.* He reached up with his right hand, ignoring the darts of agony the action sent shooting through him, and pulled Laurie down beside him.

"Keep low. Get into the car. You drive." He shoved the keys into her hand.

He caught a brief glimpse of her beautiful face, fearful but determined. She nodded once, then she was away, crawling the last few feet commando style, getting the door open and clambering into the car. Moving was torture, but Cameron managed to drag himself across to the car in her wake. He pulled himself into the passenger seat, grateful for Laurie's hands under his arms hauling him those last few inches.

Collapsing into the seat, he gasped out two words. "Let's go."

"Shouldn't we go back, get help from Vincente? Get you to a hospital?"

Cameron shook his head. "From the direction of that shot, he's between us and the apartment building. Can you outpace him if he follows us?"

Her expression hardened. "I can try." The engine gunned into life, and Cameron slewed wildly in his seat as she spun the car out of the parking lot. "Sorry." Laurie bit her lip, casting an apologetic glance in his direction.

He managed a shaky laugh. "You concentrate on the road while I focus on staying upright."

Once they were away from the riverside complex, the roads through town were quiet, and Laurie took him at his word. In her capable hands, the big vehicle maintained a sedate speed through the main street of Stillwater, then thundered onto the open road. Her eyes flicked back and forth between the road and the rearview mirror.

"Anything?" Cameron was attempting to undo his shirt.

"No. There's nothing behind us."

He managed to ease the blood-soaked garment off his left arm. It was difficult to assess the full extent of the injury in the darkness and in a fast-moving car, but he was fairly sure there was no bullet lodged in his arm. It was bad, but it could have been worse. Feeling around, he found where the bullet had passed right through the fleshy part of his upper arm. There didn't seem to be any damage to the bone. Although it hurt like hell, he'd been lucky. He had a feeling Grant had been aiming for his heart, and it was only Laurie's words about his brothers that had distracted him at the last minute, causing him to turn toward her. He had been *very* lucky.

"How bad is it?" Laurie bit her lip again as she risked a sideways glance in his direction.

"You're stuck with me a while longer." She exhaled a long sigh of relief. "There's a medical kit in the cabin. The turnoff for the Stillwater Trail is coming up…"

The flow of words dried up as he followed the direction of Laurie's intent gaze. Up ahead, flashing lights showed a police cruiser blocking the highway. A lone figure stood in the road in front of the vehicle, arms folded across a broad, unmistakable chest.

"He must have gunned that car along the back roads to get here ahead of us."

"How could he know which direction we would take?" Laurie was slowing the car. Cameron noticed that, curiously, her eyes seemed fixed on the rearview mirror rather than on Grant, who had started walking toward them.

"Logic, I suppose. It was either this way or we were headed out of Stillwater and toward Park County. What the…?"

Without warning, Laurie popped the car into Reverse and floored the throttle. "Hold tight. I'm not prepared to let him put a bullet in your head out here in the middle of nowhere and then drag me out of the car."

As the car picked up speed, she took her foot off

the gas and swung the wheel hard around to the right. It wasn't a pretty or smooth maneuver, but it did the trick. The front end of the car flew straight around so they were facing back the way they had come. Calmly, Laurie switched from Reverse to Drive and pulled away at speed.

"Where did you learn to do that?" Cameron asked, when he regained control of his breathing. Part of him expected a bullet to come through the rear windshield, but they were moving so fast, and she had performed the maneuver so quickly, he doubted Grant even had time to draw his gun.

"When I first joined the force, I did an emergency response driving course. It also helps that I have a friend who is a rally driver. He showed me a few tricks." She went back to scanning the road. "Once he's recovered from the shock of that little stunt, he'll come after us. He's armed, he's killed before and now he'll be really pissed off. You know these roads. Which way should I go?"

As he directed her, he kept his eyes on her profile. It struck him again that, apart from her looks, she was nothing like Carla. Carla had been damaged by her early experiences. A traumatic childhood had left her insecure, prone to anxieties and in constant need of reassurance and support. Theirs had been a one-sided relationship, although even as he thought it, Cameron felt a pang of guilt. He had been happy to be the provider of Carla's strength. Had known all along that was what she needed from him.

But Laurie was different. She had her own inner vitality. This woman was his equal in fortitude and courage. It was one of the many things that intrigued and excited him about her. As much as he wanted to feel her beautiful body wrapped around his again, he wanted to know more about that mind of hers. About the kind of woman who could stare down a man who wanted to kill her and calmly decide to flip a car into a J-turn. He wondered if it was to do with the route his life had taken. The man he had been when he first met Carla was not the same man he was now. A week ago, he'd have believed that thought would have brought with it a whole world of regret. Now? He examined it, prodded it, put it under the spotlight. Now it felt different, but it was too soon to say how.

He led Laurie along a series of hunting tracks, some of them only half-remembered routes from his childhood. With dipped headlights, she skillfully negotiated the rough terrain. After about half an hour of evasive tactics with no sign of Grant's vehicle in pursuit, Cameron guided her onto the main Stillwater Trail. When they reached the lockup where they could leave the vehicle, he breathed a sigh of relief.

"Can you manage this walk?" There was only the moon to light their way now. Laurie's face was a picture of concern as she gazed at him.

His injured arm had stiffened during the drive, and he flexed it with a grimace. "Since the alternative is spending the night in the car, I'm going to make sure of it."

The hike that had been nonthreatening in daylight assumed different proportions under cover of darkness. The vast beauty of the Wyoming night sky took on a new quality, one that was slightly intimidating. Throughout his life, Cameron had been used to this awesome display of stars splattering the inky darkness like diamonds scattered onto black velvet. For the first time ever, he felt in no mood to admire it. The silence should have been comforting. It meant they were alone. Parts of the trail were home to buffalo, wolves and even bears, although it was unusual for them to venture this far south. Even so, he couldn't help wishing he had a canister of bear spray. Or even better, a gun. Because it wasn't really the wildlife his ears were listening for at all. It was the possibility of a human predator stalking them that bothered him most.

Cameron knew Laurie was thinking the same thing, which was why they completed the hike in tense silence. The climbs, slides and switchbacks caused his arm to throb excruciatingly, and he was shocked at how little energy he had. Although it was summer, the temperature up here was cool. Without his shirt Cameron was soon feeling the effects of the mountain breeze, and his teeth began to chatter. By the time they drew close to the cabin, his feet felt like they were laden down with lead weights and each inward breath was an effort. He staggered, and Laurie moved to his side, getting her shoulder under his right arm and supporting him the last few steps.

She took the keys from his hand and fumbled the door open, crashing into the welcome space and kicking it closed behind them. Easing Cameron into a seat by the fire, she locked the door again before hurrying to get a blaze going. Heading into the bathroom, she returned with a bowl of warm water, washcloths and the medical kit.

"Close the curtains," Cameron said, as she prepared to get to work on his injury.

"Why?"

"Because I know how much the darkness outside bothers you." He smiled up at her.

For an instant her guard dropped, and he caught a glimpse of tears shimmering in the blue depths of her eyes. She blinked them away rapidly. "You, Cameron Delaney, are an amazing man."

"I do my best." He would have attempted a smile, but he didn't have enough energy.

Chapter 13

Biting her lip, Laurie studied the damage the bullet had done to Cameron's arm. "This needs stitches."

"If you have the stomach for it, everything you need should be in that kit. You don't take any chances on getting a hunting injury this far from town."

She swallowed hard, then nodded. There was a time and a place for being squeamish, and this was probably not it.

"Take these." She handed him two painkillers from the pack she kept in her purse, and a glass of water. "I need to clean you up before I do anything else." Soaking a washcloth in the warm water, she washed the dried blood from his chest, arm and shoulder, wincing at his indrawn breath when she touched the wound itself. "Lean forward."

He shifted position, leaning his head into the curve

of her neck, and she repeated the process with the exit wound in the back of his arm.

The bullet had torn straight through, and although it had left a bloody mess in its wake, the edges of both wounds were clean. That would make her job easier when it came to stitching them together and meant he would heal better. She took out a bottle of liquid anti-septic and poured it onto another washcloth.

"I'm going to have to hurt you."

He nodded, flinching as she applied the cloth to the open wounds, making sure she got the disinfec-tant into every part of the injured flesh. Although his face paled and his jaw tensed, he made no comment until she had finished.

"You're very thorough." His face was close to hers, those dark eyes warm on her face.

"You're not the first person to have said that about me."

Laurie turned her head slightly, and Cameron's lips brushed hers. Shouldn't this seem out of place instead of absolutely the only thing to do right now? Sighing, she leaned into the kiss, parting her lips and allowing his tongue to tangle with hers. It was a slow, soothing exchange, a give-and-take of—she searched for the right words—strength, fortification, *care*. The sear-ing heat was still there, whenever they wished to ex-plore it, but this was deeper. This had meaning. This was new. It changed everything. And it scared the hell out of her.

"I'm going to stick needles into you now." Her voice was slightly breathless as she pulled away from him.

Cameron's eyes reflected her own emotions back

at her. "I really shouldn't still be turned on when you say that, should I?"

She choked back a laugh. "If you still feel the same way when I start on the stitching, then I'll get worried about where this is going."

Inside the medical kit she found a pack containing everything she would need to suture the wound, including a syringe and a local anesthetic. Following the instructions on the packaging, she injected this into the area around the two sides of the hole in Cameron's arm.

"I haven't actually done this before, but I have been in a first responder medical emergency course." Although she tried for a reassuring tone, Laurie's hand shook slightly as she prepared the needle and suture material. "So I've been shown *how* to do it."

Cameron placed his hand over hers. "I trust you."

The warmth of his touch and the smile in his eyes gave her the courage she needed, and she nodded. With a hand that was completely steady this time, she bent over her task, completing it quickly and effectively. "There. It's not the prettiest stitching, but it'll hold you together."

Cameron flexed his arm. "It works. That's the most important thing."

Laurie finished up by placing dressings over the stitches and securing them in place. Then she collected together the used washcloths and packaging and took them to the bathroom to dispose of them. When she returned, she knelt on the rug in front of Cameron. Placing her cheek on his knee, she remained in that position for a long time. He tangled his hands in her hair, stroking and soothing.

Eventually, she lifted her head. "He tried to kill you tonight. You're one of his best friends. You said yourself you were probably his only friend throughout his childhood, yet he shot you because of me."

His hand cupped her cheek. "Laurie, this is about him. You haven't done anything. He is the one who is wrong in all of this."

She nodded, turning her face into his hand so she could press her lips to his palm. "When you fell…" The rest of the sentence refused to come. She could see from the look in Cameron's eyes that he understood. Leaning down, he pressed his lips to hers. The kiss quickly became fierce, hot and hungry, and when she drew away, Laurie was breathing hard. "We can't. You're hurt."

Cameron's expression was glazed with wanting. Danger had fired up the need in them both. "We can… if you don't mind doing most of the work."

Raising herself with her forearms along his thighs, Laurie got to work on his belt buckle. Her fingertips brushed against the rock-hard bulge in his jeans, and Cameron's hips jerked. When she had tugged his belt undone, she slid his zipper down and freed him from the restraints of his clothing. Her breath caught in her throat at the sight of him. Magnificent, proud and erect. He stripped away what was left of her breath. When she had eased his jeans and boxer briefs around his ankles, she shifted position so she was between his knees. Looking up at him with a mischievous grin, she leaned forward and took him into her mouth. Cameron's body jolted upward in response to her lips closing over his aroused length. Laurie used her tongue to coat him in wetness, at the same time wrapping her fingers around the base of his shaft.

"Do you have any idea what you are doing to me?" He caught hold of one long strand of her hair, winding it around his fingers and tugging on it.

Laurie answered by taking him farther and deeper into her mouth, leaning forward and enveloping him in heat and pleasure. As she pulled back, she tightened her lips around him and sucked hard. Cameron groaned, and she allowed herself an inward smile at the effect she was having on him.

Her head rose and fell in his lap, and she hummed softly in time with the rhythm she'd established. Using her tongue to flick the head and her hand to cup him, she could feel the intensity of Cameron's pleasure in the tension of his muscles. Before long, she felt him begin to tense and shudder. His hand tightened in her hair as his warm release filled her mouth.

"Come here." His voice was husky.

Laurie joined him on the sofa, curling into his side. Pulling her close with his good arm, Cameron drew her into a kiss that went on forever. His tongue possessed hers as he attempted to pull her shirt free from her jeans one-handed. In the end, he gave up. Laughing, he rested his forehead against hers.

"Help me out here?"

Laurie tugged her shirt free and unbuttoned it, slipping it off her shoulders. The look in Cameron's eyes made her stomach flip up and over in the giddy way only he could achieve. Purposefully, he reached up his right hand and closed it possessively around one breast, pinching lightly at her nipple through the thin, lacy fabric of her bra. She moaned softly as pleasure streaked through her. Slowly, keeping the anticipation ratcheted high, he bent lower, kissing his way down her neck.

"Now this." He plucked at her bra strap, and she reached around behind her to undo the clasp of the flimsy garment. Tossing it aside, she shivered slightly as she faced Cameron and his eyes roamed over her.

His hand cupped her breast and he bent his head, teasing her with his tongue, circling her nipple over and over. Laurie's head fell back, and she fought the impulse to dig her nails into him, deciding he'd had enough pain for one day. Instead she buried her fingers in his hair, holding him to her. His lips closed around the aching peak, and he sucked hard. A lightning bolt shot from his mouth directly to the scorching heat between her legs.

Cameron's hand found her, moving over her jeans to cup her sex. His fingers fumbled open the button on her jeans, and he got the zipper down. Laurie helped him push aside the fabric, and his hand slid inside the elastic of her underwear. He eased a finger down over her clitoris, separating her folds and pressing the tip of his finger into her sex.

"You're so hot and wet. I want to lose myself inside you."

"Please." Laurie tried to urge his finger farther, but the cloth of her jeans bunched around her hips was hampering them both. That delicious touch between her legs disappeared as Cameron removed his hand. He used his good hand to pull at her jeans, and, desperate to be free of the restrictive barrier of her clothing, Laurie wriggled free of her boots, jeans and underwear. Naked, she shifted her weight so she was straddling Cameron with her knees on either side of his thighs.

When he pressed his finger into her again, fully this time, Laurie sighed with pleasure. "So good," she whispered.

His mouth found hers, forceful and demanding in a kiss that took her breath away and set her heart racing as she rocked her hips against the pressure of his hand. He moved his finger so it just teased her opening. Around and around, with gentle flicks up to brush lightly over her clitoris. It wasn't enough. Enough to drive her wild, not enough to give her what she really wanted.

"More. Please, Cameron. I need more."

She gasped as he withdrew his finger, only to replace it with two, pressing them in as deep as they could go. She clenched around him tight, hissing in a breath.

"Like that?" Cameron murmured. Withdrawing his fingers until they were nearly all the way out, he plunged them back in, at the same time rubbing his thumb over her clitoris, setting off a chain reaction of electric shocks along her nerve endings.

Oh, dear God. Laurie had to remind herself to breathe. Tight, hot pleasure began to radiate outward from her core. Glancing down, she saw he was rock hard again, his erection straining upward toward her.

Reaching between them, Laurie gripped him, sliding her hand down his shaft. "That feels good, but this is what I really want."

Her words caused him to curse softly under his breath. She hovered on the brink of a climax. So close.

Just before she tipped over the edge, Cameron murmured softly in her ear. "Condom. Back pocket."

With a bit of skillful twisting and bending, she maintained her position and leaned down. Finding the little foil wrapper, she ripped it open and sheathed him. Raising herself above him, she guided him to her. Cameron paused with his tip pressed against her sex, rocking his hips so he tormented her, his expression telling her he was savoring the moment. Laurie moaned, and all teasing over, he pushed up, his thick heat stretching and filling her. The fingers of his right hand gripped the flesh of her buttocks hard as he thrust all the way into her.

Keeping her hands on his hips, Laurie lifted herself as Cameron pulled his hips back. She was in charge. Slowly, she controlled their movements. Feeling every inch of him sliding into her and pulling out again. Hampered by the fact that he couldn't use one arm, Cameron was forced to let her dictate the pace. He clenched his teeth, clearly wanting to go faster, to drive into her harder, to piston furiously to release the building tension.

Thrusting his hips up, he ground against her, and Laurie gave herself up to her own unstoppable need. Her whole world narrowed to the point where their bodies joined. To his heat pounding into her, to the storm of pleasure breaking over her. Her muscles clenched hard around him, drawing a groan from the depths of his chest. He thickened and jerked deep inside her as she climaxed over and over, her vision blurring and her mind reeling as she slumped on top of him. Cameron held her against his chest with his good hand, his own body shuddering to a standstill as he trailed his fingers along her spine.

"I think we should go to bed." Laurie was surprised to hear the depth of feeling that had shaken her echoed in Cameron's own voice as he murmured the words. She lifted her head from his chest to study his face. The blaze of raw emotion in his eyes stunned her. It was gone so fast she questioned whether she had seen it at all. It had been a long, hard day. Allowing her imagination to run wild probably wasn't the best way to end it.

Tomorrow would take them on the hunt for more answers and hopefully a step closer to the truth. Until then, even though her body was still shimmering with what this man could do to her, she decided the wisest course was to continue to act as though her heart was unscathed. Then Cameron smiled at her, and all her good intentions went flying to the four corners of the room.

Laurie woke just as the dawn light was creeping through the bedroom curtains. At first she wondered if it was fear of Grant that had brought her so abruptly awake, and she lay still, examining her feelings. No, she had a healthy amount of nervousness about what was to come, but she was also determined to see this through to the end and make sure Grant Becker ended up behind bars. She owed it to those women who had no one else fighting for them. It wasn't alarm that had woken her. There was a nagging doubt at the back of her mind, something she was missing that she should be seeing. Like a loose thread, there was a connection that, if she pulled it the right way, would unravel this whole case.

Carla. Laurie's unknown cousin, Cameron's lost love. She was the connection between them, the reason Laurie had come to Stillwater. She still couldn't shake the conviction that Carla was the key to this whole case. How bizarre was it that Grant had seen her for the first time one night at Dino's with Cameron and fallen for her so hard and so fast he'd started killing women who reminded him of her? Unless he didn't. *That was it.* That was what had been bugging her about this whole thing. What if that *wasn't* the first time Grant saw Carla?

"Oh, my goodness." Abruptly, she sat up, hugging her knees up to her chin.

"Hmm?" Cameron opened one eye, regarding her in surprise.

She wasn't sure how to broach this subject with him. He always seemed happy to talk about Carla… up to a point. It had never felt like Carla was a barrier between them. Oh, she was always there in the background. The woman Cameron loved, and would always love. How could she not be there in some form or another? But Laurie had never seen Carla as a problem because Cameron had not allowed her to become one. Now Laurie needed to ask some tough questions about her, and all that might change.

She sucked in a deep breath. "You told me once Carla didn't want a family life because her own childhood had been traumatic. What did you mean by that exactly?"

A frown line drew his brows together. "Where are you going with this?"

Even though they were both naked, with mere inches between them, and the memory of the passion they had shared lingered in the scent and warmth of their skin, his tone put up an instant barrier between them.

She supposed it was a fair enough question. And if she wanted answers from him, she needed to share her thought processes. However fantastic they might be.

"Bear with me on this, okay?" Her eyes pleaded with him for understanding. Cameron gave a brief but less than encouraging nod. "I was trying to make connections. You said Grant was abused as a child, and he got sent to a summer camp for underprivileged children. I also remembered you mentioned Carla's troubled childhood. I just wondered…" She broke off, shaking her head. "It's too far-fetched. Forget it."

"No, go on." Cameron's gaze had become intent.

"Okay." She plowed on, the words tumbling over each other as they came out too fast. "I wondered, was there any way they could have met each other before that night you took her to Dino's? Maybe when they were younger? Could Grant have fallen for Carla long before then? Is it possible that, instead of seeing her for the first time that night, he was *recognizing* her?"

"My God." Cameron sat up as well, leaning back against the solid-oak headboard. His expression was stunned. As he sat back, the dressing on his arm stood out stark against the smooth, tanned muscle of his bicep. The flesh around it didn't appear to be inflamed, and Laurie took a moment to feel proud of her handiwork. "If that's true, it would put a whole different light on Grant's infatuation for Carla." He frowned. "But why would Carla have told me about him asking her out without also mentioning she already knew him?"

"Just because he recognized her, doesn't mean it worked both ways," Laurie said. "This is all guesswork, but suppose they were at the same camp one summer and Grant developed a crush on Carla. Then, years later, she turned up here. But not only was she with you, she hurt him even more by not knowing who he was when he asked her out. Can you imagine how that must have felt? The girl he'd been dreaming of for all those years didn't even remember him?"

"If he had already developed an infatuation with Carla at an early age, that might explain why he wasn't interested in other women. He may have believed he'd already found the girl of his dreams." Cameron ran his right hand through his already tousled, early-morning hair. "Grant always did have something of an obsessive personality. Although his obsessions could be strange."

"In what way?" Laurie relaxed her tightly coiled position, stretching her legs in front of her.

"When we were kids it manifested itself in a desire to rescue injured animals. He had quite a menagerie. Mangy old dogs, cats with one eye, birds with broken wings. As he grew older, it became more of a crusade. Grant seemed to see himself as this white knight on a charger." He paused, scanning Laurie's face as she frowned. "What is it?"

"You reminded me of something. Carry on with what you were saying and I'll tell you when you're finished."

"That's it really. Grant always had to be rescuing someone or something. I thought it was a by-product of his childhood." Cameron attempted a shrug and grimaced as it hurt his arm. "I'm no amateur psychologist, but it seemed to me he was saving others because no one had been there to rescue him. Now tell me why the white knight thing made you frown."

"When I was hiding out in Vincente's bathroom and you came in, I had a thought that you were my knight in shining armor."

Cameron laughed. "I'm not. I was scared as hell about what might happen to you when Grant came into Vincente's apartment. I acted out of instinct, not nobility or some ancient code of honor."

"No, and that's just it. Any normal guy wouldn't want to be a knight on a white charger going around rescuing damsels in distress. Because that's a fantasy. Real life is different. You're real, and that's one of the things I—" she paused, swallowing back the word *love* "—like about you. But there is such a thing as White Knight Syndrome. I was too overwrought to capture the thought last night, but even then I guess my mind was trying to apply it to Grant."

"You mean there are guys who do see themselves in that role?"

"Very much so. I took a psychology course when I first joined the police, and there was a module on this. These guys are often loners, frequently with little experience of attracting women, who often try to compensate for that by adopting their own code of chivalry. This type of man has severe problems with self-worth, so he tries to prove his worthiness to a woman by rescuing her from a bad situation. In this day and age, that often means focusing on women who have issues."

Cameron regarded her in fascination. "And all the women who have gone missing had issues or needed to be rescued."

Laurie began to tick them off on her fingers. "Lisa Lambert definitely had issues. She was struggling with substance and alcohol abuse at the time she went missing. Kathy Sachs was unhappy here in Stillwater. She talked openly about that and also the fact that she was escaping an abusive marriage. Tanya Horton was described as a 'wild child.' I'm guessing that means she had some problems. Then we have Marie O'Donnell. Toby said she was an orphan, raised in an Irish convent by nuns. We know she and Grant became friends, although I suspect he manufactured that friendship. Chances are she confided in him about her past."

"Toby also said when Grant stepped in to save the day by taking Marie to the airport, she actually described him as a 'knight in shining armor.'"

"Imagine how much *that* comment must have fueled his ego. Then there's Carla." Laurie risked a glance at his face. "I have thought all along that she must be the key to this."

Cameron nodded, his expression grim. "You could be right. Carla certainly had problems. You already know that, like you, Carla was born in Stillwater. Her parents divorced when she was just a baby, and her mom remarried. Her stepdad was a violent drunk. Carla and her mom spent their lives on the move from place to place, trying to stay one step ahead of him. Each time they got settled somewhere, he'd find them and they'd be forced to move on again. When she was sixteen, he killed her mom in front of Carla.

Carla was placed in witness protection. From there, she went to college, learned to sail, gained her degree and made a new life for herself. She didn't talk much about her childhood, but she did mention going to summer camp."

Cameron gave a reminiscent laugh. "That was one of the reasons Carla hated Wyoming. She said the open spaces reminded her of one particular year she wanted to forget. There was nothing she disliked more than enforced fun and people she didn't know trying too hard to be her friend."

Laurie shivered. Grant? Could he have been the person who tried too hard to be Carla's friend that summer? She supposed they would never know. "Just as we've thought all along, Grant doesn't just look for the physical similarities these women have. He's looking for something deeper. They have to be vulnerable as well so he can step in and save them."

"Coming to the last two victims that we know of, Deanna Milligan certainly fits that profile. I'm not so sure about Beth Wade. She was a successful attorney."

"Beth may have had issues we're unaware of, or she may have really just packed her bags and walked out of town one day." Having seen the look in Vincente's eyes when Beth's name was mentioned, Laurie hoped for his sake that the second option was the truth. "One of the biggest frustrations for Grant must have been the fact that Carla, the person he most wanted to impress, the one all the other women were a substitute for, was no longer vulnerable. While she was with you, she didn't need him to be her white knight."

"Until he managed to get her alone. It was only

when she was with Grant that Carla was in any danger."

"Maybe he saw her go out alone on her boat that night, knew there was a storm on its way and saw his chance to be her white knight at last? He may not have known how good she was at handling a boat. When he tried to go to her rescue and Carla didn't need him, all that pent-up resentment could have boiled over."

Cameron's eyes darkened. "But what about you? You don't need him, either."

"I don't fit into his usual pattern for a number of reasons. He didn't seek me out, so I came as a shock to him when he saw me with you that night at Dino's. I'm so like Carla it's shaken him up. And he needs to get rid of me because I'm onto him." Laurie shivered. "Even so, he's done his best to *make* me vulnerable."

Cameron slid his good arm around her shoulders, drawing her closer, and she leaned against him gratefully, glad of his warmth. "By killing Moreton, you mean?"

"Yes, but also by cutting me off from every aspect of my real life. He took my laptop, hacked into my phone and then destroyed it. Then he systematically wiped out any trace that Moreton was ever in this area. Grant has covered his tracks very neatly. Any evidence Moreton had on him was destroyed in the fire. May King was the only person who knew he ordered the roses, and she is dead. If he had succeeded in his plan to kill you last night, no one would ever know who I was and why I was here in Stillwater. He could make me disappear without a trace."

"Except Vincente and Bryce know everything now."

"Would you put it past him to kill them, too?"

Cameron's jaw clenched. "I wouldn't put anything past him."

Chapter 14

Cameron couldn't get enough of watching Laurie's face as he entered her. He brushed the head of his cock over her. Even through the condom, he could feel how hot and wet she was, and it took every ounce of self-control he had to take from driving hard and fast into her. Her head was thrown back and her eyes half-closed. Lifting her knees over the crook of his arms, he pushed her legs back to her shoulders as he balanced on his knees and feasted his eyes on her body. She squirmed, readying herself for the impact of his entry as she lifted herself toward him. Cameron moved his hips forward in a single deep thrust that forced a soft cry from her. Damn, she was tight. So hot. So tight. He shuddered as her muscles gripped him and drew him deeper into her. The air left his lungs, and he fought hard to get it back again. It felt like he'd been fighting to regain control of his breathing from the first minute he'd met her.

He ran his tongue over the tender flesh of Laurie's throat, dropping fully onto her. She whimpered with pleasure, her hips lifting in time with his thrusts, and he gave himself up to the intensity of pumping deep and losing himself in her. He was engulfed in a firestorm of delight, the like of which he had never known before. This. There was nothing else. Taking everything she offered, giving everything he had. There was only this sweet surrender. All of it. Over and over. He wanted everything, nothing between them, no barriers, no pretense.

He drove into her, biting her shoulder to keep from saying out loud the words that were pounding through his head. Beneath his hands, Laurie's thighs trembled in time with his clenched muscles. When his orgasm roared through him, he collapsed onto her, gasping, feeling her clench around him. Lifting his head, he watched her face as she came, drinking in the tiny details as her eyes widened, her lips parted and a faint rosy pink stained her cheeks. Soft moans escaped her as he continued to move, forcing another wave to crash over her.

He moved to one side, covering his eyes with his arm. Hiding his feelings, because he knew she'd caught a glimpse of the intensity of his emotions last night after they'd made love. It wasn't as if he didn't want Laurie to know how much she meant to him. He wasn't hiding from *her*. After what had just happened between them? The thought almost made him laugh. He poured his soul into her with each thrust of his hips. Laurie felt it and responded. But now wasn't the time for him to say out loud how much he loved her, even though his feelings were threatening to overwhelm him with their ferocity. Now was the time to get that bastard Grant Becker out of their lives for good. Then he could deal with all the love and passion that was welling up inside him. Then he could find out if he was right in his hope—even his belief—that Laurie might feel the same.

"We should probably do something about facing the day ahead. Something that doesn't involve deciding to spend it in bed." Laurie's voice was regretful as she leaned up on one elbow and looked down at him.

"Don't tempt me." He lifted his arm and peeked at her from beneath it. She looked breathtakingly beautiful with her mussed-up dark hair falling forward to frame her face. "There's one thing I don't get. Do you think Grant kills them when they resist him, or because he wants to rescue them from the awfulness of their lives?"

A shadow flitted across her face, and he regretted asking the question. Wished he didn't have to bring Grant Becker's name up and spoil the perfection of this brief time they had together. "Who knows what goes on in his mind? That will be something for other people to unpick once he's arrested."

Sliding from the bed, she moved toward the bedroom door. Cameron watched her go, feasting his eyes on her rear view. The smooth perfection of her sculpted back, the slender waist flaring out to neat hips, those long, long legs...

She turned and grinned mischievously over her shoulder. "I know exactly what you're thinking, Mayor Delaney, but we just don't have time."

He threw back the sheets, moving purposefully toward her. Laurie's eyes widened as she took in the unmistakable evidence of his arousal. "We do if we shower together, Detective Bryan."

Laurie's senses were on even higher alert as they drove past the turnoff for Stillwater. Not only did Grant know what they were driving, but he would be more determined than ever to hunt them down and finish this. At least Cameron's arm, when she had changed the dressings, seemed to be healing well. The stitches looked secure, and there was no sign of any infection.

They were traveling along a narrow road with tall aspens rising high on each side, their gleaming white trunks flashing past like a continuous optical illusion. It was still early, and a faint golden mist lingered low on the ground. There was nothing out here. Nothing to disturb the tranquil, untamed beauty of this scenery.

"Nothing except deer, elk, some bear, maybe the odd moose and even an occasional grizzly," Cameron said.

"I may have fallen in love with Wyoming, but I'm not sure I'd want to get quite this far away from it all." Laurie was conscious of his eyes on her face and wondered what she'd said to cause such an intense stare.

Since they had reached the remote property that belonged to Mrs. Martin, she had no opportunity to find out. As she descended from the vehicle, Laurie reflected on the sort of mentality and staying power it must take to live in a place like this. And to live here alone? Miles from the power grid and the nearest convenience store? Day after day, month after lonely month. On a sunny morning like this, it didn't seem too bad, but what about in winter?

The woman who appeared on the porch of the small, cedar cabin looked as formidable as the landscape around her. Her hair was as white as the snow on the tips of the mountains and her face had the same granite hardness as the crags of Devil's Peak. She could have been any age between sixty and eighty, but her body had the lean, hard edge of someone much younger.

Mrs. Martin waited with her arms folded across her chest as they approached. She nodded in Laurie's direction, then turned her attention to Cameron.

"Mayor Delaney." There was no inflection in the words.

"Nice to see you again, Mrs. Martin. Chief Wilkinson tells me you've been troubled by some strange goings-on at the Hope Valley mine."

Her snort was a perfect indicator of her opinion of Chief Wilkinson. With one small sound she conveyed contempt, dismissal and exasperation. "You'd better come through."

They followed her into the tiny cabin and out onto the back porch. Laurie had never felt so insignificant. Beyond the huge trees she could see the tops of the towering mountains. The sky was a tiny strip of blue above them.

Mrs. Martin pointed in a straight line from where they were standing. "The mine is just beyond the trees. The crater is grassed over now, but there are no trees or shrubs growing there yet. I have to go down that way to collect water. That's how come I noticed it."

"What did you notice exactly?"

Mrs. Martin's eyes flickered over Laurie in response to her question. "Someone down there at night."

"Was it one person, or several people?"

Mrs. Martin gave it some thought. "Judging by the torchlight, I'd say one." She nodded decisively. "Yes, just one."

"Chief Wilkinson said there were strange noises," Cameron said.

Mrs. Martin snorted again. "Tell the chief to read his letters properly. Those noises were strange all right, but only because no one comes out this way at night. Not because I'm some crank who thinks there's a UFO out in the mine crater. I think I would be able to tell the difference between the sounds of a spaceship and a regular car engine."

"So the noises were the sounds of a vehicle being driven out this way at night?"

Mrs. Martin nodded. "And onto the mine crater itself. Why would anyone do that? Even those people who come down here with ropes, lamps and helmets to explore the old mineshaft do it in daylight."

She was right, of course. Laurie caught Cameron's eye and saw he was thinking the same thing. There was no legitimate reason for anyone to come out to a remote, abandoned mine at night.

"How often does this happen?" Cameron asked.

"Now and then. There may be a burst of activity and then nothing for quite some time."

Laurie shivered as she looked out at the raw, elemental beauty of the surrounding area. Vincente's words came back to her. *You mean he could have been going there as some sort of celebration?* The image of Grant coming to this untamed place to rejoice over his deeds horrified her almost as much as the murders themselves. She could almost see his face uplifted in pride to the highest point of the mountain range, the aptly named Devil's Peak. She thought of those faces on her laptop screen. Bright, smiling women with hopes and dreams and loved ones. They had woken up one morning with plans and promises, not knowing an encounter with a killer was looming.

She thought of Carla. Stubborn, beautiful Carla, who should have listened to Cameron and gone with him that night. Of Marie, who gratefully accepted a lift from a man she thought of as a friend. Of sad Deanna, wild Tanya, unhappy Kathy and tortured Lisa. And there may have been others. She reminded herself that her tentative search had found other missing women from outside Stillwater. They deserved better than this. Lying in an old mine, the broken trophies of a twisted murderer. Their families deserved better than this. They needed to know the truth.

Laurie felt a single cold tear track its way down her cheek. Determinedly, she brushed it away before her companions could see it.

"Thank you for your time, Mrs. Martin." Despite her efforts to hide it, Laurie had a feeling Cameron could sense her distress.

The old woman nodded. "If there is something bad going on out there, I want it stopped."

When they got back into the car, Cameron turned to face Laurie. "This is your call. Do you want to keep going along this road and see if there is anything at all to link Grant and the murders to the mine? Or do we turn around, drive into Stillwater and lay everything we know before Chief Wilkinson?"

She wanted to rest her head on his chest and feel his strong arms around her. She knew why he was offering her these options. He could see how profoundly this lonely place had affected her, and he was trying once again to protect her from the awful reality of it all. But she didn't have a choice.

"Everything we know is nothing at all in the eyes of the law, Cameron. We don't have anything to link Grant to any of these murders." She managed a shaky laugh. "We still don't have proof any murders have taken place. We could buy ourselves some breathing space from Grant by going to the chief, but he would catch up with us eventually."

He started up the car. "So we keep going?"

She nodded. "We keep going."

In spite of his father's threats, Cameron had risked coming out to the mine once or twice when he was younger. As a daredevil kid, it wasn't so much the fear of his father's reaction that had kept him away. It was more this place itself. It was bleak and depressing, and the work done on it several years ago to make it safe hadn't changed that underlying feeling. "Abandoned" described it in more ways than one. Birds didn't sing here. Even though nature had begun to reclaim the scarred landscape, animals didn't come to forage inside the crater the mining activity had left behind. There was an acrid, dusty smell of disuse hanging low in the air that made Laurie wrinkle her nose and lift her face in search of the cleaner, fresher breeze higher up. Even as a kid, Cameron had never been able to understand why Grant found it so enticing here. If you wanted danger in Stillwater, there were plenty of prettier ways to find it. He had always preferred to dive into the icy lake waters or scale the sheer peaks of the high points on the trail.

They left the SUV at the edge of the crater and made their way down the slope into the roughly circular basin. Although scrubby grass had grown over the area, the striations were still clear, the different levels of excavation showing through. The silence was eerie, and Cameron thought of the barroom stories of long ago that were still told about this place. Even though it was a small mine, it had once been thriving, with a prosperous workforce. When it dwindled and eventually closed, some of the lifeblood had drained out of Stillwater.

"There was originally an underground mine on this site." Cameron pointed to the shaft entrance at the opposite side of the crater. "It was closed after a series of accidents when too many men lost their lives, but there was still a lucrative coal bed here, and a surface mine was opened instead. Gradually, production wound down and it closed completely about forty years ago. Before the work was done to make it safe, there was still old, broken machinery lying around. You could kill yourself on rusted metal just walking around here," Cameron said.

They moved around the edge of the crater, keeping close together, unsure of what they were seeking until they found it. Without discussing it, they scoured the ground for indications anything might have been buried, any suggestion that something was out of place. Although the landscape was uneven, there was no sign that anything had disturbed the surface of the grass. Cameron's eyes were constantly drawn back toward the top of the crater itself, as if at any moment he expected to see a familiar, muscle-bound figure appear on its rim. Since he wasn't given to imaginative flights of fancy, he decided it was proof of the strength of the grip Grant had them in. It was a grip Cameron intended to break.

Grimacing, he flexed his injured left arm. It felt better than he had expected, but it was stiff and aching. He hoped he wouldn't have to get into a fight with Grant. The other man was built like a bear and fought like a tiger. Even as a kid he'd been possessed of a phenomenal strength. Cameron remembered one-sided wrestling matches with a grimace. Both men were members of the same gym in town, but while Cameron used it as a means of staying fit, Grant subjected his body to a schedule that would make a professional athlete's eyes water. Even without his injury, Cameron knew he was at a disadvantage. He comforted himself with the thought that Laurie had her gun tucked into the inner pocket of her jacket, and the determined look in her eye left him no doubt she would use it if she needed to.

Her courage astounded him, along with her compassion. He understood the look he had glimpsed in her eyes back at Mrs. Martin's place. Even with her own life in peril, Laurie had taken time out to spare a thought for the women who had died, to hate that this could be their final resting place. Just when he thought he couldn't love her any more, she blew him away with her grace and strength. He had never experienced passion like that which surged through him at her touch, had never known peace like he felt in her arms. He had to get this right, not because he was under some white knight or crusader delusion. This was about making sure the woman he loved was okay.

They reached the main shaft at one end of the crater. When Cameron was a kid, his overactive imagination used to try to tell him that square black hole was the doorway into hell itself. Now? As they approached, it didn't look any more appealing. The original timber beams were in place supporting the cave-like entrance to the shaft. Each one carefully sawn off and hammered into place, their workmanship standing the test of time. At one side an old, rusted railway cart stood, leaning gently to one side. It looked lost without any tracks to run on, but it was many years since the railway line had extended this far out of town.

"Did they forget to take this away when they cleared the debris from this piece of land?" Laurie asked.

"A few years ago, there was some talk about opening a mining museum out here in Hope Valley. A local history group petitioned the council because this was one of the first underground mines in the state, but they didn't have the funds or the public interest to do anything about it. I guess this was a relic that got left behind."

They were a few feet from the mine entrance now, and Laurie's hand stole into his. "Do you think…?"

He followed her gaze into the inky mouth of the shaft, following her thoughts. Could this be where the missing women had ended up? "I don't know."

It was the truth. Would anyone choose this place to dispose of a body, let alone more than one? It was certainly remote, but, as a hiding place, was it practical? Mine explorers, those hardy souls who found enjoyment delving into abandoned industrial sites, occasionally came out here to seek adventure. It had presented the town council with a dilemma. They couldn't say for sure the mine wasn't dangerous, because, once inside, there were so many interconnecting tunnels, each with its own set of hazards. At the same time, they couldn't say for sure it *was* dangerous. Eventually, they had compromised, issuing a statement advising mine explorers to stay away and disclaiming responsibility if anyone chose to ignore that recommendation. Once inside, Grant would have solitude in which to hide the bodies, but he would have to know his way around the tunnels to be sure of getting in and out safely.

"We can go in a few feet." Cameron pulled the small flashlight he'd brought from the cabin out of his pocket. "But it's not safe to venture too far inside."

Laurie's face told him she wasn't keen on the idea of going in at all, but her fingers tightened on his and she stepped into the darkness at his side. Once they had taken a few steps, the flashlight beam became insignificant against the utter blackness. The tunnel smelled of darkness. Of rotten earth and burrowing creatures and dusty rock. Underfoot, loose stones slithered and crunched, making the path ahead of them tricky. It couldn't possibly have become as cold as he imagined it was after just a few short feet from the entrance.

"He's not going to be stupid enough to leave any clues right here as we walk in." Laurie's dispirited voice echoed in the gloom. "And it comes back to the old problem. No one will search this place just because we have a hunch he may have killed these women and brought their bodies here."

They walked on a few more feet. The smell had changed, become unpleasant. Not that it had been pleasant before. Now it made his stomach clench. It was a sweet, rotten odor, making him think of unwashed toilets and rotten meat.

Cameron directed the flashlight along the ground ahead of them, halting when its beam illuminated a familiar object. "No, but I think it's fairly safe to say our hunch was right."

Lying on the ground to their right, faded because the colors were distorted by the unnatural light and also because it was no longer fresh—the supplier had, after all, met with an untimely death a few days ago— was a heart-shaped arrangement of roses.

Chapter 15

Laurie's breath seemed to be trapped somewhere between her chest and her mouth, so no matter how hard she tried, she couldn't release the inhalation she'd just taken. Bursting out of the mineshaft at a run, she doubled over and the air finally left her lungs with a *whoosh*. When she straightened, the sunlight seemed too bright, and she blinked hard at Cameron, who was just behind her.

"Okay?" His face was concerned. Clearly, he thought she might be about to faint. *And he could be right.*

Laurie nodded, leaning back against the side of the rusted railway cart for support, her head tilted back against it. "It was seeing the flowers there, you know? Suspecting is one thing, but knowing is another." She looked out at the desolate expanse of land. "He sent them flowers when they were alive. Why would he leave them here when they were dead?"

Cameron came to lean next to her, his broad shoulder pressed against hers. She knew the touch was deliberate. He was using his body to give her strength and support. "Who knows? Maybe he still feels responsible for them? Or it's his twisted way of showing respect. I don't want to probe his mind any further than I have to. All I do know is that this means you were right all along, and now we do have to take all of this to Chief Wilkinson."

Laurie turned her head to the side to look at him, grounding herself by drinking in the details of his face. Even though she knew his features so well, he still took her breath away. His high, carved cheekbones and aristocratic nose could have made his face harsh, but, in contrast, his lips were full. Those incredible, deep-set dark eyes enchanted her. It was a strong face, an unforgettable face. Then something about it changed. As she gazed up at him, he lurched and an unexpected expression of surprise crossed his face before the light in his eyes dulled and Cameron pitched forward onto the ground.

Laurie stared at him in shock, taking in the blood that was welling rapidly at the back of his head. Something had hit him from behind and hit him hard. Looking up to find the source of what had caused his sudden fall, her eyes encountered the triumphant, light blue gaze of Grant Becker. He was standing inside the old railway cart, holding in his hand the bloodstained rock he had just used to bash Cameron over the back of the head.

Laurie began to reach inside her jacket, but shock

slowed her down and Grant moved faster. Throwing down the rock, he had his own gun out before she could make a move to get hers. Surprisingly nimble for such a large man, he vaulted over the edge of the cart, landing neatly on his feet beside Cameron's unconscious body. Prodding his one-time friend's body with the toe of his boot, he seemed satisfied Cameron wasn't coming around anytime soon.

"Is he okay?" Laurie hated the wobble in her voice, but the wound in the back of Cameron's head was bleeding badly. Somehow a dangerous killer training a gun on her was less important than the fact Cameron was lying injured at her feet.

"Hopefully not." In contrast, Grant's voice was cheerful, his smile unconcerned. "Throw down your gun."

With a hand that shook wildly, Laurie did as he asked. Her gun landed close to Cameron's outstretched fingers. No matter how hard she willed him to move them, to pick up the gun, nothing happened. *Things like that only happen in movies.*

"Can't we call someone? Let them know where he is?" She wouldn't plead with Grant for herself. For Cameron, she would go down on her hands and knees and beg.

His smile vanished abruptly. "Who? Bryce? Vincente? The Delaney brothers to the rescue?" Grant spat the words at her as he stepped forward to grab her. His hand was so big it encircled her upper arm. "You think I'm going to fall for that?"

"But Cameron is your friend."

"No." He started to drag her away. Laurie tried to dig her heels in, but she had no chance against his superior strength. Relentlessly, Grant propelled her forward. Desperately she looked over her shoulder at Cameron. *Be alive. Don't die.* "He was my friend once. Before he stole the only thing that ever mattered to me."

The only thing that ever mattered to him. *Carla.* She tried to focus. In the hands of a disturbed and ruthless killer, the only weapons Laurie had at her disposal now were her wits and the snippets of knowledge she had about this man. She had to try to use those to her advantage. Her biggest problem was she didn't know what role she should play. For someone whose job involved playing a part, it was intensely frustrating. If Grant killed these women because they resisted him, then she had to avoid coming across as antagonistic. But if he killed them because he believed he was rescuing them from the awfulness of their existence, then she had to try not to appear vulnerable and in need of his heroism.

Those were the thoughts that flashed through her mind as Grant hauled her across the crater to his patrol car. In the end, her deliberations led her to the conclusion that, for the time being at least, she should keep quiet and read the situation. Years of undercover work had taught her how to think on her feet. She hoped it would stand her in good stead during this, the most perilous situation she had ever faced.

He really should lift his head, but it was easier to stay like this with his nose pressed so far into the sparse grass that he was inhaling dirt. The strangest thing was the lack of pain. There was pressure in the back of his skull, but nothing hurt. Even so, his brain registered that he *should* be hurting. He could feel the blood, sticky and warm, oozing from the wound at the back of his skull. That couldn't be good, and…

Laurie!

Clutching at the tufts of grass in his hands, Cameron attempted to claw himself upright. It felt like the biggest mistake of his life. Like someone was using a power tool to fire six-inch nails directly into the back of his head. He didn't just see stars; whole galaxies swam before his eyes. Gasping for breath, unable to even utter the groan that wanted to rise from his lips, he collapsed back onto the grass. Waves of nausea and dizziness rolled over him, and he closed his eyes until the sensation passed.

Cameron forced himself to think. Even with his head hammering out the devil's own drumbeat, he could work out what must have happened. Grant must have been waiting for them when they came out of the mineshaft. Probably, he had watched them go in. How had he managed to hide from them so he could sneak up behind them and hit Cameron on the head? He replayed the minutes before that excruciating pain had struck him. As they exited the shaft, Laurie had been white as a sheet. She'd leaned up against the old railway cart and Cameron had joined her.

My God, he was hiding in there! We gave him the perfect opportunity. Grant probably couldn't believe his luck when we turned our backs on him.

Cameron had no idea how long he had been unconscious. Laurie could have been in Grant's power for a few minutes or for longer. He doubted it was hours. The feel of the sunlight on his back and shoulders told him it wasn't yet noon. *It can't be hours.* He had to keep telling himself that. If he let himself give in to the feelings of despair that were threatening to overwhelm him along with the pain, he would lie here wallowing while Grant killed her.

Take it slowly this time. Keeping his grip on the grass, he managed to claw his way to his knees. The world swam out of focus a few times, but, panting with the effort, he took a moment to celebrate. It felt like he had climbed a mountain, but he hadn't passed out or lost the contents of his stomach. And so far, his head was still in place. A bloodstained rock was on the ground inches away from him, and his gaze caught Laurie's gun where it lay close to his fingers. Cameron's lips tightened. The knowledge she was defenseless spurred him on, and with another agonizingly slow movement, he got himself into a sitting position with his back against a wheel of the railway cart. Reaching out, he snagged Laurie's gun and held it in his lap. Not that Grant was going to be coming back for him. He had what he wanted. He had Laurie.

Reaching into his pocket, he fumbled his cell phone free. Feeling like he was performing every action in slow motion, he got into his contacts. *Don't be busy, Bryce.* It went straight to voice mail.

Almost sobbing with frustration, Cameron tried Vincente's number. The feeling of relief that flooded through him when he heard his brother's voice was so intense he almost passed out again.

"Cam? We did it. Warren and Nichols are officially out of here—"

"Listen to me." As he cut across Vincente's celebratory tones, Cameron's own voice sounded like sandpaper rasping over gravel.

"My God, Cam, you sound like shit. What happened?"

"I don't have time to explain. Grant has Laurie. Get Bryce and come out to the Hope Valley coal mine right now."

"Should I call the police?"

"Not yet." He was about to end the call when he thought of something else. "And Vincente?"

"Yes?" It was strange how, even in a phone call, you could hear concern in another person's voice.

"Bring me a clean shirt, plenty of water and some extra-strength painkillers."

Cameron was counting on one thing. He knew exactly how Grant planned to kill Laurie. He was so sure, he was prepared to stake everything on it. Pinning all he had on it. If he was wrong... He squeezed his eyes shut. He couldn't be wrong. If he was wrong, then Laurie was already dead, and that, well, that just couldn't be. No, Grant would want to savor killing her. Cameron didn't believe a bullet to Laurie's head would be enough for him. The thought made him wince. Since wincing sent a thunderbolt of pain through his skull, he decided it was an activity he should try to avoid.

Reaching up a tentative hand, he made an attempt to feel the back of his head. It wasn't a good idea. There was too much blood to feel anything much, and the action caused an immediate return of his former giddiness. Sighing, he waited for some sign of his brothers' arrival.

They didn't let him down. He didn't know what Vincente had told Bryce, but the two of them must have broken records to get from the transportation depot on the other side of town to the mine in the time it took them. Bryce was driving Cameron's car, and it bounced wildly across the uneven surface of the crater before coming to a halt a few yards from where he was sitting.

"If the suspension on my car is ruined, I'll know where to send the bill," Cameron said, as they hurried toward him.

"Did Grant do this?" Bryce's eyes skimmed the blood that had soaked the collar and shoulders of Cameron's shirt.

As Vincente held out a bottle of water, Cameron saw the flash of anger in his older brother's eyes. He accepted the water gratefully, drinking long and hard before he spoke. "Yes. Not content with shooting me last night, he decided to try to bash my brains out this morning."

Bryce looked ready to explode with rage. "That bastard shot you? Why the hell didn't you tell us?"

It was obvious that Vincente, although equally angry, was going to keep a grip on his fury and be more useful than Bryce, whose anger was in danger of raging out of control. Laurie needed them to be focused. Cameron held out a hand to Vincente. "Help me get up."

Moving position so he could get a better look at the back of his brother's head, Vincente drew in a sharp breath. "We need to get you to a hospital, Cam."

"Can't." Cameron couldn't risk shaking his head. "I told you. Grant has Laurie."

"Tell us where he is. We'll go after him."

Cameron gripped Vincente's hand briefly. This was the brother who had always thwarted him, driven him to distraction, given him every possible reason to dislike and distrust him. Now, without asking questions, Vincente was prepared to put himself in Cameron's place and face danger on his behalf. The love he had never before been able to feel for his older brother rose up now, powerful and compelling, tightening his throat.

"The three of us will do it. Together."

Reading the determination in his eyes, Vincente nodded to Bryce. Together they moved into position on either side of Cameron. Hooking their arms through his, they raised him to his feet. The world swam out of focus again and he sagged against their support, before forcing himself to remain upright.

"If you won't let us take you to a hospital, where do you want to go?" Vincente asked as they moved slowly toward the car.

"Tell me it'll be somewhere I can get my hands around Grant Becker's throat." Bryce seemed to be holding his whole body rigid.

"Eventually, yes. But for now, take me to the lake house."

Vincente frowned as he helped to ease Cameron into the back of the car. "The lake house? Don't you want us to start searching for Laurie?"

"I know where he'll take her." As Bryce started the engine, Cameron did his best to concentrate on staying upright in his seat. "He'll wait until dark before he makes a move. If we're going to follow them, we'll need a boat."

Laurie had been in enough jail cells to know she wasn't getting out of this one through her own efforts. Of course, she'd never actually been locked inside one before. This cell was about six feet by eight, with brick walls and a solid metal door. Light came in through a barred window set high up out of reach at one end. The only items in the room were the bed, which was free of bedding, and a bucket. This place was old. Laurie, used to seeing cells with observation windows and stainless steel commodes, sensed its age in something other than the lack of modern facilities. There was a feeling of disuse about it. This was not a cell that was occupied regularly.

Since she had made the journey here in the trunk of Grant's patrol car, she'd had no idea where she was geographically. Attempting to judge the time she had been lying there, bumping around in the darkness, hadn't been easy, but she thought it was about an hour. Approximately sixty minutes from the time Grant had shoved her roughly into the trunk at gunpoint at the old mine. Which meant she could be anywhere. Laurie summoned up a mental map of the region. He could have stayed on his home territory and driven west, remaining in West County. Or he could have been heading into Park County, even, judging by the speed he was driving, possibly making it as far south as Teton County. It wasn't impossible that he'd taken her across the state line and gone north into Montana. Since there was no way out of this cell, there was no real point in speculating. She supposed she would find out soon enough once Grant returned. Her whereabouts mattered only in the sense that she felt a powerful need to know where she was in relation to Cameron.

The image of him lying facedown on the ground, bleeding from the wound in his head, rose up in her mind, and panic threatened to overwhelm her. She wasn't gagged—*what use is a gag when there's no one around to hear your cries for help?* were the words Grant had used when he'd left her here—and a strangled sob escaped her lips. *Cameron has to be okay.* Stubbornly she forced herself to refuse to acknowledge there could be any other possibility. *We'll get out of this somehow.* At the moment, she was struggling to see how, but she was determined to keep fighting to find a way. Anything else wasn't in her nature. Dragging herself back to the present, she went back over the details of her arrival at this place.

When the car had halted and the trunk popped open, Laurie's eyes had taken a few seconds to adjust to the bright sunlight. Grant's bulky figure looming over her had caused her to automatically shrink back into the cramped space of the trunk. Muttering a curse, he had hooked one arm under her legs and, with the other around her waist, swung her out of there as easily as if she had been a reluctant child.

Laurie had gained only a brief impression of her surroundings before he had set her on the ground and brought her into this building, but the phrase "miles from nowhere" seemed apt. They weren't in a town, that was all she could say for sure. There were no defining features to the landscape, just a few hills in the near ground and a hint of mountains in the distance. The building itself gave her no clues. She got the impression of an institutional structure, squat and square. There was no one else around as Grant led her to a side entrance, along a corridor and into this cell.

"Where are we?" She had tried for a pleasant, conversational tone.

He hadn't replied. His face had remained expressionless. "When I come back, you need to be wearing those clothes."

He pointed to a neatly folded pile on the bed. Without another word, he turned and left the room. Laurie heard the grate of the key in the lock and his booted footsteps fading as he walked back the way they had come. Since then, she had heard nothing. There were no sounds of traffic, no noises from within the building to indicate anyone else was inside here, not even any animal noises or birdsong outside. It was as if she was the last person left alive in this godforsaken place.

But she *was* still alive, and even though Grant clearly had plans for her, she clung to that like a drowning woman clinging to a lifeline. *Drowning.* The word made her think of Carla, and she shivered. The clothes he had left were basic enough. Knee-length shorts, T-shirt, flannel shirt and sneakers with a lightweight waterproof jacket. It felt creepy to wear clothes Grant Becker had chosen for her, and Laurie thought long and hard about not changing into them. What would happen if she defied him? The cold light in those blue eyes was probably a good enough indication. She got the feeling she would be wearing these clothes one way or another and decided she would rather put them on herself than have him do it for her.

It was only when she had finished changing that she considered her outfit. The colors were bright, the overall effect too young. The bubblegum-pink sneakers too cloyingly attention seeking. *I'm dressed like a teenage girl rather than a grown woman.* The thought sent a shiver of discomfort up her spine. *Am I dressed the way Carla was when he met her at summer camp?*

The shiver up her spine became a hateful clawing finger, prodding her and convincing her she was right.

Hard on the heels of her last thought came another. Did Grant bring the other women here? Did he dress them all this way? Was he, every single time, trying to resurrect his teenage romance with Carla? Laurie drew a deep breath. If that was the case, at least she finally knew what she had to do.

She had come to Stillwater to be a substitute for Carla Bryan. Now she had to play the hell out of the role.

Chapter 16

Although Cameron still had the headache from hell, the nausea and dizziness had receded and the pain-killers were starting to take the edge off. He could even move his head without getting the impression the pain elves were digging tunnels into his brain. Feeling like he had aged twenty years in the last few hours, he shrugged off his brothers' offers of help and made his way through to his bedroom. Once he had gotten out of his clothes, he stood under the shower for a long time, leaning his right forearm against the tiled wall and letting the lukewarm water wash away the blood.

If he was right—*please let me be right*—Grant would seize this opportunity. Within his distorted mind, he had been given a second chance to rescue Carla. He had failed the first time. Carla herself hadn't needed his help. She had thwarted his attempt to be her white knight and paid for her independence with her life. Now he got to do it all again. How many killers got lucky this way? Cameron believed Grant would try to re-create the scene exactly; only this time he would want to succeed. He would make sure he figured as the heroic rescuer.

Cameron was counting on Laurie having the same thoughts as him and playing along with Grant. If she antagonized him…the thought made him shudder. No, Laurie wasn't that stupid. She was strong and smart, and she had her police training, including years of undercover experience, to draw on. If anyone could get through this, it was Laurie.

For Grant to stage things exactly as they had been with Carla, he would have to wait for nightfall and get Laurie out onto the middle of the lake. Since he had no control over the weather conditions, and couldn't summon the same storm that had blown up that night, Cameron figured Grant would make sure she got into difficulties some other way. Sneaking up on him wasn't going to be easy, especially with an injured arm and what felt like a giant hole in the back of his head. Although he might not have been in any fit state to convey his gratitude to them when they turned up at the old mine, Cameron was glad to have Vincente and Bryce with him.

The waterproof dressing Laurie had applied to his arm that morning survived the shower. A memory of her wrapped in a towel, laughing as she dodged his attempts to remove it, came into his mind, sharp and bright. Why hadn't he grabbed hold of her then and told her how much he loved her? Why had he been so concerned about trivial things like timing and whether she would want to stay in Stillwater? One thing was for sure: if they came through this and out the other side, Laurie would never again be in any doubt about his feelings for her. Not if. *When* they came out the other side of this.

Getting into clean clothes was a struggle, but with a fair amount of stumbling and cursing, he managed it. When he got back into the kitchen, there was a smell of coffee. His stomach surprised him by welcoming it. Vincente was getting bacon and eggs out of the refrigerator, and Bryce was looking sheepish.

"Tell him," Vincente said. "At least this house doesn't have carpet. So, when he kills you, the blood will be easy to clean up." Realizing his attempt at humor was misplaced, he grimaced. "Sorry."

"I called Leon Sinclair and asked him to come and take a look at your head."

Cameron had been easing himself gradually onto one of the high stools that flanked the central island, but those words made him pause halfway. "Why would you invite the town drunk over to look at my head?"

"Because before the town drunk, as you so charmingly call him, got a medical discharge, he was an army doctor." Bryce's fine, dark eyes held a measure of condemnation. "And he is a recovering alcoholic who has been in rehab."

Accepting the mug of strong black coffee Vincente held out to him, Cameron mumbled an apology. Although he wasn't clear what he was apologizing for exactly. All he really knew about Leon Sinclair was the guy knew how to party. Hard. There weren't many bars in Stillwater, but in the twelve months since he'd arrived in the town, Sinclair had managed to get himself thrown out of every one of them. Army doctor or not, Cameron wasn't sure he wanted him anywhere near his head.

He was about to say as much when Bryce's cell phone pinged with an incoming message. "He's here. Give the guy a chance. Okay?"

He went to get the door, and Cameron eyed Vincente over the top of his coffee mug. "This is my skull we're talking about, so why am I being made to feel guilty because I don't want it experimented on by a vagabond stranger?"

"How about you reserve judgment and see if he can patch you up? We don't want your brain falling out just as we go in all guns ablazing later."

Cameron joined in Vincente's laughter, pleased he could do it without feeling like he was going to collapse. "You always were the poetic brother."

It was into this scene of hilarity that Bryce walked a few moments later accompanied by a tall, rangy man with dark blond hair and a beard. Leon Sinclair generally had an unkempt look about him, but he appeared to have made something of an effort on this occasion. His flannel shirt, although crumpled, was clean, and it was the first time Cameron could recall ever seeing him sober. He carried a medical bag, which he set on the counter.

"Mayor Delaney." Cameron noticed a slight hesitation in his speech, as though he might once have had a stammer he'd worked hard to overcome.

He held out his hand. "It's Cameron. You've met my brother Vincente?"

Leon regarded his outstretched hand for a moment in surprise before shaking it. He seemed to be waging some sort of internal battle. When he spoke again, the falter in his voice was even more pronounced. "Before I take a look at you, there's something you should know. Although I still have my medical license to practice, I was given a medical discharge from the army for mental health reasons." He gulped in air as though he hadn't breathed during his previous statements. "Do you want to proceed?"

This was Cameron's chance to avoid having to tolerate having this clearly disturbed and probably incompetent man anywhere near his injury. Yet, as he looked into Leon Sinclair's intense green eyes, he found himself nodding. *I need my head examined.* He almost groaned aloud at his own bad joke.

"Do you know what you were hit with?" Leon became businesslike as he opened his bag and donned disposable gloves.

"A rock."

"And where was your assailant in relation to you?"

"Above and behind." Cameron felt anger bubble up inside him once again. "I was standing on the ground and he was hiding in a railway cart behind me." He mimed the action of Grant lifting the rock above his own head with two hands and bringing it down with force. "He brought it down on my head from above, like so."

Leon began to examine the wound on Cameron's head. "Did you black out?"

"Yes." Cameron flinched at the pain induced as the other man probed his skull.

"How long were you out for?"

"I don't know. Long enough for him to abduct the woman I was with."

Leon evinced no surprise at this comment. Cameron got the feeling he'd lived the sort of life where little shocked him. "Okay. This is a nasty head wound and I'd advise you to get to an accident and emergency facility as soon as possible. There is no obvious skull fracture, but that doesn't mean there isn't a hairline break I can't see."

"That's it?" Bryce sounded slightly belligerent. "That's all you can do?"

"This wound needs stitches and your brother needs an X-ray to determine whether there is, indeed, any fracture." Now he was on familiar ground, Leon's former nervousness had disappeared. "This sort of blunt force trauma can cause damage that isn't obvious with a simple physical examination."

"I can't get to a hospital right now. Can you glue me together until I can?" Cameron saw the surprise on his brothers' faces. In the space of minutes, he'd gone from not wanting Leon near him to placing complete trust in him.

A slight smile touched Leon's lips. It was an unexpectedly engaging expression. "Glue won't work on a wound this deep. I'll stitch it."

Cameron groaned and flexed his arm. "My second lot of stitches in twenty-four hours."

"Someone really doesn't like you, does he?" Leon laid out his anesthetic and suture kit and spoke in the voice of a man who didn't expect an answer.

"Believe me, the feeling is mutual." Cameron suffered in silence as Leon meticulously cleaned the wound, injected his scalp with anesthetic and carefully stitched the edges of the cut together. It took a long time, and no one seemed inclined to make small talk.

"You still need to get yourself some emergency care as soon as you've done whatever it is you have to do," Leon told him when he'd finished.

Cameron managed a nod without feeling like his head was coming off. He felt able to tentatively touch his head. There seemed to be a lot of stitches back there. "What do I owe you?"

Leon flapped a hand. "Buy me a drink sometime."

Bryce frowned. "I thought you were on the wagon?"

"If I could find that damn wagon, I might just clamber on board." Leon waved a hand as he left. "I hope you get to rescue her."

"What's his story?" Cameron asked when Bryce returned from showing Leon out. His brother seemed to have become the designated contact for troubled veterans in the area. That was all very well, but who was helping Bryce?

"The answer to that question always seems to be 'don't ask.'" Bryce looked out of the window. The afternoon was already well advanced. "So what's the plan?"

Cameron nodded at the bacon and eggs Vincente had taken out of the refrigerator. He was suddenly desperately hungry. "How about you cook while we talk?"

Because of the silence, Laurie heard the car approaching when it was still a long way off. She had watched the light change through the prison bars and knew it must be early evening. Using a mindfulness technique she had always found helpful, she closed her eyes and focused on her breathing. Letting go of her thoughts and allowing her breath to flow freely and naturally. When Grant's boots echoed on the tiled corridor, she was able to accept the sound, even welcome it. It was the next stage in what had to happen.

The door opened slowly as though he wasn't sure what to expect. Laurie supposed each woman he had locked in here must have reacted in her unique way. She hoped some of them had given him a hard time. Her own act of rebellion had been a subtle one. She had removed the bow from her gold-colored bra and slid it behind one of the legs of the bed. It would be proof she had been here. She only hoped she would still be around to identify it.

If Grant was surprised to see her sitting calmly on the bed, he showed no sign of it. His eyes skimmed over her, taking in the change of clothing. She had donned the waterproof jacket now, noting with surprise it didn't fit with the rest of the outfit. It was clearly a man's garment. Way too big for her, it hung almost to her knees, and she'd had to fold the sleeves back several times. And it was old, the surface cracked and worn in places.

Coming fully into the room, Grant held out a plastic garbage sack. "Put your clothes in here and tie the top."

Clever. He hadn't touched her belongings. She assumed he would burn them at the first opportunity. When Laurie had followed his instructions, Grant stooped to pick up the bag. The temptation to bring her knee up under his chin was overwhelming, but she forced herself to resist it. The best she could hope for with that was to unbalance him. She had to play a long game here. The only chance she had was to try to outwit him.

He pressed his gun into her ribs. "Carry your

clothes to the car. Walk out ahead of me. Don't do anything stupid."

She nodded. As they reached the cell door, she drew a breath. Turning her head to look at him over her shoulder, Laurie tried for a soft, slightly husky voice. Nervousness made her lip quiver slightly, but she didn't think that was a bad thing. "It was scary in there on my own. Thank you for coming back for me."

Something shifted in his eyes, and for a moment she thought she'd blown it. Had he seen through her? Could he guess what she was attempting to do? He hesitated, then gave a curt nod and gestured for her to continue. With a heart pounding so loudly she thought he must be able to hear it, Laurie walked ahead of him along the corridor and out into the open air. When they reached the car, Grant opened the trunk and gestured for her to climb inside.

Having stored the bag containing her clothes, Laurie placed her hands on the edge of the trunk. She lifted her left leg, resting her knee on the edge in preparation for hoisting herself in, but, before she did, she allowed her right leg to slide out from under her so she fell backward. Giving a soft cry, she clawed desperately at the trunk. Once again, she was surprised by Grant's fast reaction. For such a big man, he had lightning reflexes and could put them into practice at whiplash speed. Catching her around the waist, he scooped her up into his arms. It was exactly the reaction she'd been hoping for when she'd faked the fall.

Laurie linked her arms around his neck, feeling his indrawn breath reverberate right through her whole body. *Gotcha.* Even though touching him made her skin crawl, she had to convince him she saw him as her white knight.

"Thank you." *For saving me?* Should she utter those words? She didn't want to push things too far too soon, so she decided against it. Her judgment had always served her well. She trusted it now, adding the single word she believed would resonate most with him. "Grant."

Although he didn't speak, his chest expanded even farther and his eyes raked her face hungrily. She had been right to use his name. It had created a connection between them. She was sure she didn't imagine the trace of regret in his expression as he lowered her carefully into the trunk. Laurie curled up in the tight space. As Grant lifted a hand to bring the lid down, she fixed him with the full force of her gaze, a gaze she knew was almost identical to Carla's.

"Is there any way to leave a light on in here?"

He frowned. "I don't think so."

"Oh." She bit her lip. "It's just so dark and—" she managed to introduce a creditable wobble to her next words "—I don't like the dark."

Laurie had been hoping this damsel in distress act would get her a ride in the car with him. It was going to be hard to work on his chivalrous instincts when she wasn't actually in his company. It looked for a moment or two as though her ploy might have worked. She could see the conflicting emotions flitting across his face. Valor was fighting common sense. In the end, she also saw the moment when self-preservation won. Grant was too good at protecting his own back to drive around with a future murder victim sitting up next to him in the passenger seat. The shutters came down on his expression once more and he slammed the lid of the trunk down hard.

Laurie cried out loud enough for him to hear, hoping to feed his White Knight Syndrome a healthy dose of guilt for the journey. The thought almost made her laugh. *You seriously think you can guilt-trip a serial killer? That he's sitting up there worrying because you're scared of the dark? Get real, Laurie. He's sitting up there fantasizing about how much he's going to enjoy killing you.*

Riding in a trunk was never going to be a pleasant experience. Laurie was cramped and uncomfortable, jolted up and down most of the time and sometimes thrown around wildly. The only thing that didn't bother her was the darkness she had claimed to be fearful of. She supposed anyone who had ever been unfortunate enough to find themselves in this position went through the same range of emotions. Seesawing back and forth from numb helplessness to terror and everything in between. The experience of being in the trunk was bad enough, but the dread of what would happen at the end of the journey was even worse. Laurie didn't know whether her situation was easier or harder than most. She had a good idea of what was coming next. She was fairly sure it would involve a boat.

Sitting in that cell, there had been plenty of time to think. She had reasoned Grant would want to use her to turn back time. If the picture she had built up of him was correct, he had met Carla when they were both troubled teenagers and had developed a crush on her that had rapidly become an obsession. It was so powerful, he had never forgotten her, to the point where he had never dated or even, it seemed, looked at another woman. Laurie wondered why he had never made a push to seek Carla out once he was an adult. Maybe it didn't fit with his idealized view of romance; possibly he preferred worship from afar? Then she remembered what Cameron had said about Carla going into witness protection at the age of sixteen. What if Grant *had* tried to find her, but failed? His passion would have intensified even more if the object of his desire had disappeared without a trace.

Then, of course, there had been that memorable night when Carla had appeared, as if by magic, in Grant's hometown. In the restaurant he frequented every Saturday night. It must have seemed as if fate had stepped in to make all his dreams come true. Except fate had a habit of being cruel. Not only was Carla on a date with his best friend, when Grant got her alone and asked her out, she didn't even recognize him. This was the woman he had dreamed of every night for at least—Laurie tried to calculate the timescales—twelve years. If she hadn't been lying in his trunk, if she didn't know he was a killer, she could almost have felt sorry for Grant Becker. Then, after the shock of that encounter, he had to suffer the humiliation of watching her fall in love with Cameron, had to witness their very public happiness. It was no wonder a mind traumatized by childhood abuse had become completely unhinged.

Within six months Grant had killed—or in his twisted view of the world, *rescued*—Lisa Lambert. He went on to kill three other women in West County, and possibly others beyond that immediate area, before Carla's death. But Laurie still didn't believe he intended for Carla to die that night. She was convinced he had followed Carla's every move from a distance. Laurie could picture Grant's agitated state of mind: knowing Cameron was away from home, aware she intended to take her boat out alone and apprehensive about the approaching storm. He would *have* to step in and stage a rescue. His need to be the knight in shining armor would not allow him to stand back and let events unfold. And the damsel in distress on this occasion was the woman who had haunted his dreams since he was a lonely, impressionable adolescent. What had Carla's reaction been when he brought his boat alongside hers? Had she been annoyed? Dismissive? Scornful? Maybe she'd even been angry at the interruption to her training schedule.

The coroner's report said Carla had suffered "a blow to the back of the head and bruising to the throat consistent with strangulation" before she drowned. Lying in the darkness of the trunk, Laurie pictured the scene. Carla, her impatience thinly disguised, making some offhand remark to get rid of Grant so she didn't waste any more valuable training time. Grant, his face suffused with rage, hands reaching for her slender throat. Carla hitting her head as she fell overboard into the stormy waters... Maybe that wasn't exactly how it happened, but she was sure the scenario playing out in her head wasn't a million miles from the truth.

Laurie didn't know how deep Grant's emotions went. She could only guess at what he felt next. Grief? Remorse? Fear? She was sure all of those things played a part in his life during the aftermath of Carla's death. But the killing spree continued soon after. His compunction to play the white knight hadn't gone away, even though Carla was out of his life. Within weeks of her death, Grant was lining Deanna Milligan up as the next person in need of rescue.

Then, twelve months after Carla's death, Laurie had turned up and turned his whole world upside down. She had been so focused on Cameron that night at Dino's, she had spared only a passing glance for Grant. Looking back, she remembered he had looked at her intently. But so had Vincente. So had everyone. As far as the close-knit community of Stillwater was concerned, she was the biggest news they'd had in a very long time. For Grant, she was so much more than news. Although she didn't know it, Laurie was having the same sort of effect on him she had on Cameron. But with far more sinister consequences. Sitting in Dino's that night, she had not only re-created the scene four years earlier when Grant had first seen Carla with Cameron, but Laurie had also given him a glimmer of hope. If she was right, in his damaged mind, he was seeing her as a chance to undo the events of that night on the lake. Rushing out of Dino's, he had done what any chivalrous knight would do. Grant had sent her a token of his esteem. A heart-shaped arrangement of red roses.

If I'm right. Those words were the key to everything. She was second-guessing a killer, trying to apply logic to an unstable mind. If she was right, Grant would want to place her on the lake tonight. Somehow, she would have to be in trouble so he could rescue her. This time, it would all end differently. Laurie— or Carla, as she was sure he really thought of her— would not be capable and confident and annoyed at his interference. She would melt into her rescuer's arms and show her eternal gratitude. Laurie resisted the impulse to shudder at the thought. It was an outcome that would keep her alive, and right now, she was prepared to call it a happy ending. But there were so many unknowns between now and then, the biggest one of all being the mind of the murderer driving this car. What if she had this all wrong? What if his real plan was to put a bullet in her head before turning the gun on himself?

Even if she was right, at any point along the way, she could slip up just as Carla had done and enrage him. Panic was threatening to engulf her, and she battled it back down just as the car drew to a halt. She heard the door slam and forced herself into a state of calm as she waited for Grant to come for her.

It was dark now, and Grant was holding a flashlight as he opened the trunk. He reached out a hand to assist her in a curiously courteous gesture. Laurie forced herself to place her hand in his, uncurling her cramped limbs and clambering out.

"I'm sorry I had to leave you in the dark." She was surprised to hear the note of genuine regret in his voice.

Soft sounds of water lapping on rocks confirmed one thing at least. She was right. He had brought her to the lake.

Chapter 17

Because he lived on its shore and it bordered his home, Cameron had become used to thinking of it as *his* lake. Now he realized it was a dangerous habit. He had been lulled into a feeling of false security. Stillwater Lake was a huge body of water, mostly encircled by pine forest with a dramatic backdrop of mountains. The twin discs of the moon, one in the sky and the other shimmering on the lake's surface, provided the only light. They made his lake seem, for the first time, a menacing place. It mocked him with its cold, raw beauty.

His advantage was he knew this area just about as well as anyone could. There weren't many places on this lake from which it was safe to put a boat out. There was this area closest to his house—Cameron's own private property—but he was guessing Grant would be clever enough to keep away from here. Then there was the leisure marina across on the far side, the place that had become popular with water-skiers and speedboat enthusiasts. Now and then there was a party or barbecue down on the marina that went on well into the night. Grant would know that as well as Cameron did. He was unlikely to take the risk of running into a group of drunken windsurfers. Finally, there was the spot known as Catfish Point. It had been named by the fishing enthusiasts after the most popular activity over on that, the quietest part of the lake. Cameron had decided Catfish Point was the place from which they needed to start out.

Vincente and Bryce had gone to make all the necessary preparations, leaving him alone with his thoughts. While they were gone, Cameron had swallowed more painkillers, changed into dark clothing—the activity getting easier as he learned new ways of coping with his injuries—and come out here onto the deck to look at the familiar scene. He couldn't lose two women he loved in this place he loved. That wasn't a plea. He wasn't going to beg or try to bargain with fate. He was making a promise to himself and to Laurie. They hadn't talked about the future, but he wanted to make damn sure there was one to talk about.

The sounds of his brothers returning roused him from his thoughts, and he went back inside.

"Anything going on out there?"

"Quiet as a grave." Vincente winced. He seemed to have developed a knack for saying the wrong thing today.

Cameron didn't have the time or the energy to be concerned by careless remarks. He picked up Laurie's gun and tucked it into the waistband of his jeans. Having it with him mattered more than taking the other, more powerful guns that Bryce and Vincente had stowed in the car. It was his link to Laurie.

"Let's go."

It was only a ten-minute drive to Catfish Point, but Bryce stopped the car short of the lakeshore, pulling the vehicle off the road and into a clump of trees where it couldn't be seen by anyone approaching. They left the car and, gathering the equipment they had brought with them, made their way to the lake. Moonlight shimmered on the dark water, and the star-splattered sky seemed much lighter here than back at the house.

In daylight, there was a good view of the whole lake from here, and Cameron had brought Toby's binoculars with him. He raised them now, scanning the expanse of dark water. There was nothing disturbing the calm of the surface, and he muttered a quiet curse of frustration. He wasn't sure he had enough patience to wait it out, but what was the alternative? Where else could Grant have gone? Vincente had suggested they should head out to the Hope Valley mine, but Cameron's gut told him this was where Grant would come.

Just as he was about to lower the binoculars, a movement on the extreme left of his vision caught his attention, and he swung around to look in that direction. *There!* A sailboat was just setting out from the edge of the lake. Even in the darkness, he could tell from its silhouette it was almost identical to Carla's beloved *Firefly*. It was too far away for him to make out who was in it, but he thought there might be two figures.

Handing the binoculars to Bryce, he turned to Vincente. "Where did you leave the boat?"

Vincente pointed to the right. "Not far. Explain to me again why we have to use a rowboat."

"We can't risk him hearing our approach." He was counting on the cover of darkness and Grant's focus on Laurie meaning he wouldn't see them until they were close enough to get Laurie away from him. If he did see them coming? They would deal with that problem when they had to.

They made their way along the lake edge to the rowboat that Cameron normally kept at the lake house. Vincente had rowed it across here earlier while Bryce drove around to meet him and bring him back to the house. The Delaney brothers had figured out how to work as a team just as Cameron needed them to do. The thought did him a whole powerful lot of good.

Vincente gestured for his brothers to get into the boat. Pushing it into the water, he waded partway in, ignoring the lake water filling his boots, before jumping nimbly into the little craft with them. Bryce took up the oars and, skirting the edge of the lake instead of heading out to the middle, took them toward the sailboat.

Cameron kept the binoculars to his eyes. Shifting away from the other boat briefly, he scoured the darkened forest close to where he had seen the sailboat start out. A flash of something that shouldn't be there caught his attention. He concentrated on it, trying to bring it into focus.

When he was sure he knew what it was, he nodded with grim satisfaction. "It's them. Grant's patrol car is in those trees."

* * *

"Are you cold?"

Although there was a light breeze out here on the lake, the chill in the air wasn't the reason Laurie had shivered. She was about to deny it, then she remembered her vulnerable act and she nodded. "A little."

"You were cold that night, too, do you remember?" Grant's voice had a faraway quality to it that scared her almost as much as the thought of what would happen when he stopped this boat. The fact he had been calling her Carla since he had helped her out of the trunk was doing nothing to alleviate her concerns. Add in the fact he had brought with him a long steel spike—the sort of thing camping enthusiasts might use to secure a tent awning, the sort of thing that would be just perfect for driving holes through the hull of a boat—and it would be fair to say Laurie's anxiety levels were sky-high.

Which night? Was he talking about the night Carla took her boat out on this lake, or a different night? Her mind raced with possible options. "Of course I remember."

It was too dark to see his face, but he turned toward her. "You do?"

"I remember everything." Oh, she was treading such a fine line here. One wrong answer and she would lose the tenuous advantage she thought she might have built up. Push him too far and she would have more in common with Carla than just her looks. She would be going over the edge of this lightweight sailboat and feeling those deep, dark waters closing over her head.

"But when I saw you again in Dino's all those years

later you didn't know me. Even when I reminded you, you said you had no recollection of me or that night."

Think fast, Laurie. Play your part. Vulnerable. In need of a hero.

"I was shocked, scared. Seeing you again after all that time… I didn't know what to do. I wanted that commission from Cameron to build his house so badly. It was the boost I needed to launch my career." She drew in a deep, shuddering breath that owed nothing to her acting skills. "I'm sorry I hurt you."

"Why did you stay with him for three damn years if it was all about your career?" Clearly he wasn't so far gone down the route of believing she was Carla that she could dupe him completely.

"After that night, when I told you I didn't know who you were, I thought I'd blown any chance we might have had. And Cameron was good to me." Should she push this theme? Was it worth the risk? They were nearing the middle of the lake and he had taken hold of the spike, testing its point against the wooden planks at the bottom of the boat. She decided she had nothing to lose. "But he wasn't you, Grant."

Although she sensed his tension, he remained silent for long nerve-racking minutes. There was a hint of tears in his voice when he finally did speak. "That night at summer camp, I gave you my coat to keep you warm. I kept that coat as a reminder of you, Carla."

His words explained why she was wearing a man's jacket now. Laurie drew it tighter around her. "You came to my rescue."

She sensed the movement of his head as he nodded. "We talked for hours. I remember every word you said. What food you liked, the music you listened to, your favorite flowers."

Those words nearly undid her. "Dark red roses."

"Did you know they were from me, Carla?"

"Of course I did." Her eyes caught the merest hint of movement on the water behind him, and her breath caught in her throat. She had to keep him talking, keep his attention on her. "After camp was over and we went home, I thought about you all the time."

Grant was crying openly now. Although he still held the spike, his hand was limp and he seemed to have forgotten about it. "So did I. Your face was before me every minute of every day. I went to sleep with your image in my mind, dreamed of you each night and woke up thinking about you each morning. I worked so hard to make a success of my life so I could find you and build a home for us. I wanted to rescue you from the hell you were going through. But when I came looking, it was like you had disappeared off the face of the earth."

Two damaged kids had found comfort in each other's company one night, setting off a chain of events that had led to murder and destruction on an unimaginable scale. Laurie felt the tears on her own cheeks. She wasn't crying for the man before her now, the man who still held that spike dangerously poised over the boards of the boat. No, she was crying for the sad, hurt boy he had been back then.

The dark shape on the water behind Grant glided closer. She could see two figures in the boat that approached, but there was no way of making out who they were. The fact that anyone was there at all had to mean Cameron had survived the blow to his head, and in spite of everything, her heart achieved a joyful leap at the thought.

"I was in witness protection. I saw my stepfather kill my mom."

At the same moment he leaned toward her, groping for her hand in the darkness, everything sped up to double time. As Grant's lips touched her cheek and Laurie betrayed herself by recoiling from him, Cameron hauled himself out of the lake and onto the sailboat, causing the little craft to rock precariously.

Grant's grip on her hand tightened, and Laurie struggled against him as he tried to haul her upright. The swaying of the boat worked in her favor, and Grant failed to move her from her seated position. Moonlight gleamed on Cameron's wet clothing as he steadied himself by rolling with the boat's movement. Laurie's initial joy at seeing him gave way to fear. He had sustained so many injuries over the past few days, how could he possibly survive another confrontation with Grant?

"Tell him, Carla." Grant's voice was hoarse. "Tell him it was always me you loved."

Laurie pulled her hand free of his. Rising to her feet, when she spoke, the words were clear and confident. Although she said them for herself, she was also saying them for the other women. "I'm not Carla."

The double-time sensation went into reverse. Everything slowed. Grant's bellow of rage seemed to go on forever. As he fumbled for his gun, strong hands grabbed Laurie around the waist and pulled her backward into a waiting rowboat. The moonlight showed her everything. As she fell, she saw Cameron pull a gun from his waistband. A perfect circle appeared in the center of Grant's forehead. She didn't see him fall, but, even as Vincente and Bryce moved to cover her body with theirs, she heard the sound of Grant Becker's body hitting the water.

Chief Wilkinson accepted Laurie's offer of toast and coffee with real gratitude. "They pulled his body out of the lake this morning, not an easy thing, as you'll remember from…" His voice tailed away in embarrassment. "…The last time. That was quite a shot."

"It was a miraculous shot, considering it was dark and the way that boat was bobbing around," Cameron said. He and Laurie were dealing with this in their own way, but he was already growing tired of other people making judgments about how much they could cope with. Tact wasn't Chief Wilkinson's style, and Cameron took pity on the other man. "I have Carla to thank for the fact I can stay steady on a boat in extreme conditions. I spent enough time as her first mate. I'm glad the practice finally came in useful for something." He hoped the message was clear. *I can speak and hear her name without coming undone.*

Some of the tension left the chief's frame, but he still looked shell-shocked over the revelations of the past forty-eight hours. He nodded in Laurie's direction. "They found your clothes in his trunk. Using your description of the place you were locked up, I followed a hunch and went out to the disused jail near Elmville. Remember that place, Cam?" Cameron nodded. "Enough to give a man the creeps." The chief held up a plastic evidence bag containing the gold-colored bow from Laurie's bra. "Recognize this?"

"It was the only thing I could think of." Her mischievous grin peeped out briefly, and Cameron was fiercely glad to see it. "If he was still alive, I'd be sending Grant Becker the bill for my most expensive piece of lingerie."

Chief Wilkinson looked slightly baffled, but Cameron covered her hand with his. "I'll buy you a replacement."

The warmth in her eyes made his heart flip upside down. He wished all these formalities were over so they could be alone. Properly alone. Ever since that dramatic scene out at the lake, they had spent their time going over the story first with police officers, then all over again with FBI agents, including Mike Samuels. Cameron, in spite of his protests, had been kept in the hospital for twenty-four hours under observation. Although Laurie had remained at his bedside, the constant stream of visitors had ensured they had barely exchanged more than two sentences in private.

They both knew there would be more talking to come. There would be formal statements and they would both need counseling. Despite his exhaustion and his physical injuries, Cameron could already feel the emotional impact of what had happened out on the lake. Alongside the image of that bullet hitting Grant, and his body toppling into the water, others were forcing their way into his mind.

He had memory of him and Grant skimming stones across the lake on a bright, sunny afternoon. Then there was the sound of Grant's laughter on the day they had made a makeshift sled out of an old dog bed and gone scooting down the hillside, sending drifts of snow flying up in their wake. He had never envisaged himself taking a life. Killing one of his oldest friends?

Even though it had been necessary, he was going to need some help to deal with the trauma he knew would come his way in the coming weeks and months.

But he also knew he would get over it…because he had Laurie at his side. Last night, on his discharge, they had tumbled into bed, sleeping in each other's arms for twelve hours straight, waking only when Chief Wilkinson pounded on the door to bring them more news about the case.

"The press are sniffing around like bloodhounds on a scent. I feel sorry for Glen Harvey. Poor guy is having to deal with the fallout of all of this and take on the sheriff's duties. Turns out Grant hadn't been at the top of his game for some time."

"In what way?" Cameron asked.

"Turning up late, not showing up at all sometimes, not keeping in contact with Harvey. Now we know why, it makes sense. He had a whole other life that had nothing to do with law enforcement. Quite the opposite. Harvey, being a loyal deputy, covered for him, but things weren't good by all accounts. The whole department was a mess." The chief cast a sidelong look from Cameron to Laurie. There it was again. That measured look. Deciding how much they could take. "They've started the search for bodies out at the mine."

"Your face tells me they've found something."

"Three females and a male. So far. The male is very recent." He coughed apologetically. "His throat had been cut."

Laurie's hand reached for Cameron's. He closed his fingers tightly around hers. "Moreton." Her voice was a whisper.

Chief Wilkinson nodded. "Your friend Samuels has already identified the body. The darnedest thing is, even though they haven't been formally identified yet, each of the females was wearing the same footwear. The same brand of bright pink sneakers. Even looks like they may have been dressed in the same clothes."

Cameron caught hold of Laurie as she swayed toward him. She rested her head on his shoulder for a moment before collecting herself. The police had taken away the clothing she was wearing when she was rescued for forensic examination. When she lifted her face to his now, her eyes were dark with pain. "I never want to see them again. If they ever give those clothes back, promise me you'll burn them."

"I promise." He wanted to make more promises to her. That the dark days were behind them and they had sunshine to look forward to. That, no matter how strong she was, he would be there beside her, holding her and supporting her. That everything coming their way, good and bad, they would face together, side by side. He contented himself with smiling into her eyes and got his reward when she relaxed against him.

"We had a few problems out at the mine with a very persistent snooper." Chief Wilkinson claimed his attention again. "At first I thought he was press, but he claimed to know you, Cam. He kept insisting we should be looking through the belongings for an Irish passport. Funny thing is, he was right. We found a passport in the mineshaft in the name of Marie O'Donnell."

"Your snooper's name is Toby Murray," Cameron said. "His girlfriend went missing after Grant Becker gave her a lift to the airport eighteen months ago."

Chief Wilkinson scratched his head, and Cameron suspected he might be regretting not listening to Toby. He experienced a pang of sympathy for the chief. He knew from experience just how infuriating Toby could be.

"While you were in the hospital, Vincente and Bryce spoke to Samuels about this other business." Chief Wilkinson changed the subject, shaking his head mournfully. "Drug smuggling is bad enough, but human trafficking? That's about as low as it gets."

"What happened?"

"Your brothers gave Samuels all the information they had on Warren and Nichols and the drivers who were working for them. I got a call last night to say Warren had been arrested in Colorado. Samuels is confident he'll get a confession from him and he'll take Nichols down with him. From there, he's sure they'll smash that whole human trafficking and drug smuggling ring wide open." He picked up his hat, preparing to depart. "Samuels told me to tell you Delaney Transportation will be okay, Cam. Vincente said that was what you were worried about." He sighed, shaking his head. "I don't know if I've mentioned this, but I'm getting too old for this job. It's time I retired."

Cameron showed him out and then returned to Laurie. He held out his arms, and she walked into them as if it was the most natural thing in the world. "I can't believe it's over."

"Believe it."

"How's your head, Mayor Delaney?"

"Still there."

"Good." She took his hand and led him toward the bedroom.

"Don't tell me you're still tired?"

She laughed. "I wasn't planning on sleeping."

"After the few days we've had, I'm not sure surprises are my thing." Laurie studied Cameron's profile as he drove, but he still wasn't giving anything away.

"Be patient."

She sighed. "That's never been my thing."

After the chief had gone, they had spent most of the day in bed. Not talking. Not with words. Now it was late afternoon and Cameron had decided they needed to go for a drive. Laurie could sense something in him, a sudden, burning restlessness that scared her. *When are we going to talk about us?* Oh, God, that was such a cliché. But she loved him with an intensity that scared her. Now the immediacy of the danger was over, it was time to find out where, if anywhere, this was going. *Because I can't be a Carla substitute. I thought perhaps I could, but my heart won't take it. I'm too selfish. I need all of him...or I need to walk away.*

To be fair to Cameron, she knew he had never cast her in that role. She was the one who had come here to play a part. He had always made it clear he saw her as Laurie, not Carla. The first time they made love, he had told her he wanted her, no one else. But the question was still there in her mind. *Could he ever love me the way he loved her?* And every time she asked it, she disliked herself for her selfishness.

Now she didn't know where this burst of energy, this need to drive out of town, had come from. His fingers drummed constantly on the steering wheel and a slight smile played about his lips, but she could almost feel his nervousness. It was directed at her. *What the hell is this all about?*

"Almost there." He turned off the highway, taking the narrow track that led to the old Dawson ranch.

Laurie had seen this place only once, and that had been from the ridge above. Now, as Cameron halted the car, she was able to appreciate the full splendor of the ranch. Encircled by majestic mountains, the ranch house itself lay within a circle of verdant green. Although it had been neglected, the beauty of the natural stone and golden wood house shone through. Catching hold of Laurie's hand, Cameron led her up to the front porch.

"My dad used to bring us out to visit Culver Dawson now and then. They'd sit on this porch and talk, and I always thought this was the most beautiful view in the world." He swept a hand out, indicating the vista before them.

Laurie turned and saw what he meant. It had everything, with the grass and wildflowers in the near ground rising up to meet the pine-topped ridge and the snow-capped mountains in the distance. For a moment, she forgot her anxiety and sighed with pleasure. "Imagine waking up to see that every morning."

"Can you?"

She turned her head, a slight frown in her eyes. "Sorry?"

He laughed, his nervousness even more apparent now. "I'm making a mess of this, aren't I?"

"You're certainly not making any sense." But her heart was beginning to thud wildly, because the look in his eyes was so warm, so loving...

"Laurie, I'm trying—but very badly—to ask if you could see yourself living here, with me, as my wife."

"But you have a house." Dear God, was that all she could think of to say?

Cameron shook his head. "I've been thinking of selling the lake house for some time. It was mine and Carla's, and when she died, it never felt the same." He was silent for a moment, and she sensed him searching for the right words. She knew it was because he'd mentioned Carla.

Laurie reached out a hand and placed it over his on the porch rail. "I know how much you loved her. I would never try to take that away."

He smiled. "I did. And now I love you. The two things are separate. There is no overlap between them. When she died I thought there would never be room in my heart to love someone else, but I've learned hearts are amazing things. They expand to fit the love you need. Oh, I know what people will say, but I don't care. You look like her, she was your cousin, she's only been dead a year, we've only known each other just over a week. None of those things matter. We've packed a hell of a lot of loving and living into that week, Laurie. Enough for me to know my own heart." He was watching her face carefully as he spoke. "I'd like to think I know yours, as well."

She felt the tears she'd been holding back spill over. "I don't usually cry." It was an anguished wail.

"Is that a yes?"

She hurled herself into his arms, clutching the front of his shirt tightly and nodding into his chest. "I love you so much. I couldn't bear the thought of leaving you."

"And I was right about this place? You'd be happy to stay in Wyoming?" Cameron's face was anxious as he waited for her answer.

Laurie's smile reassured him. "I would be happy to stay anywhere as long as you were there."

* * * * *

We hope you enjoyed this first installment in Jane Godman's thrilling new miniseries.

Don't miss book two, available in July 2017 from Harlequin Romantic Suspense!

"Is that…" Thorne's voice was husky and Maggie realized he was now standing next to the bed. She'd been so focused on the screen she hadn't even noticed his approach. "Is that the nose?"

Maggie's gaze traveled back to the head, which was shown in profile. She ran her eyes along the line of the baby's face, from forehead to chin. How could something so small already look so perfect?

"Yes. And here are the lips." Dr. Walsh moved an arrow along the image, pointing out features in a running commentary. "Here is the heart, and this is the stomach and kidneys." She moved the wand lower on Maggie's belly. "Here you can see the long bones of the legs forming. And this is the placenta."

Maggie hung on her every word, hardly daring to breathe for fear of missing anything she might say. She glanced over and found Thorne leaning forward, his expression rapt as he took everything in. He must have felt her gaze because he turned to look at her, and in that moment, all Maggie's hurt feelings and disappointment were buried in an avalanche of joy over the shared experience of seeing their baby for the first time. No matter what might happen between them, they had created this miracle together. They were no longer just Maggie and Thorne; they had new roles to play now. Mother and father.

"Congratulations," he whispered, his brown eyes shining with emotion.

"Congratulations," she whispered back. Her heart was so full she could barely speak, but words weren't needed right now.

Thorne took her hand in his own, his warm, calloused fingers wrapping around hers. In silent agreement, they turned back to the monitor to watch their baby squirm and kick, safe inside her body and blissfully unaware of today's dangerous encounter.

I will keep you safe, Maggie vowed silently.
Always.

Don't miss
PREGNANT BY THE COLTON COWBOY
by Lara Lacombe, available May 2017 wherever
Harlequin® Romantic Suspense books
and ebooks are sold.

www.Harlequin.com

THE WORLD IS BETTER WITH

Romance

Harlequin has everything from contemporary, passionate and heartwarming to suspenseful and inspirational stories.

Whatever your mood, we have a romance just for you!

Connect with us to find your next great read, special offers and more.

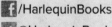

Turn your love of reading into rewards you'll love with
Harlequin My Rewards

**Join for FREE today at
www.HarlequinMyRewards.com**

Earn **FREE BOOKS** of your choice.

Experience **EXCLUSIVE OFFERS** and contests.

Enjoy **BOOK RECOMMENDATIONS**
selected just for you.

PLUS! Sign up now
and get **500** points
right away!

Earn
FREE
REWARDS
HarlequinMyRewards.com
Join
Today!

MYR16R